GLORYBOUND

JESSIE VAN EERDEN

Glorybound

a novel

*To Catherine,
with excitement
for what this new
season of your life
will bring —Jessie
Oct 2013*

WordFarm

SEATTLE, WASHINGTON

WordFarm
2816 East Spring Street
Seattle, WA 98122
www.wordfarm.net

Cover Images: iStockphoto, iStockpro
Cover Design: Andrew Craft
Book text is set in 11 point Monotype Dante

USA ISBN-13: 978-1-60226-010-8
USA ISBN-10: 1-60226-010-9
Printed in the United States of America

First Edition: 2012

Library of Congress Cataloging-in-Publication Data

Van Eerden, Jessie, 1979-
Glorybound : a novel / Jessie van Eerden. -- 1st ed.
  p. cm.
ISBN-13: 978-1-60226-010-8 (pbk.)
ISBN-10: 1-60226-010-9 (pbk.)
I. Title.
PS3622.A585486G58 2011
813'.6--dc23

                                                          2011035221

P 12 11 10 9 8 7 6 5 4 3 2 1
Y 18 17 16 15 14 13 12

for Mike

Prologue

....

SLEET-BLURRED VISION. Fewer headlights. It was the young driver's first run, and he distrusted the truck's bulk in weather. He edged his rig off the road, a shortcut north of the Pennsylvania Turnpike, and into a diner's parking lot, wary of the wheels sluicing the gray slush. He eased to a stop beside a white delivery truck and stepped out of the cab into darkness thick as pond water; he had to swim toward surface, toward moon: the diner's *Coors* sign.

A bell shook when he opened the door, and he walked up to the bar where a tall man sat hunched. A wide waitress showed her face, and the driver asked for anything the kitchen was willing to serve up this late. She nodded, bobbing her high, bleached hair, and disappeared. He sat three stools down from the bent man and took up a pen sitting by the register, a fake flower glued on top. He fingered the petals and looked down the counter. The man was backlit by the window's neon sign, mostly silhouette. Black, wavy hair, black jeans and black, wool shirt. His face was cloudy, indistinct, and the driver rubbed his eyes as though still seeing through sleet.

"Bad out," the driver said, after awhile. He waited and spun the pen petals, skittish, the loneliness of his cab more palpable beside this shadow man. "Too much weather. Thought I'd get a bite and wait it out. I'm hauling lumber up to Buffalo, gone down to Georgia and back. The South gives me the creeps." The flower tore loose, so he took up a salt shaker. "I've got a girl in Buffalo I stay with. Glad to be clear of that curvy route, but slick highway can kill whether it's straight or not."

The waitress brought out a Reuben and some chips, along with his bill to say she wouldn't be open long. She glanced at the man in black, but his bill lay unnoticed, no cash on the counter. The chips were stale.

"Where you from?" the driver asked the slumped man.

"No home to speak of. I lay my head where it's fit." The man didn't turn, just scooted his plate away, untouched eggs and toast. Slow movement, like moving in his sleep. Talking in his sleep, too, his voice hollow and dreamlike.

"You been south?"

"Yessir. I been south a everyplace. But you go to the far reaches, and God still there."

Sauerkraut stuck in the driver's teeth. He felt cold. "Must be your delivery truck out there. What is it you deliver?"

"Used to be the word a God. Truck's near empty." The man unbuttoned his cuffs and rolled up his black sleeves, studying the clock. He rubbed his hands together, as if at a spigot. He turned, coal-black eyes set in a ghost's face, and the driver's cold sank into bone. The man raised his voice: "'I'll pour out my spirit,' sayeth the Lord. 'Your old men will dream dreams, your young men will see visions.' Blood and fire and billows of smoke. Day's a coming." His deep voice nearly sang, such timbre.

The driver thought him drunk, but saw only a coffee mug by the plate of food.

"I see things." The man looked up at the clock again, as though expecting someone. "I see dark things, boy. Coming at me, like"—he took a quick swipe with his right hand. "I see the cat's dumb, ain't mewling no song, right there in the straw." He pointed to the floor, under the stools between them. "Little bird caged up. Don't nobody know to splint its wing? But nobody doing it. And that ain't all." He slid off the stool, wagging his finger, and walked over to the driver, who'd quit chewing. "I seen a serpent, by and by, one a them thick, rope bodies you could pull out the ground to no end. It's waiting in a burlap sack—hot. Mean. It waits for a fool to take it up in the name a hisself. You deal in fire again' God, you get paid in burns." Rubbing his arms up and down, eyes black, but each swirling, the white of them like ice vapor. "I see it, I can almost reckon the hands who's doing it. Now you tell me"—he slapped the counter hard—"is them visions, or is them dreams? Young men'll see visions, and old men'll dream dreams—which is it, boy?"

Sirens sounded right outside the diner, and the driver jumped, police lights bluing the walls and the man's pale, steady face.

"No telling which," the man said. "I ain't young, I ain't old. I see more besides, some from the past: a baby dead 'fore it got born. I still see that, and some still to come. All of it bitter." He pulled a key from his jeans pocket and set it on the driver's scribbled bill. Car doors slammed shut outside. "You take the truck. Them sirens for me. Day's come." He walked slowly to the door, muttering,

"Sun shall be turned to darkness on that day, alright, and the moon to blood."

"What's your name?" the driver blurted.

"Got no name." The man didn't turn. "You call on the Lord's name, son. Them that call out shall be saved."

The bell shivered, and the waitress came out from the kitchen with her hand on her hair. She and the driver watched the window as the man raised his arms in surrender, his sleeves still rolled. He raised them high and outspread, the way the driver had once seen a TV preacher, sweaty and gold-toothed, lift his hands to shout praises, to say *Glory*.

Aimee

....

THE LEMLEY SISTERS HAD DECIDED they would drive to the prison on the first Monday in August, but on that morning Aimee woke with bad pain. It was still dark—not yet five. She peeled off her blanket and top sheet, rolled to her side and drew up her body. She pulled her knees to her chin like a child, her cotton nightgown worn sheer.

Aimee wondered if she would be able to go through with it, and if she did, if she stood before him like some shy, sweet thing in the doorway, what would she say? She felt her hair, the black waves just long enough to fall onto her lips as she lay there. Would he say something about it being cut short? Would he say anything at all?

Aimee unbent herself and rose from bed, walked barefoot down the hallway laid with yellow linoleum. She splashed her face at the kitchen sink, since you could hear the bathroom faucet rattle the pipes from any room in the doublewide, and she didn't want to wake Crystal yet, or their mom, Dotte. She touched her abdomen, hot through the gown, where the pain slowly lazed into her with bitterness—a cramp that would set in. She ate a slice of American cheese and left the wrapper, started coffee. She put her hand to the warped window-screen above the sink, trying to feel a breeze that would not come. These endless days of drought seemed to Aimee like a punishment, for though the sky was burdened with rain, it refused relief. If that thick air could somehow be gathered like a dishrag, then she—Aimee Jo Lemley—would wring the rain from it, would bring on more rain than had flooded the Donnie Manse River in 1985.

A car passed on the road, throwing its lights against her. In the flash, Aimee looked to the back of her hand, trailed her eyes up her arm, then down to her breasts, to her belly rising with breath under the thin cotton, that pink-white skin showing through. She fixed her eyes on her flesh in the brief light, memorizing what she saw like it was Scripture. Then it went dark.

Crystal came into the kitchen through that long-chute hallway, silent as a ghost in the doorframe. Color-poor and mannish, she had already dressed in their daddy's old work jeans, same as the day before, and a throwaway blouse with a soiled front missing the fifth button.

"Shouldn't go to such trouble to dress up," Aimee said to her, meaner than she meant. Behind Crystal, she could see a smoky light float out from under Dotte's door at the end of the hall, but nobody came out.

Aimee drove the white pickup north on Route 40 and carried on her usual one-sided conversation. Crystal hadn't spoken in ten years, and silence had changed her. For the most part, she moved more like other people's shadows than like her own self.

They had never seen the Cuzzert Correctional Facility, but they knew where it was. A big sign marked the turnoff, but even without the sign you could tell when you were getting close, because the pavement on the road in was all new, starting right around King's Service Station. Pitch-black asphalt and perfect, like no other road in the county. When Cuzzert people talked about the prison, they talked about the road that got paved, not the facility itself. In truth, hardly any of them had seen it—it was a country, or maybe a whole world, apart.

"Aubrey ain't there yet," Aimee said. "He don't teach till nine. Should probably wait till he's there, so he can set up everything. We go this early, and we gonna sit and wait it out. Too damn early, 'fore work like this. Crys, you bring cigarettes? I need a damn cigarette." She rolled down the window and propped her arm up to feel the wind. When Aimee swore, she still sounded new at it. She said only a few words—*damn, shit, hell*. She never swore to God or said *goddamn* or even *for Christ's sake*; she'd say *for Pete's sake, for goodness' sake,* which put her swearing off-kilter. But she'd heard once that taking the Lord's name in vain was a new nail in Jesus' palm, and besides Crystal and maybe Aubrey Falls, Jesus was the one Aimee adored and protected. She knew Crystal hated filthy talk, and she knew Crystal had no Pall Malls. She also knew—because Crystal sat with her left hand in an absolute, unyielding fist like a knot of pine—that it would not be easy for Aimee to turn around and drive right back home, which she very much meant to do.

"Hershel Dunmire come into the shop the other day, give me grape Bubble Tape. That stuff'll cost a buck-fifty at the Family Dollar. Well, I chewed it all morning, and it turned to paste on my teeth, so I look at him pouty, you know, and give it back to him. 'I can't have this,' I told him, 'it'll make my teeth ugly.' He looked about to bawl, but he took it back. Sat in his chair the rest the day holding it. His poor mind's so balled up, Crys. He don't always wash, you know. He shit his pants that once, but I act like I don't know nothing. Can't do nothing else. I done told his sister-in-law who keeps him, but she's up in her seventies like him, so she can't do him no better."

Aimee bounced her hand on the gear shift as she talked. Crystal was looking out the window, toward the fence posts along the road, their rusted barbwire lost to thicket. She nodded to Aimee now and again, seeming not to affirm any one part of the monologue, but it was clear she listened. Even more than that, she suffered Aimee's meandering and heard the deepest tones beneath, like the unsung harmonies of a hymn. Aimee never thought Crystal vacant, but that didn't mean she didn't feel lonely in the truck cab with her sister's silence and her fist, with that calm way she slipped her yellow hair behind her ear.

"Hershel's stuck on me like a fly on barn tape," Aimee chattered on, "and Jimmy don't care if he's there, 'cause he's back in the garage all day. None of them guys mind him. They think he's a piece of furniture, 'cept for Aubrey. Sweet Aubrey Falls buys him a Coke every time he comes in, opens the damn can for him. If Aubrey ain't showed up to teach, then we probably can't get in anyhow. Probably need permission from some guard. Whole world's drying up, seems like. Hotter than the hubs of hell, and it ain't even six, yet. Shit, Crys, this ain't getting no better—my stomach's killing me."

Crystal looked over at her, and Aimee thought she saw something give, a small flow of pity spurting forth that would surely grow to a gushing and allow her to turn the truck around. But Crystal's fist stayed tight on her thigh. She looked past Aimee then, out the driver-side window. Aimee followed the path of her eyes to the Cuzzert Pike sign as they passed it, to the turnoff down a gravel road overhung with the shaggy gray of barren crabapple trees. To the goldenrod, dying of thirst but almost pretty, lining the pike's ditch. To Glorybound Holiness Tabernacle where they knew it sat, six miles down the gravel road, out of sight. And beyond that, to the strip mine. After the Cuzzert Pike junction, the only breaks in the fencerow with its attending brier bushes were the occasional dirt drives and a few right-of-way swaths for power lines.

Aimee kept quiet for awhile and tugged at the collar of her long-sleeved top. She'd taken it from Dotte's closet the night before, along with a skirt to her ankles. Her mom wouldn't miss the clothes, since she'd grown too broad to wear them.

Aimee had no dresses of her own that would suit a prison visit. She no longer kept the high collars and long skirts. Dotte used to make all the girls' dresses, stiff calico prints, blouses buttoned to the top or hooked into an eye in back, close to the neck as a choker chain. Aimee's dresses were flimsy now, not like the ones handsewn. She'd just bought a mint sundress, low-cut almost to her navel. She safety-pinned it some, but that made little difference in what it showed off. Her dresses were mint, now, and black and hard yellow and indigo; they fell mid-thigh in a ruffle. They were red-ribboned, like a bleeding fish in water. In the truck cab, she pulled at her collar and flipped the visor down then up, traced the circle of the steering wheel round and round. Crystal kept looking out the window. Her cornsilk hair, tied back, lay limp across her left shoulder. Beside Crystal's drab stillness, beside the fist she kept firm in her lap, Aimee's constant hand movements, with her nails painted red, were wild and frantic, as though she were trying to get unstuck from a web of wet spider thread. Flamboyant. Even her despair was flamboyant.

As soon as the road looked smooth up ahead, Aimee held her breath long enough to hear the tires hit the seam in the asphalt where the new paving started. Then she saw the steel sign grow from the berm as they rounded the bend: *Cuzzert Correctional Facility for Men, 15 Miles.* So strange and foreign, bright heavy letters coming out of nowhere like that. The old wood fence posts bowed low before the sign.

Aimee took an immediate left and pulled into the lot at King's Service Station. She let the engine idle, then stall, and she didn't start it again. *In service to the King*, it said on the awning over the single gas pump. And beside the pump, on a new sign staked in the gravel: *Year 2000 Coming Soon—R U Ready 4 Jesus?* in big black letters. At one time, a sign like that would have pricked Aimee like a thorn and made her anxious, but this morning she read it with a stone face and squinted at the service station window, looking for the poster that announced the price of cigarettes. She adored Jesus, but she felt he would take his good-old time coming back to this world, and she wasn't too sure he'd be looking for her when he came.

King's wasn't open yet. The sky was barely turning light, but the August heat already brought sweat to Aimee's underarms. She propped her left arm on the door again to let herself breathe.

"You know the prison people bought the Sisler farm for like half of what they shoulda paid? Aubrey told me that; I don't know how he found it out. He just knows things 'cause he's college educated. It was still a shitload of money, though. Was Ronnie Sisler between us in school? I think he was. Remember how foul he was 'fore he got saved? That boy liked to butcher with his daddy when they did the broilers. Pushed on their bellies to make 'em squawk through their windpipe when they didn't have no heads. He brought a chicken head to school one time, I remember that. Then his daddy died, and he met the Lord. Just like that—gentle as a pup."

Aimee looked out the window as Agnes Felton pulled into the lot. Agnes took her time gathering herself and her purse from the car, plucking at her perfect crown of black curls before unlocking the front door of the station. The lights came on, and the *Open* sign burned bright green. Aimee wanted to buy a pack of Pall Malls, but she didn't get out.

"Ronnie quit school when we did—or did he finish? I think he finished maybe, 'fore his mom shipped him out. Buddy, he learned that church guitar quick, after he got saved, had that sweet voice. You two was right much the song-birds." She looked hard at Crystal, harder than she meant. It was cruel to speak of Ronnie, but she needed Crystal to break apart, to let their old pickup turn back toward home and let that prison stay fifteen miles out, a world unto itself.

"You know, you never wore no filthy blouse like that when he was around, and them big jeans. You almost twenty-six years old, and you dressing like a damn hobo." Crystal didn't look over, but she held her fist in her other hand, cradled it. "Ronnie done went down to the city, right? Down Charleston? I remember Mom said he took up snakes down there—down in the city! Doing strychnine and everything, copperheads. It's the damn nineties for Pete's sake, they living in the dark ages. And people say *we're* backward holy rollers and shit. I never thought Ronnie'd turn like that—too soft. I expect he's probably dead—you know if he's dead?"

Crystal unlatched her door and got out of the truck. She stood facing Route 40, her fist at her side like she was ready to take a swing, and Aimee suddenly wanted to feel that fist hit her mouth. She clutched the steering wheel and felt mean and sank down into the meanness—not sure how else to be—the way she sank down onto her pile of cheap dresses on the floor of her room, all those dresses she heaped around herself like costumes, none of them fitting right. Even though she picked them off the store racks herself, somebody else was pulling them onto her doll-pretty body. Aimee knew Crystal knew everything she did about Ronnie Sisler and more besides. And they'd both heard the stories Dotte told from inside her cloud of smoke, her new glory—a Pall Mall glory—in her cardigan sweater tied with a skirt belt overtop of her nightgown. Dotte had just started dressing like that when this Ronnie Sisler episode came across the church prayer chain over the phone with a call from Miriam Louks. The way their mom told it, with her yellowed eyes, put it in Aimee's mind like a movie scene, and she dreamt about Ronnie that night, his neck lined with a coil of innumerable snakes, and he was singing "Victory in Jesus." She never told Crystal that dream because she was afraid it was a prophecy, and she knew Crystal loved him.

"I do wonder if Ronnie Sisler's dead," Aimee said to herself. "Might as well be. People that up and leave us, they might as well be dead." She got out of the truck and went around the front end to where her sister faced the road.

"You really wanna go?" Aimee asked.

Crystal kept fixed on the road, on where it disappeared around a bend up ahead, black and wavy like thick oil.

"If you wanna go, you can walk from here."

Crystal didn't budge.

"If you want to go, say so, dammit!" Aimee laughed a dry laugh then sent her voice into a deeper pitch, loud like a preacher's, like their daddy's preaching voice.

"See here, Sister, I see signs that it ain't yet time," and she made a big mocking sweep with her arm toward Route 40, as though showing Crystal the breadth of the given signs. "No, it ain't yet time."

Aimee laughed again, softer, and let her voice slide back into a plainer register. "I for one ain't ready, Crys. I ain't ready to look at Daddy's face through a piece of damn glass and say who the hell knows what."

Crystal finally looked at her then, and Aimee felt see-through and let herself stay that way for as long as Crystal looked. When she looked back at the road again, Aimee whispered, "Please. Can't we just wait till tomorrow? I promise I'll go tomorrow." She went back to the truck and got in the driver seat.

Crystal turned from the road and climbed back into the other side of the cab. She put her hands in her lap, her fist relaxing, opening upward in a pale cup. When Aimee saw it, she felt the submission, and she turned the key. They were two weak sticks—bent then stepped on. They cracked so easy.

But it was going to be hard to explain to Aubrey why they hadn't shown. He would be watching for them, a boy too sweet for his own good. He'd be eager for the reunion of the daughters with their convict daddy, pretty as a picture.

"You see that heat lightning, Crys? Just now? Weird in the morning like that. 'Course it won't rain, though." She shifted into first and pulled out, taking a right, back the way they'd come.

"We dying for the rain. But I got wash to do anyhow. I'm so cramped up, I'll call Jimmy and take off sick. And I'll do the wash."

Aubrey

....

THE FIRST TIME AUBREY HAD MET HER, he'd called her by the name embroidered above *The Muffler Barn* on her shirt. *Aimee* in yellow curlicues. The shirt hugged tightly to her chest, unbuttoned low in the front. Aubrey looked everywhere except down that shirt, then tried to buy the first pack of cigarettes of his life.

It was the fall of 1998, and Aubrey had just moved to Cuzzert, West Virginia. He felt reborn and purposeful, or at least tried to convince himself he felt that way. He was about to start up classes in town and at the nearby prison. He'd also started drinking percolated coffee that made his head buzz as he would repeat to himself, "I'm really doing something here," a mantra that helped him overcome his shyness. He was muttering this affirmation as he walked into the Muffler Barn with a flier about the GED class and saw Aimee pull a wholesale carton of Camels from behind the counter. She slid them over the dirty Formica to a shuffling woman who wore house slippers and whose hair, when Aubrey got in line behind her, smelled like motor oil and sulfurous water.

"Sign here, Esther," Aimee said. She glanced at Aubrey, then slipped her short black hair behind her ear to show a naked lobe, no earring. She shifted her weight and flicked at the counter with her red fingernails. Her eyes were such a pretty black—almost too pretty—and Aubrey had to look everywhere but at those eyes and at that shirt that clung to her. But nothing he looked at in the room registered, except for an old man sitting on a wooden office chair next to the counter, fiddling with a collection of rubber bands around his wrist.

Esther took what felt to Aubrey like a decade to sign the yellow paper that had written on the top—he had plenty of time to read—"IOU for 1 box," and across from it on the right-hand side, "$17.00." No date and no shop insignia of any sort, nothing else at all but Esther's painstaking, childlike signature.

"See you next month, then," Aimee said, and the old woman scuffed out with the Camels pinned under her armpit and her hand in her slacks pocket, the way a businessman carries a newspaper on the street.

"You got a car needs worked on?" Aimee asked Aubrey without looking at him as she stuck the signed slip onto a nail behind her, on top of a collection of identical slips punched through with the nail.

He blanked, forgot about the flier he held at his side.

She turned around. "I ain't got all day," said her perfect mouth.

Then he said, too loud, "I'll have a pack of cigarettes please, Aimee." Either her face or the thought of smoking a cigarette, or both, produced an acrid taste in his mouth like metal.

"We don't sell cigarettes here," she said. "If you want a oil change or a tune up, or you want Jimmy to look under your hood, that we do."

Aubrey felt her black eyes studying him, looking him over; he thought she lingered on the white *Loyola* on his green T-shirt neatly tucked in. She slurred the word "oil" into a single syllable—"ole change," she said it, so sweetly. He thought she was making fun of him, or herself, as though she were acting out a caricature. Still, he liked the way it sounded.

"But you just sold that lady a whole carton," he said, aware of his own crisp voice.

"To Esther Moats, yessir, every first of the month on credit. What you got there?" She nodded at the flier in his hand.

The old man on the wooden office chair beside the counter quit playing with the rubber bands on his wrist. He looked up and said, "Esther Moats, first of the month. And Gary Wayne, but he come in for chew." And he bowed again over the rubber bands, reordering them or counting them like a rosary.

"Well," said Aubrey, feeling his body go stiff.

"What you got, I asked?" Aimee started to smile.

"A flier." He handed it to her. "We're starting a GED class and job training in town. Maybe you could post this on your door."

"I got a job and don't need no GED."

"It's a high school equivalency. For people who didn't graduate."

"What're you assuming?"

"Nothing. I'm not assuming anything. I just thought you could hang it up, for customers."

"This made on a computer?"

"Yes."

"You don't need no diploma if you gonna be a woman-prophet of God."

"Excuse me?"

"You done heard me."

"A prophet of God. Are you—a prophet?" He was ready to laugh, but not until she did first, and once she laughed, then he'd be able to leave and spit out this metal secreting from his gums.

"I will be," she said, straight-faced. Even her smile disappeared.

"But you're not yet?"

"Nope, not yet."

"What are you waiting for?"

"God's time."

"How long have you been waiting?"

"Almost ten years."

"Ten years?"

"You asking a hell of a lot of questions."

"Sorry." Aubrey could see the dull silvery top of her camisole as she leaned forward, lower and lower, over the counter. "Sorry," he said again.

"What for?" Her smile crept back into her mouth.

"Why'd you quit, Aimee?"

"Quit what?"

"School."

"'Cause my daddy died, and the sun come up. Why you looking down my shirt?" She wasn't wearing a bra, and he couldn't look anywhere anymore except at that silver camisole. "You're slick with my name, so what's your name, guy?"

"Aubrey Falls."

"He falls, indeed. You tell me, Mr. Aubrey Falls, do you know the Lord Jesus in a personal way? As the Lord of your salvation?"

He said nothing to that, just exhaled a quick, metal-coated breath. He retreated quickly into himself. He felt like a character in some ridiculous movie, playing the butt of the joke, how he'd always felt when he left his college friends' late parties alone and walked down the streets in Chicago, looking at his face in shop windows, in search of someone who took him seriously. This strange woman, this angel-faced girl with a skimpy work shirt and a voice that slipped its long fingers around him, did not take him seriously.

"Come here," Aimee said quietly, glancing over at the rubber-band man who didn't seem to be watching. "Lean on over here for a girl gonna be a woman-prophet."

Aubrey couldn't move. He heard his dad's voice in his head, that doctor-voice speaking under an icy sheet of irony when they had once watched a televangelist endorse a city councilman on his show, the two suited men shaking hands on the screen. "Politicians and prophets," his dad had said. "Two roles played by the same clown." When Aubrey's dad had died, another physician had offered the eulogy in that same clinical voice.

"Come on," Aimee said, and Aubrey leaned in with some effort, his body like lead.

"Little closer," she said. He was close enough to taste the smoke and, underneath, the black coffee of her mouth, and she whispered, "Do you know that I'm a virgin, and I plan to stay one till I'm a prophet, till after the trials and the tribulation and the Battle of Armageddon, when the trump shall sound?" She reached down in a flash and swiped her hand hard over the front of his pants, and he leaped back stunned.

"Ain't nobody who flinches worth the powder to blow him up!" she said and started laughing, and the rubber-band man, who had in fact been watching, cackled harshly. Aubrey backed up to the shop door, feeling his whole body turn red, feeling the buzz in his head swell with his purposeful mantra and this woman's gaping shirtfront and his dad's voice, and it all burst into tiny shards of laughter that pounced on him from everywhere in the shop. He felt his own recognition of himself dissolve into the black pools of Aimee's eyes as she laughed.

"Yeah," she said. "I'll stick this here flier up for you, Aw-brey." And she pierced the flier onto the nail, on top of Esther Moats' credit records.

Aimee

....

IT WAS STILL EARLY MORNING when Aimee pulled the wet laundry from the washer on the back screen porch. After she and Crystal had come home from King's and emptied out of the truck cab like heavy water, Crystal had left for work on foot. Aimee had watched her out the window until the pale ponytail went blurry. Now, Aimee hefted the basket to her hip with one arm, pulled on Tingley overshoes without her canvas shoes underneath and slipped out the screen door, careful, out of habit, not to make the spring whine.

Morning fog was burned off already. A few of the trailers in the Painted Rocks Estates park had lights on, enough to show Aimee a number of faces still creased with sleep, and they could see her if they looked out. The Lemleys' was the only doublewide in the park, the first place on the left as you pulled in. When the park had been new, theirs was the showcase trailer you could walk through, and then you put your name on the list for one of the others. The guy would say, "Remember it'll be half this size," but people most likely forgot. The Lemleys got the place years later, after the bank foreclosed on whoever had the doublewide at that time. It was no longer a showcase by then, but blue lattice framed the front door and front cinder-block steps, and Aimee and Crystal had found that pretty, along with the rocks at the park's entrance, with red paintings on them. Indian paintings, the bank man had said, unearthed when they'd dug for the park's septic tanks. Later, Joshie Dixon, who lived one trailer back, told Aimee the paintings weren't done by Indians at all. "Girl, everything 'round here's a sham." He had looked sad for a second, then he'd twisted his face up and pinched her.

Aimee started with the underwear on the clothesline at the back of the three lines that ran the length of the trailer, post to post, gathered and propped in the middle by a long stick cut like a slingshot. The lines were shared by the eight trailers on the Lemleys' half of the park. She started with the underwear on that line, farthest from the road that pulled in from Route 40, closest to the Dixons' kitchen window, but their blinds were down.

She pulled each piece from the broken Rubbermaid basket, shook it once, clasped it to the line, and let the wind slip through and around. She hung the towels in a solid sheet of terry, the socks haphazard among the work pants and blocky shirts that Crystal wore and the few underthings that Dotte had put in the wash. Not much else from Dotte, since she hardly ever dressed. And then Aimee's own dresses, upside down with the slight sleeves or straps dangling.

Before starting the green washing machine, Aimee had changed from the blouse and the long skirt, though she didn't return them, and wouldn't till midday, when Dotte would come out of her bedroom and drink her coffee cold. Aimee had peeled her slip from her sweaty body and found a spot of blood on the back, her period coming early. So that's what had summoned the pain in her abdomen. She had put the slip in the wash and kept near-naked for three cool minutes. She'd chosen her new, short, mint dress, hadn't safety-pinned it, low in the front and all but backless, made of T-shirt cotton.

Now, between her legs, a hum—always there when she hung the dresses. She felt her body when she pinned them up. She felt a peculiar union between her body and her spirit and her wet dresses, all three flying just a little off the ground, wild but held fixed by two clothespins.

She pulled her peach-colored dress from the pile and shook it. It was the only dress in the basket that her mom had made for her. It was simple and unadorned, yoked at the waist; she'd had it since high school, but her figure hadn't changed much even into her early twenties, so it still fit. On Sundays, she wore the dress to Glorybound Holiness Tabernacle. The short sleeves of the dress ended blunt. The neckline veed just to her collarbone—no lower—and into a line of pearl-headed buttons rimmed with fake silver. Aimee despised the dress but loved the buttons—always had. She fingered them and saw that one was coming loose. They were hard to keep on the dress, the kind of button sewn on through the post sticking out the back not through a pair of holes or a set of four with a sure crisscross of thread. The buttons flopped and could catch easy on a table if she bumped it, but they were elegant if you didn't look too close.

"These buttons would break your heart, Daddy," she said out loud. And her body hummed; it hummed deep. Her cramps still twisted inside her, but the hum was more and more, the hum that was always responding, like a hymn of response after a Word, responding to a nonspecific shame.

"Break your heart, bray-ek your heart," in a sort of airy song she said it. The tiny straps of an upside-down dress caught at her bare leg. "Nunh-unh," she said. "No you don't," and she kicked them away. She looked at the peach dress with the pearls going down single file, and she gently plucked a button from it.

"And this is for old June, may she rest in peace," making like she was placing it on a gravestone in front of her. "We still breaking hearts." And she laughed and threw the pearl button hard toward the road. It skittered to a secret spot in the ditch, and the humming slid all up inside her. Her love for June was a bronzed, blessed thing that she reached for when she couldn't shake off the shame.

June Tatum was dead now four years, but during services at Glorybound her chair was still unfolded with the rest and set with white asters, or dried bittersweet if it was winter.

When Aimee had been a child and had looked at June, she'd felt hints of things she hadn't understood: sympathy, gratefulness, awe, blackness, a mean little joy.

June Tatum had been a regular at Glorybound, considered by the small congregation to be a woman-prophet, different from men-prophets in that she had been allowed to prophesy but not to lead from up front. It was the men who led. It was Aimee's daddy, Reverend Cord Lemley, who led.

June was both revered and pitied. She sat in the front row of metal folding chairs beside the altar bench and *amen*ed and *praisejesus*ed with her deep-toned voice when Aimee's daddy would get preaching. June was a big woman, and she wore the same dress every week: a two-piece skirt and top, dark blue with huge white lilies all over it, with strained elastic around the skirt's waist, short sleeves that puffed then narrowed just above the elbow where her fleshy arms bulged out. And the dress top had five big buttons down the front, each a diamond set in a rim of metal—maybe pewter—in a pattern that reminded Aimee of the wrought-iron railing on the Tabernacle steps. Five fat jewels down June's mountainous front. The buttons sparkled if the Sunday light found them through the single window.

As a little girl, Aimee sat with Crystal in the second row, opposite June, beside their mom and behind their daddy's preaching chair, where he sat before worship began. Once it began, he stood up front and paced and swaggered and jumped like an acrobat on fire. The people of Glorybound Holiness Tabernacle met in the redone basement of a coal company house, owned by Miriam Louks' aunt before she died and donated it for the church. It was built in the thirties, when Cuzzert was a coal mining town and every man was either a miner or under the age of fifteen.

Miriam, skinny and tough as a strip of leather, lived upstairs and kept the basement clean. She broom-swept the green carpet that covered the cement floor, the carpet worn thin from the stomping and dancing that people did when they rose from their folding chairs. Miriam washed down the bathroom where, beside the toilet, she'd written on a card in neat cursive: "Please don't flush tissue down unless you truly must." She had plugged a Glade potpourri fixture into the wall outlet, but she'd never replaced it; it had browned, and it clung there like a locust hull. She and Dotte had decorated the Tabernacle with various framed pictures of Jesus: him under rays of light or in bronze shadow, with the thorny crown and then without, with the beads of blood-sweat and then a clean, pale-marble forehead. Miriam also managed what Aimee and Crystal called "the numbers." On a board she got from the Methodists—a hanging board with slats and movable numbers—she recorded the weekly attendance, the record attendance, the love-offering amounts. None of the numbers she posted ever went above thirty.

The girls braided each other's hair or rooted around in their mom's purse for the first half of every service, until Cord's preaching went loud and the electric faith of the Glorybound worshippers shot around the room. Then the girls sat up and watched and raised their hands and waved the handkerchiefs they'd pulled from the pockets of Dotte's purse. They watched June Tatum as she rocked, second row back, as her buttons glinted then went dull. Aimee wondered—though she never asked—how June Tatum, who wore the same dress every week, could have those special buttons.

June walked with a cane. She was a couple hundred pounds overweight and blind, which was one reason why they said she was a woman-prophet, because a prophet has to go without something, and she went without sight. Even though she was blind, people said she could open the Bible and speak the Word on that page, and Aimee and Crystal believed it was true though they'd never seen her do it. June wore her gray hair back in a ratty ponytail, in a white scrunchy, like the kind Aimee saw the high school girls wear. What drew Aimee's gaze, besides the buttons, was June's grizzled face. June shaved her upper lip and jaw and chin, just like a man. She was the only woman with stubble that Aimee had ever seen, so she obsessed over June, wondered when she had started shaving and why. If she was blind, and she felt hair on her face, then how did she know women shouldn't have hair there? Did she go around feeling other women's faces for comparison? Or did somebody tell her about it—Aimee suspected that the leathery Miriam Louks was the kind of person who would tell her about it. And since June was blind, did she cut herself ever? Aimee knew June missed some parts altogether; some patches were thicker than others, varied like a cut field. She couldn't have shaved very often, because the stubble was thick whenever Aimee saw her, on Sundays and on days when they spotted June at the Save-a-Lot grocery and Dotte made a point to speak to her.

When June rocked forward into a shout and back into a murmur, the chair strained under her. Aimee watched and wanted more than anything to touch June's face. She knew a prophet was meant for something, and in secret she thought maybe the stubble proved June was meant to be a man, a man who would lead from up front, different from the way her daddy did. And she wondered if the stubble would be soft. Not like Daddy's—sandpaper half a day after he shaved.

One Sunday, Crystal leaned over to Aimee's ear, just before the hymn of invitation when the church would get wavery and hot, and she whispered: "Dare you to touch June Tatum's face." That was all she said; then she straightened her sock on her right foot to make it look like that's why she had leaned over. Aimee sat very still. She had never breathed a word about June's face to Crystal, but Crystal always knew more than she said, even before she stopped speaking. Aimee nodded her head down as their daddy moved into a prayer of preparation and getting-right before the hymn started, but she nodded back up and shot a glance at June.

June's eyes, mostly white like a poached egg, were wide open, and her head, instead of bowed, was facing up, blotchy red with sweat and shining some. The mixed feelings sputtered up in Aimee: she felt so sorry for the huge woman, and she felt so cruel, but she also felt so much hope. She touched her own face absently, a face she knew to be pear-colored and smooth and rosy in the right spots. Lovely. She knew it even young—before everyone said so—a face framed by her long, black hair that held its waves like shelves for the light to sit on. She could not interpose herself, she knew—could not take on June's self and give June her own doll self. But that is what she wanted. Out of pity and envy both.

"Okay, I'll do it," she whispered, "but next week."

Crystal grinned with her eyes squinted shut.

The following Sunday, as the people filed in, Aimee sat in the chair beside June's. June tapped her way to the chair and sat, seemingly unaware of Aimee's presence. June had worn the same dress, of course. This was the closest Aimee had ever been, and the buttons lured her. She sat close enough to see June's nostrils flare as she breathed heavy—close enough to see that the diamonds in the buttons of the dark blue dress were fake—maybe even plastic—glued cockeyed in their mounts of dull, tin grate, which looked itself to be gray plastic, but she couldn't tell without touching. And she remembered that's why she was there—she'd planned all week to touch June's stubbled jaw line during the opening prayer when everybody would be bowed down and no one would see her do it.

Aimee felt hot as her daddy started with a prayer murmur, a murmur that she knew would crescendo into a calling-down of the Spirit to anoint him with a Word to say in the name of Jesus. She felt the heat drift down from June's body, too, and drape her face, her bare ankles below her dress and her hands, like a hot mist. Both of June's hands perched on her cane in front of her. They were pale and helpless, strangely small compared to the rest of her, and they quivered to the rhythms of her watery breathing. June's hands looked to Aimee like the small minnows she'd caught when she had gone fishing with Crystal once at their cousin's pond, and they'd not pulled the line quick enough, and the minnows had swallowed the oversized hooks. Their stomachs tore when Aimee and Crystal pulled; the girls knew no way to get the hooks out. Crystal cut the lines on both of their poles and lay the fish side by side on the bank of the pond. One flopped over on top of the other, as though to die in a small heap were a comfort.

"Might we be supple in your hands, O God—break us and make us, O God, O glory, *break* our hearts and make us again, like clay in your hands." Her daddy was praying, getting louder now, with the soft, cooing, *yes-oh-yes* chorus of the people in the folding chairs gathering after his words like the little minnows in Aimee's mind, swimming after baited hooks.

"Make us bold, Lord God, in the Holy Ghost power." Cord stomped, then. "Yes, Lord, I say 'yes,' and we ain't leaving till you do, I say." He stomped twice, and a cry came from the back, a shrill echo, *"Ain't leaving,"* and Cord answered the cry, "We say, 'ain't leaving,'" and some chairs grated on the thin carpet as a few people stood. The final "amen" was nearing when Aimee knew all would stand and swerve and sweat and the basement would tremble, so, with no further meditation, she reached up to June Tatum's face and stroked the thick jaw with her fingertips.

At Aimee's touch, June shot up out of the chair quicker than Aimee would have thought possible. Crystal laughed a choked laugh from the other side of the room. June's empty eyes looked wildly around, obeying instinct. When she stood up, the third fake-diamond button on her dress caught on the back lip of the chair in front of her, and the button shot off onto the green carpet in the corner. June wheeled around, pivoted on her cane looking lost and walked out of the basement as quickly as she could, which was a halted and awkward operation even so. The "amen" must have come by then, because eyes were open and looking at the door that June left ajar behind her. Aimee held her left hand in her right and searched for any eyes that had seen what she'd done. She found Miriam Louks watching her from a few seats back, that prim mouth in a sour pucker. Aimee's daddy emerged from his prayer as though from a deep cave and plowed right into the Word without looking up. Later in the service, maybe missing June's usual affirmations, he glanced at her empty seat, and then at Aimee hugging herself and crying silently. Then he went on.

After the service, Miriam Louks scuttled around picking up, and she found the escaped dress button that Aimee had watched sparkle and dull intermittently in that corner all morning, a tiny reprimand. Miriam turned to two of the other women who were trying to figure out what had set June off—the Spirit? The toilet? Some kind of coughing fit coming? Aimee stood apart from the huddle of women, and Crystal slipped up beside her.

"What on earth moved her?" one of the women said, meaning to ask what had moved her heart but conjuring up in Aimee's mind the difficulty of moving a mountain.

"Mercy, that dress," Miriam said in a voice people reserved for prophets. A voice that coated over the mixed feelings that prophets drummed up in you, the pity and the jealousy, the gratitude and the horror, coated it all like Pepto-Bismol coats a sick stomach. Miriam closed the button into the skinny folds of her old-skin palm and looked at Aimee, saying, "Don't those buttons just break your heart? Don't they?" The other women *yes*ed her, with the same coating-over the remorse and contempt and fear, but Aimee didn't understand. How could buttons break your heart? Like her daddy had prayed to God to break their hearts—she'd heard him pray that a lot—to be *supple* was the word he used, and sometimes when he said it he made movements with his big hands like he was molding a pliable clay himself. *A button's a button,* she wanted to say to Miriam Louks, and she wanted it back. It didn't belong to Miriam, and Aimee suspected she would not give it to June to sew back on. And why didn't her own buttons break Miriam's heart? She thought, then, *Maybe they do.*

"What'd it feel like, Aimee? A porcupine face?" Crystal whispered.

"I don't know. It felt wet," Aimee said. "Maybe like grass."

"I think she was crying when she went." Crystal looked down, and Aimee could tell she was sorry she had laughed out loud right when the button had flown off.

"It felt like moss," Aimee said. It felt rough but soft, and she couldn't decide between the two sensations. It did not feel like her daddy's face when it was close to hers. Was it the only time June had ever been touched on the face? Sometimes people held her by the elbow and guided her—Aimee had seen that—but on her face, that was different. Surely someone touched her when she was little. Surely. And Aimee shut her eyes, tried to imagine what it might be like, hearing voices but feeling nothing for so long, seeing nothing and then, out of that nothing, the feel of fingers on her face.

Aimee shivered. She did not like to be touched or looked on as something lovely. Everyone touched her. Even now, Miriam reached for Aimee, stroked her long black hair as though petting a horse. People treated her like she was a pretty hollow bone, with no spirit whistling around inside, no prophet's ache, just sawdust and a doll's fiberfill stuffing.

Now you see what it's like, is what she thought. It was a punishment for June, or an initiation. Or a gift.

Aimee imagined that June would feel her dress button missing, the threads spilling out loose like sprigs of a plant. June would have to get a new dress.

But the next week, the same dress had a new button—dull copper from a pair of jeans. When Aimee looked close, she read *Riders* on it. It somehow made June look more like a wild woman-prophet than ever. It made Aimee love her and follow her out of the basement that morning, to the edge of the road, like a disciple.

Cord

....

#96309

May 12, 1999

Describe a time when you made a change in your life for the better.

This is my cursive letters. Let me know if you want print. You can maybe read it better. We do not make the changes. God does and I can tell you I been changed. I was born in 1958 close here, about a hours drive south in Roane. I lost my Mama when I was 7 and my Daddy was a drunk and growed me up to be a drunk. When I was 15 I was in sin with a girl of simple mind and I was half the day drunk and the other half fighting to no purpose. I got my girl pregnant. She was 15 also and we neither of us had money to feed a child. There aint no way to change that but by the power of the Lord. I can tell you the day and the hour when He saved me. July 14 of 1973 when the power went out.

It was storming and lightning something fierce. There was a Tent Preacher who come from someplace north we aint been at before. The thing was he went on preaching through the storm. That made people sit up and take notice, cause he could have been struck dead in the tent right there. Nobody went out to him. He just preached all night to empty chairs, but he knew people was watching from their windows. My girl and me did not stay near where the tent was set up, we stayed in the basement at her aunts house a mile out, but we was in town that night for a drink, even her pregnant and we could have drowned the baby in what we drank that night—mercy of God we did not. We got to watching the Tent Preacher from the bar window, we started laughing at him. It was raining hard, but we lifted up the window and started cursing at him. We called him a ugly old buzzard, cause he was bent over. He did not act like he heard for a long time, we just got louder, acting foul as we could, drunk out of our heads. Then he done something. He looked right to my eyes through that open window and he quit preaching. He had the Bible open, he stuck his finger in it to mark the page when he shut it and he started walking to me. It was raining so hard everything went flat, all his hair I mean and his suit clothes. He come up to the window, not even to the door, he had his eyes on me. He did not say nothing at first. He opened up the Word of God where he had it marked, there on the sill right in front of me, and he reached and took hold of my hand rougher than any man ever done me. He stretched my point finger and laid it on the open page of the Word and said—Read this here Son. I do not know what happened to me, I was mighty mad he called me Son, but I was scared too, cause I knew I was in sin and deserved to die. I looked down and I read out loud where my finger laid. I still know it by rote, from the 8 chapter of Luke—A woman having a issue of blood twelve years which had spent all her living upon physicians, neither could be healed of any, came behind Him, and touched the border of His garment, and immediately her issue of blood stanched. And Jesus said, Who touched Me? When all denied, Peter and they that were with him said, Master, the multitude throng Thee and press Thee, and sayest Thou, Who touched Me? And Jesus said, Somebody hath touched Me, for I perceived power going out from Me.—And Buddy right then—glory to God—when I read the Power Going Out, the power in that bar done went out. Black as pitch. I mean black in that place. I lost all feeling in my fingers, my mouth went stone dry and nothing was realer to me than Jesus in that room. I started bawling like a baby and that Preacher prayed with me. God saved me right there. I was all His, I quit drinking cold turkey, I was changed inside and out. I had long hair at that time and I cut it short. My girl and me got married by the Tent Preacher, even though she was not right in the head. They said later on that lightning come in on the breaker and blew it, but that do not make it any less a sign. I spoke the Power Going Out like God calling that lightning down to me and I can tell you Buddy, God is keen to send His lightning. Do not be fooled. And up before that, about the woman having issues of blood, she was a bleeder and my Mama was too. That is what they told me when she died when I was 7—She was a bleeder, my Uncle Jack is one who said it. Then they buried her. So that was one sign. I read the signs. All of it is true. I would put my hand on the Bible and swear.

(Boy you the only one reading this. I do not care to reveal my name here. Only that I am a earthen vessel for Gods glory. I am not one to say much to testify, cause I got a

heap of shame right now, but you need the Lord. I will die here as I deserve. But we all here for glory. When I die you glorify God. This is too long now to redo the cursive in print. But let me know, I can do the next one in print.)

Crystal

....

EARLIER THAT MONDAY MORNING, Crystal had stirred from bed before Aimee. She woke in a sweat, confusing the sounds of braking tractor trailers on Route 40 with the chorus of locusts that plagued her dream. She felt about her neck and thighs unconsciously for any locusts that might have pulled through the eddies between dream world and waking. She sat up and let the locusts' breath of fire go blue and cold.

Crystal did not sort through the vision. She dressed in the jeans and blouse hanging on the spike nail in the wall and sat on her bed, waiting in the dark. She heard Aimee's bed breathe open when her lovely body lifted from it, heard her get up and walk barefoot on the linoleum. So easy to hear through the makeshift wall of two-by-fours and particle board their daddy had put up to divide them when Crystal was fourteen and Aimee twelve. He'd promised to put up solid sheetrock when they could afford it and to paint the walls any color they wanted. Now, Crystal was nearly twenty-six, and she still lived by the rhythmic breathing-open and breathing-shut of Aimee's bed. The particle board was beginning to bow, curving slightly away. It cupped Aimee's sound and sent it through to Crystal so she could hear her sister's sleeping all the better.

When she foresaw her sister's figure at the sink—slight in the nightgown sewn for a teen girl—Crystal went to the hallway and looked down it to where the kitchen floor opened up. She remembered their daddy's tall frame and broad build, how he'd filled the long, narrow hall, blocking out the light behind him so she couldn't see his face when he spoke. She had never been sure, in those moments, whether the words had come from his mouth or from someplace else.

She walked to the kitchen, expecting Aimee to go back on her word, though Crystal hadn't decided whether or not she would let her call off the trip to the prison. Crystal also expected Aimee to say something mean and unintended to her, as one expects a strike from a snake with its belly cut open and nothing to shield it.

Later, when they got back home from King's and closed the doors of the white pickup behind them, Crystal let Aimee go into the trailer first. She let the front screen door slap and then followed, up the two cinder-block steps. Her sleeve snagged on the faded blue lattice. Harsh splinters tore a tiny hole in the sleeve where it puffed out a little and showed the blouse to be feminine despite its work-filthy front. These splinters looked fresh, like someone had busted a piece in the lattice recently—could be the Dixon boys were throwing stones. The lattice needed fixing in other places, too, and Crystal would work at it when she got home from Cool Springs in the evening.

In her room, she changed the blouse for an old-but-clean white T-shirt of her daddy's, with *Jesus Saves* airbrushed in purple and gold. It hung loose on her torso. Her body was still young, her breasts like child breasts. She undid her hair and then tied it again, pulling its thin strings back from her plain broad face. She glanced in the mirror and closed her mouth to hide the teeth too large. With her mouth shut, she looked like she held marbles or barreled-up curses in there, ready to be spit. She left for work on foot, carrying nothing.

Crystal took a left on Route 40 for the half-hour walk into town, passing the field that served as grounds for the annual Coal Heritage Fair. It was early morning yet, and the rides were still closed up on themselves like jacks-in-the-box. Men had the tents spread flat on the patchy grass so thirsty for dew.

In town, she turned right on Manheim Road, which followed the Donnie Manse River. She walked past the cemetery, where the treeless river bank showed her the orange rocks and the sick sulfur water. The cemetery was only half real, people in Cuzzert said, since, when the river had flooded in 1985, it had unearthed the coffins and swept the headstones and the bodies of the dead downriver. The only grave it had left standing was that of Janey Close's stillborn baby, marked with a big stone cross, even though the baby had been buried for less than a year and its ground had not yet settled. People had reassembled the order of the graves as best they could. They'd put up new stones and chiseled epitaphs that, in spite of things, still began, *Here lies so-and-so.*

She walked past the Methodist church, with its vinyl-sided addition that had housed a number of things, one of which was a crisis pregnancy center started up by the Methodist preacher's wife. Crystal walked past where Aubrey Falls stayed in the one-room cabin he rented from the preacher. She used to pass his cabin without waving when he'd first come to Cuzzert. Now, even though she suspected he would leave soon enough, she waved and looked to his window. But he would be teaching his class at the prison by now.

She walked faster when the unlit *Eat* sign at Cool Springs came into view around the bend.

A slow morning breeze tried to comfort Crystal through the threadbare under-arm in her T-shirt as she plucked the feeding bucket from the wall of the shed out behind the shop-and-diner. Balaam stood by the locomotive husk, rubbing his neck against the hard iron. He turned toward her when she stirred a cup of molasses in with the oats chop. She held out some chop in her palm, and he raised his head, then dropped it down in a mope. She'd named him Balaam after the Old Testament seer, from the Book of Numbers, who was sent to speak a curse over Israel but who spoke a blessing instead, after his donkey saw an angel and opened its mouth and spoke.

Her Balaam and a standoffish peacock were all that remained of the petting zoo at Cool Springs. The place had been a real attraction in Cuzzert back when the town had thrived, with its petting zoo and mountain crafts for sale—quilts and cherrywood rockers, guardian angels carved of coal—and with its show-case of obsolete train and tractor engines from the thirties. Kids could climb into a caboose for the camera. They could buy a balsa-wood postcard stamped *Cuzzert, West Virginia*, or a panorama photo of the hairpin curve just past Cool Springs on Manheim Road.

Once the mines had mechanized and gone to strip, towns like Cuzzert were gutted. A Wal-Mart went up in Biggs, the town twenty minutes to the west that got lucky and kept alive, maybe because it sat where the Donnie Manse River emptied into the Monongahela—joined to something of greater speed and force. Kids wanted Wal-Mart's cheap toys and the water park that opened next door. A daytrip to climb on train skeletons didn't stand a chance.

Cool Springs had been reduced to a truck stop for drivers headed to Biggs or down to Charleston. It had attracted some prison traffic too, when the facility had first come in, but that had dwindled once the novelty of the place wore off. The owner kept Cool Springs open for the profit he made selling lottery tickets; he ordered the other merchandise at random, as if for a joke. He'd gone absentee, moved to Ohio, and hired Crystal as caretaker—she'd still been speaking then—and to serve up the coffee and cones. Some local people came to Cool Springs for buckwheat flour and the peaches from Romney, cheap at fourteen-fifty a bushel. Some came for a leather jacket with fringes, a rubber tomahawk or a half-moon outhouse miniature. And some came for a look at the Lemley girl who'd quit talking; they came out of reverence and contempt both.

Crystal stroked Balaam's ears till he jerked away in a huff. Idle, she couldn't help but think about her daddy in a prison cell. It was a place she couldn't envision, except that she imagined everything steel gray. Aubrey had told her and Aimee a week before that their daddy was there. He'd been sentenced in April of that year, to serve time just an hour's drive from Painted Rocks, for hitting a woman on a north Pennsylvania highway. And he had stopped taking meals. He had hit a woman with his truck and become as though dead, near starved, and all but nameless until that past week when he had written in a paper for Aubrey's class his name, Cord Lemley, and his claim that, yes, he had a wife and two girls heir to his shame. Two girls he had not sent a word to of his own volition.

Crystal could almost hear his voice, the way he must whisper his prayers from his bed. Could almost feel the words strike the cold, blank walls and return to him void, filling his own ears till he couldn't stand the sound. She shook his voice from her head, but it hovered above her, first his praying voice, then his preaching voice, hard and pointed. She felt the quivering spot inside her, pulsing with Word of the Lord, the jabber of tongues she had uttered, hymns she had sung low and true at each Glorybound Holiness Tabernacle service. She willed it all inside the rough gray hide of the donkey, as though sewing a pouch of money inside a pillow. She marveled that Balaam could bear it. She nearly expected him to speak.

The peacock came around the shed's corner, its tail dragging like a fine broom. It pecked the kernels Crystal tossed it but wouldn't fan its broad beauty for her. She stood and walked the path back to the shop-and-diner, through the antique tractors and train cars, machines sprouting from the ground, truncated. A pony farm tractor had turned brown like the tree leaves in drought, along with a Shay engine that had been overworked with glory and fire. It was a museum or a graveyard. Little difference between the two.

A man-dug stream cut through the path, calling for an arched bridge, perhaps pretty once. A lethargic trout swam the stream as though the water were tar. At one time, kids must have tried to fish out the trout, because someone had padlocked a wire mesh over the stream so that only coins could drop through to line the cement streambed. These were the cool springs. Hardly the pool of Bethesda where the angel's finger stirs. Hardly enough water that the trout didn't drag its belly.

A blue station wagon pulled in as Crystal reached the front door. She turned to see the butt of the car wag as Arlene Sisler and her kids piled out. Crystal felt the sun, then, in all its force, and thought it cruel, somehow making a fool of everyone who woke with it.

"Get your sister a Hershey's," Arlene called, pulling her large self out the driver-side door, then pulling out her foster girl by the arm. The youngest boy, Chris, hollered his items at Crystal: pig's-ear treats for his dog, so many lengths of heavy chain and some live bait. The older one, Loyal, had come with more Mountain Dew can rockers, peeled and twisted into shape with his pocketknife—wanting to know if she could maybe get ten dollars for one. Arlene cursed the heat, cursed her kids and their talk as it scattered like buckshot. Crystal held the door open to the shop-and-diner as the Sislers rattled inside.

"Kay!" Arlene said with a pinched moan, and Kay emerged from the extra-large hunting jackets, smearing melted Hershey's on a sleeve. The child was nearly three and still walked naked from the waist down, wearing only a short black T-shirt that said *Princess* in faded blond print. Kay was a smaller version of Arlene, all of one piece, with a stunted neck and feet that splayed under her weight. The child answered Arlene's call with a vague cock of her head.

Arlene began a disheveled pile by the cash register on the counter: a red oil lantern, a cedar birdhouse painted with the words *Bird Hotel*, a dozen fly traps. After years of getting a welfare check at the first of the month, she kept up her habit of doing her shopping then, even though she no longer received her government check. Since the prison had settled with them for their farm in 1994, the Sislers, by Cuzzert standards, had become well off.

"Nothing worse than trash coming into money," Miriam Louks had said to Dotte out at Glorybound once, and Crystal had heard. Dotte had hushed Miriam because Arlene was her cousin by marriage—married her second-cousin Hiram Sisler who'd died in the mines the year their oldest son Ronnie was saved at one of Cord's revivals. Ronnie Sisler started coming to Glorybound by himself, a thirteen-year-old quick to get the Spirit. During the hymns, his face broke out in a sweat, as though with fever, and Crystal had spent a lot of time watching his watery eyes that rolled up to the basement ceiling.

The first thing Arlene had done with the prison money was buy a satellite dish and plastic patio furniture for her new front yard on the east edge of town, just past Jimmy Shrout's Muffler Barn on Manheim Road.

The second thing was to send Ronnie down to Charleston for auto-mechanic school, trying to get him away from Glorybound, because Arlene deemed the path of the Spirit the path of fools. When he got into the snake-handling church down there, he wrote to her and said he had quit school and found the Lord's work. He'd given all his tuition money to the Whosoever Will Worship Center of the True Pentecost, and he'd taken up serpents.

The third thing she'd done was put five hundred dollars cash inside a greeting card with a teddy bear on it and left it on Dotte's front steps. On the inside, Arlene had written: "I blame your crazy preacher husband for taking my Ronald from me. It ain't your fault. But you ought leave that church behind you." Then, underneath the card's message, *Sending you a teddy bear hug,* she'd finished with: "Husbands don't leave nothing but bills and mouths to feed. Get you and the girls something nice. Love, Arlene."

"This here's the best of the bunch," said Loyal, his pale, freckled face beaming. He set the Mountain Dew rocker on the counter and rocked it back and forth. It sat a little crooked, but Crystal picked it up, stuck a piece of masking tape on its seat and wrote "$10." She held the pen out to Loyal with the roll of tape.

"What she want, Mom?" he said, scratching his freckles like they were a rash.

Arlene grabbed the pen and tape and told him he was to write his own ten-dollar tags. "God, girl, it'd be easier if you just said things outright." Crystal offered no apology for herself. Arlene was on edge; she was usually kinder, or at least she didn't usually aim her meanness at Crystal.

"Man alive, if life ain't already sucked from you, you'd better die soon 'fore people take hold." Arlene shook her head, went to the door and fingered the variegated leaves on a topiary tree sitting just outside. Ivy climbed its central pole, and pink petunias vined down from a plastic pot on top. She sighed and slapped at a fly. Crystal waited at the counter for Arlene's litany of complaints and cursings, ready to absorb them like a rag wiping up a spill. Dusty miller and lobelia bushed from the big bottom pot of the topiary. The tree was ridiculous, priced at twenty-five dollars, the most whimsical thing in the row of plants that lined the storefront, wilting its fine leaves in the heat. Arlene had Chris drag the tree to the counter.

"Thing is," Arlene said, heaving herself back over toward Crystal, "my sister told me she saw my Ronnie's truck drive up by her place just south of here a couple days back. Can't mistake it for another 'cause the doors don't match, green and black on red. I ain't seen hide nor hair of him since he went down for school—five years now and I ain't had one letter or check, not even one of them damn gospel tracts he give me when he was wrapped up with your daddy."

Crystal's face flushed hot. She started itemizing the purchases on a Cool Springs carbon paper receipt.

"I was pretty damn shore he done died from snakebite or poison, one, and I wasn't too sorry 'cause the boy robbed me blind for them fanatics down there, after I tried to do right by him and send him to school. Thing is, Miss Crystal, if he's back, I don't want him taking up with you church people again." Arlene reached for Crystal's hand and stopped her awkward cursive flow.

"Thing is, I got money hid where nobody knows it, not even these two boys here, and they ain't got sense enough to find it, but some of it come up missing yesterday. I won't say how much. Ronnie's in thick with you holy rollers, for some goddamn reason. I don't blame you, you're a victim of your daddy's foolishness. But I ain't in favor of him taking up with you again, and your loose sister and your poor mama. You all a pack of crazies." Arlene bit her lip, looked steady at Crystal and swatted at Kay who was pulling on her pant leg.

"I know your church been hard up ever since your daddy left. 'Course Miriam Louks got enough money to feed the lot of you and pay for a new preacher both, if she weren't so damn tight. It might be that Ronnie'd come by here. Maybe tell you things, or give you a little something to take care of. Seeing's how you're so nice and quiet."

Crystal looked down and drew her hand back. Arlene waited, seemed to expect her to speak her mind, but silence allowed Crystal no defense and no corroboration. She hovered, ever appearing as one without judgment. The silence hung between them and soon grew uncomfortable enough for Arlene to start bagging her own heap of fly traps and Skittles and pig's-ears. She set out a wad of cash for payment, and Crystal finished itemizing the receipt.

"Shit," Arlene exhaled. She plucked a Slim Jim from a pack she'd bought and slid it to Crystal across the counter. Maybe a sort of bribe, maybe an apology. She took on a hard pity in her voice: "What do you think about, girl? Where do you go? Don't you got words for nobody?" Crystal detached the customer copy of the receipt and handed it to Arlene.

Loyal gathered up the sacks, and Chris dragged the tree to the car. Crystal followed them out to the gravel lot, watched Kay smear the Hershey's into her hair until Arlene took and threw it in the gravel. The station wagon signaled and pulled out for the two-mile drive down Manheim to their place on the edge of Cuzzert. Crystal pictured the car for the length of the drive, the length of the worn-out mountain town that lay beside a river flowing with rust and acidic mine soup. She stood by the door in the dark wet circle where the topiary tree had sat on the ground. She squatted like a catcher and put the Slim Jim in her mouth, to suck on the salt and smoke before she chewed it.

It had been a long time since Crystal had felt the need to defend someone besides Aimee or Dotte. Before Ronnie had left five years ago, he had taken two sixteen-penny nails and put them together in a cross, had wound it with copper wire and given it to Crystal after the sending service they'd called for him at Glorybound. He'd given it to her without touching her; she'd kept her silence and felt like she was drowning. She hadn't even shown the cross of nails to Aimee. After Ronnie had gone, Crystal had hid it under a loose corner of carpet in her room and cried.

That's what people do in Cuzzert, she understood within her silent self. They leave. They go without saying goodbye. But she stayed, that's what she did. She touched the sharpness of their small secret gifts, and she inhabited their old clothes, as she did her daddy's jeans that she bunched with a belt, his airbrushed T-shirt. When Ronnie left, she had expected it, since the tiny church was dying already. All the young people, except for her and Aimee and Ronnie at that time, had already left Glorybound for the Methodist church across from the cemetery. The Methodists had an electric guitar player, not just the acoustic and tambourines. And some drove all the way to Biggs because a church there had a whole rock band, and the young folks could forget their small assembly in the basement of Miriam Louks' dead aunt's house. Could leave behind the strange, thick vapor of waiting that the church still soaked in, as though, after so many years, they thought Reverend Cord Lemley would return. Or maybe Jesus.

Crystal rose from her squat and clapped at Balaam, who had come along the path behind her. He was chewing on the potted junipers near the door. She faced up the road, toward its hairpin turn nearly smothering under the shag of dry trees. She saw Aimee's face in it, pictured her for a moment.

That morning, when Aimee had pulled their white pickup into its dirt spot beside the blue lattice, when they'd sat there in silence before getting out—the first silence of the day after all of Aimee's hectic talk—the quiet had rung out in the cab and out the windows, had hit the remote things strewn around Painted Rocks like toys in a child's playpen and had ricocheted back in, vibrating and welling up, till Aimee spoke: "I been saying Daddy's dead for so long, I almost made myself believe it." Then they'd gotten out, Crystal letting Aimee go a few steps ahead.

Reverend Cord Paul Lemley—titled "Reverend" by self-appointment, and Holy-Spirit-anointed as a prophet of God, not ordained by any official church—had left them ten years before. He had taken over the preaching at Glorybound Holiness Tabernacle at age seventeen. Marty Noose, the tent revivalist who had led Cord and Dotte to the Lord and to that tiny basement church in Cuzzert, had laid hands on Cord and willed the church leadership to him just before Marty followed his wife into Glory.

Dotte made dresses to sell and did some mending for people, and Cord got a job driving a truck for Biggs Wholesale during the week, delivering cases of Doritos and Fritos to the gas stations in the county, boxes of peanuts, tinfoil, Sunkist pop, everything. He preached for love-offerings at Glorybound, mostly pocket change, but he considered his preaching the work of the Lord, and he trusted the Lord to provide. Cord preached at Glorybound for fourteen years, then left in his delivery truck one morning at dawn with a suitcase and a bag of peanut butter and bread, after he predicted the Second Coming of Jesus and Jesus did not come.

It had to do with the signs. Crystal kept records of the signs in the black-cover notebook she loved, which she later stowed under the loose corner of carpet with Ronnie Sisler's nail cross.

The first sign came just after the flood of the Donnie Manse River in 1985. Every man in Cuzzert was called upon to help restore the cemetery that had lost all its dead except the stillborn baby of Janey Close. Driving there on a morning soon after the waters receded, Cord was listening to a radio preacher speaking on Ezekiel 37 and the signs of the end times and the coming-back of Jesus Christ. As he pulled off Manheim Road, where the crowd with shovels and pickaxes congregated, the radio preacher read verses 13 and 14: "And ye shall know that I am the Lord, when I have opened your graves, O my people, and brought you up out of your graves, and shall put my spirit in you, and ye shall live." Cord turned off the ignition and sat and listened for the voice of God to keep on.

That night, he opened his leather-bound Bible to Ezekiel 37 and read more about the opened graves and, earlier in the same chapter, about Ezekiel being set down in the valley of bones, and God telling him to breathe into those dry bones, that they may rise up and live, and sinews and flesh may come upon them. Cord was reading the words in the back room he called his study, and he heard a rustle outside his window, between their trailer and the Dixons'. He switched off his light, looked out the window and saw the Dixons' skinny husky wrestling with a dried deer carcass. The dog had broken his chain and the part of it he dragged behind him was tangled in the deer's rib cage.

Crystal was in the living room outside the door of Cord's study, and he called her in to show her the passage in Ezekiel and the carcass the dog had brought over to his window. He told her about the preacher on the radio that morning and said, "You know what this means, Crystal Lee Ann?" She said she did not. "It's the signs of his coming. Our Jesus coming for us, to take us to the Overjordan. You watch."

Later that night, she slipped out the door of the back screen-porch and rounded the corner to the pile of bones abandoned by the Dixons' dog. She touched a tiny bone, one that had broken like a stick, not at the joint but in the middle so that it had splintered. She kept it and put it under her corner of carpet.

Cord watched for signs for the next three years, but God kept silent. Crystal began to fill her notebook with other things. A letter to Ronnie Sisler. A poem she read at school that she hand-copied into her notebook because it sounded like a hymn. A list of things to do before the rapture—she made the list with Aimee on the back porch with their voices in a hush and their knees drawn up to let air in under their skirts.

"He's a coming," Cord preached at Glorybound on Sunday mornings and at the Wednesday night prayer services he started up. "The end times is upon us; is your heart ready? How's your heart tonight? Is it saying, 'Come, Lord Jesus, come'?" Crystal closed her eyes at the services and prayed and called up a face in her mind that might be Jesus' face, but sometimes it was Ronnie's, and sometimes, at home, she got out the splintery bone of the deer from underneath the carpet, and she pricked herself to know it was real.

Then the second sign struck. One night Cord didn't come home from his delivery run for the wholesale. It was past supper already, and Dotte was jittery. She sat at the table, taking in a skirt at the waist from a bag of secondhand clothes Miriam Louks had given her for the girls. A storm had come up in a rush, moving northward from the river and from town, a harsh choir of rain then hail on the trailer's thin roof. It didn't last more than twenty minutes, but when Crystal opened the door afterward, looked out to the road and saw a tree down on a power line and limbs strewn all over Route 40, she knew something had happened to her daddy.

She ran back through the long hallway of the doublewide, out the back door and up the front steps of the Dixons' trailer, pounding on the door till Joshie Dixon opened up.

"Gimme your bike," Crystal said to him, and he picked his face acne and said something foul, but she ran around to the side where his mountain bike leaned against the trailer. Before he could stop her, she was riding south on Route 40, around the downed branches, headed toward Biggs where Cord was supposed to be coming from.

She found him about half a mile from Painted Rocks, in the hayfield that opened up from the road, the field used as a fairground every summer. The wholesale truck sat pulled off to the shoulder, its door hanging open. She left the bike and ran out toward a lump of dark clothes lying in the middle of the grass like something dead, but it moved, and she saw it was him. She called for him, and he lifted his arm, lifted his body almost, then collapsed again.

He had a small black line on his neck, in a crooked slice, and blood sat on it but didn't flow out. The chain he wore around his neck with a copper cross pendant was charcoal black, and the skin beneath it red and raw, but it was his side that he held as he moaned. A hole had burned into his work shirt there, and the skin beneath bore a black mark like the one on his neck, this one in the shape of a fern.

"I saw him, Crys," he murmured, and some of the skin of his lips peeled off like paper from a candy. "A blue robe, and his hair like gold. I saw him in the open field, beckoning to me, and I had nothing but to leave the truck and run to him, though I heard the thunder come up like a wave."

Crystal cleared the grass by his head of the old litter from last year's Heritage Fair. A popcorn cup and a cotton candy bag, the half-eaten candy wisps gone gray. A bird circled, soundless, overhead. She touched her daddy's hand, the one that didn't grasp his side but lay open on the coarse grass. It was so rare that they touched. She was surprised to find his hand cold and not much bigger than her own.

The lightning had entered the right side of his neck and exited out the right side of his torso, a curve of electrical fire. The shock had traveled around his neck in that chain, too, and the doctors at the Biggs hospital had no idea how Cord had survived. Cord knew exactly how, and he wasn't shy to tell it to the whole burn ward of the hospital. His wounded side, like that of Jesus, was confirmation enough of the coming day of Christ—Jesus coming up even in Cord's own body and showing himself in the fern-shaped bruise. He recounted for the nurses the story of how he was saved when lightning had struck that bar years ago, how the tent preacher had looked him in the eye, and the rain had poured, and how that was no coincidence, no sir.

"And my life done been spared," he claimed, "so's I can testify, buddy," and he went on for awhile, his black hair and black eyes wild against the whiteness of the hospital walls and beds and faces. He went on till he was released, and he went on at Glorybound after that.

"I can still taste the copper in my mouth from that lightning bolt," he said to the faithful standing up on the green carpet of that basement floor and clapping. "And I can taste glory, I can taste me that milk and honey Overjordan, yes, and I say *glory*, can you say it with me, *glory*?"

Crystal had gone back to that field the evening after the storm, and on the far edge where the tree line started, on a pile of picked rocks, she'd found a blue kite that had broken loose from its string. It had a tail of white and yellow plastic streamers, and she tore a white one off and put it in her pocket. At home, she got out her notebook and started a clean page. "August 9, 1988," she wrote, "I saw the Lord's hand on my daddy. I am some scared, but it must be that the Lord does not make a mistake. I will make my heart ready. I will make my robe white, mine and Aimee Jo's."

In her long skirts that her mom made and her ankle socks and canvas shoes, with her hair braided and her neckline snug, Crystal paid strict attention to her daddy's words after the sign of the lightning. She ate his words and lived by them. Almost sixteen years old, she became an apprentice to Cord in his prophesying of the coming of Christ. She had always sung strong in the service, but now he called on her to pray, even though she was shy and she was not sure what Ronnie Sisler thought of her praying. She tried not to think much about Ronnie Sisler at all.

Cord seated Crystal beside him at the Tabernacle to read Scripture and bounce the tambourine with the heel of her hand, leaving Aimee seated back beside Dotte. Aimee was fourteen years old and so much like a child to Crystal then, a sheep for her tending, a lost sheep, for Crystal had begun to glimpse in her sister's dark eyes a worrisome fear. Crystal's own eyes would smart if she looked on Aimee for too long, so she allowed a separation. She shut her eyes and prayed hard, prayed a circle of protection like a split-rail fence around her lost-lamb sister.

Crystal had learned to read with the Bible as her primer. She'd learned by the rhythms of the King James Version, the images of the seven lamps of the seven churches, the lake of fire, the dry bones coming into sinew, the woman and the beast with horns. And now in the rhythms of her daddy's voice, she knew the words already in her mind. She repeated them under her breath as he spoke, and she expected it all, as though she foresaw it, this thing that was coming upon them. It was no longer Ronnie's face she conjured in her mind's eye when she prayed and sang and swayed. It was her daddy's face—she willed herself to see it—his face sweating from the lightning's fierce brand. That lightning that surely meant her daddy was a holy prophet of God.

The next year, in July of 1989, the strip mine out on Cuzzert Pike, a few miles west of where the Tabernacle met in Miriam Louks' basement, broke a water seam and leaked coal sludge into the well water of twelve households surrounding the mine, three of which were households of Glorybound members. The ruined water was the third and final sign Cord needed to make his prediction.

Such disasters had happened before, even to Cord's own family when he was a boy, but not on such a scale. This was the pinnacle, Cord said and Crystal recorded. The mining company, a CONROY branch run by a proprietor in Biggs, without so much as an apology put a notice in the residents' mailboxes announcing they would bring in five thousand-gallon water reservoirs on trucks to serve as the new water supply, to be refilled monthly at the company's expense. It was not a temporary remedy. Big, white, plastic tanks sitting along the road and snaking into houses through hoses.

No one filed a complaint. Crystal had learned young, like everyone in Cuzzert: people wronged by CONROY, they go without their due, and they go without a fuss, and they wait for someone like her daddy to find a holy purpose in it. Her daddy obliged.

The trucks would come on July twelfth. So Cord set the date: Jesus was to return on August 21, 1989, forty days after they'd pull the water tanks in, forty days of desert and tanked-in water that would quench no thirst.

"For the second angel sounded," Cord preached to his people, and especially to the Feltons, the Shrouts, and Ashby and Tim Welch whose wells the mine had poisoned. "And, in Revelation 8 now, 'as it were a great mountain burning with fire was cast into the sea, and the third part of the sea became blood.' And Verse 10, 'the third angel sounded, and there fell a great star from heaven, burning as it were a lamp, and it fell upon the third part of the rivers, and upon the fountains of waters. And the name of the star is called Wormwood, and the third part of the waters became wormwood, and many men died of the waters, because they were made bitter.' Here speaks the Lord, people, here is the signs that he give us. Here is the signs."

Cord claimed to know the day though not the hour. August 21. It was also Crystal's sixteenth birthday. He asked his congregation to pack a suitcase, in the event that the battle of Armageddon began and they had to flee. He planned the caravan route to run north toward Pennsylvania, and he had Dotte stock his delivery truck with water, gospel tracts, peanut butter and white bread.

But he didn't call the saints to a mount, nor even to the basement church with its green carpet and metal smell of folding chairs. Instead, he instructed all to turn on their televisions to the local network on the twenty-first—that was the way Christ would come in modern times. On the screen of the TVs that sat in every household of the high and the low, so all the world would see the glory coming, as it said in Revelation 13: "And he doeth great wonders, so that he maketh fire come down from heaven on the earth in the sight of men." No way for it to happen in the sight of all men, said Cord, unless it's on the TV screen.

The Lemleys sat in their doublewide and watched the television that day from 4 a.m. on—leaving the living room only to pee, muting the sound during the soap operas—till the screen turned to snow at 2 or 3 the next morning. Dotte finally turned the TV off and started sobbing. She was wearing a new dress she'd made, all white with white, rose-shaped buttons up the back. The air in the trailer was hot, and Cord sat with his shirt unbuttoned down to his chest, his black, coiled hair tufting out like field grass, and he ran his fingers through it. He rubbed his side where the fern-shaped bruise showed through his thin shirt, and he said nothing except, "I done my part."

He looked at no one and peeled himself from his armchair. Crystal had fallen asleep on the couch with Aimee's head in her lap. She jolted awake when she heard the trailer's front screen door slam shut, and she slid out from under Aimee to follow her daddy.

She watched his oversized feet drag as he staggered to the delivery truck. He was, of a sudden, like a piece of burning paper to her. She saw him curl to black in a fire, as though the lightning's heat had never completely gone out of him. Some of it had stayed inside him and burned him up slow. He chose fire for his own portion, the price, he'd told her—and she'd written down in her notebook—for being able to speak the prophecies of God and the unforeseen. She was half dreaming, wiping the sleep from her eyes with the white sleeve of her blouse. In the dark, dust swarmed like smoke after the wholesale truck when he pulled out of Painted Rocks. Crystal watched from under the holey shelter of the blue lattice. She tasted the dust. That night in her notebook she wrote: "I have eaten the ashes of my daddy's fire."

Jesus didn't come. Her birthday, August twenty-first, turned still and soured like milk in the heat. And her daddy left.

Cord

....

#96309

May 19, 1999

What advice would you give your son?

I got no witness left in this place. A radio preacher I heard one time said a mans sin done spoilt his testimony. It is a rug stained by blood and dirt. The second thing is I never had no son. I had 2 girls and my wife had a miscarry between them 2 and was flat in bed for a month. What come out of her did not take on shape. It was just blood, but from being begot we believed it had the Lord Gods breath in its nostrils, so we named it for a boy, name of Amos from the Word. If he was living I would say to him by way of advice—Amos do not go a hard way to God like I done. And I knew real young that I would go that harder way. I got a shadow of it when I was a boy at my Uncle Jacks farm. He and my Aunt Gail lived close us in Roane about 5 mile off. He raised me up part time after Mama past. When my Daddy got so drunk he slept in town on the bar floor and did not come home. Me and my sisters went back and forth them 5 miles between till we was grown.

I got the shadow of my future way at Uncle Jacks when he was preaching holiness to me. He was a <u>sanctified</u> man, I mean that he walked the Straight and Narrow. Uncle Jack took me out on the porch, it was a cold night and he said to me—Boy our bodies like a jailhouse for the Soul, these here skins keep our Souls trapped up in sin. Apostle Paul said to keep down your body and bring it thus to subjection so you can be purified, and be ye holy as I am holy, God said. He shook me and ask if I heard and yes I did. Then he put me on the prayer stool he made. Maybe you never seen one—a 2 by

4 pointed downward in front with two legs nailed on the end like a bench. Uncle Jack made me kneel there—you put your legs back through underneath and sit on the 2 by 4—I stayed like that. Uncle Jack said one more thing—When your Mama birthed you your Soul got full distorted, if you want it should be purified for glory one appointed day then you work the sinhold free in the fear of God.

Then Uncle Jack went in the house and switched the light off, I was there kneeling on the stool in the dark. I could not see nothing, but I knowed the edge of the porch with a great precipice off it and the ground underneath slanting to the wood shed, which I knowed where it was cause the wind was beating the door again the metal wall of the shed. I sat there for close 4 hours and the temptations rose up. Like I wanted to hate my Uncle Jack and I wanted my Daddy to die instead of my Mama. After a time I could not feel my legs and I cried out to God and repented for my being so full of hatred. But I done cried out silent. I struck my legs to feel them but I could not. Then I repented out loud, after that I went quiet and fell forward off the stool. At that time Aunt Gail come out the house with a quilt and wrapped me in it and took me inside by the fire. I see this now like a shadow of my coming a hard way to the Lord, cause it took me so long to repent out loud to Him. Then I forgot the Lord for many years after, like I done wrote in my last paper.

One thing more I would say to Amos if he was living—Amos do not put idols up above the Lord God even if they are kin to you. Jesus said in the 10 chapter of Matthew—A mans foes shall be they of his own household. He that loveth father or mother more than Me is not worthy of Me, and he that loveth son or daughter more than Me is not worthy of Me. That is a hard Word but it is the true Word. I know it cause it come upon me to follow it. And he might be called upon to follow it. That is what I have to say to Amos. To God be glory.

(Boy you done wrote a note on my last paper—Did I ever find out more why my Mama died beside the fact of her being a bleeder—and Did I want to write more description of her. For the first, I know all I need to. I seen how much blood can come from a woman, cause of my wifes miscarry like I write here. It is only by Gods hand she did not die like Mama. For the second part, Mamas name was Sissy, though not her real name but what people called her. You might not believe but she had 3 dresses only, and she kept them fit. I <u>never</u> saw no tear on her dress nor no stain. She filled her supper plate after Daddy and me and my sisters done filled ours. You do not notice these type things as a young boy but I do remember now.)

Dotte

....

DOTTE HAD HEARD HER GIRLS LEAVE in the white pickup when Monday morning still hung dark. The pickup sounded like a man with a chest cough that rattled him through.

After they went, she raised her heavy self from bed and lit a cigarette. She had smoked since she was twelve, when her older brother had made her. After she and Cord got saved she gave it up, but she was back at it now, even first thing in the morning. The new smoke mixed with the old. The air in her room was thick curtains of smoke.

Dotte left her room in bare feet and just her big nightgown with the top buttons undone. The top of the gown sagged in a permanent way. She got her black sweater from off the back of the kitchen chair and pulled it around her like a shawl, without filling the arms up. She saw a cheese wrapper on the counter and the half pot of coffee turned off to drink when she wanted.

She knew it was too early, but she dialed up Miriam Louks on the wall phone. It was Monday, and that week was the Coal Heritage Fair in Cuzzert, put on by CONROY. The Monday paper from Biggs would announce the high school girl who got Queen Coal in Sunday's pageant at the VFW, the girl who proved she could hang an evening dress on her body so the straps stayed put when she danced onto the stage. Dotte didn't get the paper.

"Who is it this year, Miriam?" she whispered into the phone when the other end picked up. "You look at your *Weekly Register*?" It was a little after five in the morning. She talked soft, like she didn't want to wake Miriam all the way.

"Who? Who you say? Is that Dotte?"

"Yes, it's Dotte," even softer. "Could you tell me who got queen this year? Could you read from the *Register*?"

"Mercy. These is God's hours, Dotte. Not mine."

"Please, could you look for me?"

"Right now?"

"Could you please?"

"Mercy."

Dotte heard *mercy* again, then a grunt. Then, "Hang on."

Dotte waited, listening to Miriam set down the phone, pull a housecoat onto her skinny body and go down her stairs. Then she heard nothing when Miriam must have gone out to the plastic box by the Cuzzert Pike. It said *Biggs Weekly Register* on it, beside two black mailboxes, one Miriam's and one the Tabernacle's mailbox that never got any mail. In time, Dotte heard her climb back up the stairs and pick up the phone, out of breath.

"Here on the front, Dotte. It says, 'Charlene Marie Sparr.' Not a girl you know at all, from Biggs High School. She's got some pretty teeth, though. Daughter of Richard Sparr and the late Maude Sparr. Poor girl's mama died, looks like. No one to keep her from the vain things."

"Where's it say she gets the dress from?"

"Same as every year, Dotte. That outfit out in Maryland, Stephanie's Bridal."

"Do they have a pitcher of the dress?"

"No."

"Thank you, Miriam. I hate to trouble you."

"Why do you want to know, Dotte? It's a vain thing."

"I hate to trouble you. I thank you." Dotte still kept to a whisper. She hung up the phone and draped her sweater over the chair where it had been. Its sleeves touched the floor. She retraced her path on the yellow linoleum that was gray in the dawn light barely coming down on it. She moved toward her room to lie down till noon, moved slow and with a rocking of her body back and forth. She said the name as she went, "Charlene Sparr. Charlene Marie Sparr."

It used to be that she made all the dresses for the fair except the queen's. Four dresses, and they all four matched. Two for the older girls, the pageant runners-up to the queen, and then two for the young girls, about eight years old. That was like making dresses for dolls, they were so small.

When she made a dress, she took the measurements in her living room with the girl standing on an overturned pail. Bust and waist, neck, width of her back between the armholes, front and back skirt length. Girls came with their mamas to the trailer in Painted Rocks. They stood for their measurements and left without much talk or a look-around.

Dotte was barely twenty when she started doing the dresses for the fair, but already had both her daughters. She used to embroider her initials inside the skirt hem: D. J. S. L. Dorothy Jean Sisler Lemley, with the letters curling into each other. The bottom tip of the S swooped up into the curl of the L top. Cord saw her doing it once because she did her sewing in the open corner of the living room on her electric-power Singer. He made her stop doing the initials, to root out pridefulness.

Cord never liked that she made the pretty dresses in the first place. The ones she made for her girls had to be plain. Except for their baptism dress because that one was for the Lord's favor and not for men's. Crystal wore it first, as a little girl, then Aimee. The lightest pink cotton, down to the ankle, lace trim on the square neck and the skirt hem, and a pink belt in a bow. Dotte made the long sleeves from a see-through material, like veil cloth. My, the girls looked like little angels flapping wings when Cord leaned them back into the Donnie Manse River. Every baptism he saw through was dunked under, except for the saddest one: Ronnie Sisler's. That boy couldn't go under. They all rejoiced him coming to the Lord, but sadness won out in his soul. It was the year his daddy died in the mine.

Dotte recalled it like a picture in front of her. Cord took Ronnie out into the river, right behind Paint Davis' bar. Ronnie's mama, Arlene, kept to the railing in back of Paint's and would not come down to the river bank. She was not willing that Ronnie come to Jesus. She stood alone up there with Loyal Dye crawling on her, just a baby then. It was the first river baptism since the big flood. The water still looked mean, like it would take you out.

Cord said, "He is Lord over the waters, Boy," because Ronnie looked so scared. "In the name of Father, Son, and sweet Holy Ghost," and he leaned the boy back. But Ronnie would not go. He thrashed up and near climbed Cord like a pole.

"Not like you, Daddy!" the boy yelled and started to cry. It was for fear of dying like his daddy, Dotte's cousin Hiram, who'd smothered in that mine shaft. Cord never thought a baptism was of the Lord if it was not a dunk-baptism. He tried it again, and Ronnie thrashed. He could not put his face under. After a time, Cord just laid the boy back in a deadman's float and said that counted.

It was always up to Cord how things got done, so Dotte had never made a lacy dress for her girls besides that pink one. The only reason he let her make pretty dresses for the fair was since they needed the money. One hundred dollars a dress she got paid. Besides that, the girl's family bought the material, mail-ordered by the school-teacher pageant chair in Biggs. Dotte didn't get to choose the fabric, but she always loved it, even when it was the wrong kind for the pattern. She wouldn't tell them when she knew a different material would hang better, a silkier or stouter one, depending on the pattern they sent her to cut out.

Besides telling him how they needed the money from the dressmaking, she said to Cord, "Esther was a beautiful queen in the Word." And she guessed that helped make the work okay in the eyes of God and of her husband. The tent preacher, Brother Noose, who was old and bent over, had said that about her looks as he married them. Esther, in her kin Mordecai's care, used her queen-beauty to God's glory. So it was good that she, Dotte, could make the beautiful dresses for the Coal Heritage Fair. She knew Brother Noose was being kind when he said that to her because she herself was not beautiful, even as a child bride at fifteen.

But she did make her own wedding dress, and it turned out. She made it out of eyelet curtains that Brother Noose's wife gave her. She drafted it with a yoke and a fitted bodice, but when they got married she was starting to show, four months pregnant with Crystal. She had to let it out some, and it looked more like a nightgown shape, but she'd planned it to be prettier, and did that without a pattern. She'd dreamed it off a magazine picture.

Esther was a beautiful queen who did right. Beauty itself was no sin, so it was okay for Dotte to make the dresses. She thought maybe beauty was a blessing of God's, and sometimes she thought that's why Crystal wasn't pretty, since she was conceived in sin. But she was a healthy girl because they were saved before she was born into the world.

Aimee got the beauty. God allowed it because their lives were right with him when she got conceived. About Aimee, Dotte said to Cord, "She is like a queen." But he didn't ever speak to it.

The last dresses she made for the fair, in 1989, were plum velveteen with a lighter plum-tint taffeta inlay for the bodice and the skirt both. Puffed-out sleeves that tapered to the wrist where the corsage would be worn. Gathered at the bust, like she could never do for the dresses she made her girls. Twenty-six buttons up the back for the high school girls, and eighteen for the small ones. Taffeta hair bows to match. Prettiest dresses she ever made, them and the pink baptism dress. The plum dresses were special because she knew they were the last ones she would ever make, for the Lord was coming back that summer, or that's what she thought then. And she did sew in a D. just for *Dorothy,* just for *Dotte,* since they were the last ones.

Now, Dotte shuffled into her bedroom at the end of the hallway.

"Charlene Sparr, daughter of the late Maude Sparr," she said low. She said the name once more, then clicked the door shut on the hallway and on the kitchen at the end of it and on the Dixon dog outside as he started barking at the still-dark world.

Crystal

....

BALAAM WAS INTO THE JUNIPERS AGAIN, facing Crystal in the gravel lot with guilty eyes that made her almost laugh. She shooed the sluggish donkey back along the path, around the rusted trains, and she followed him in a kind of stupor. If she were to speak, she would tell Balaam to leave that place where everything was rusted out and dying in the heat. She could say it so easy, breaking her ten-year vow of silence with a whisper to a beast of labor. She crawled onto a bench in the caboose car that was peeling green metal and giving way to briers.

She saw more folks pulling into the lot, walking through the screen door after cheap peaches or soft-serve ice cream. They all made up a body of waiting. They waited for doom or rapture at the Tabernacle, for the welfare check on the screen-porch, for enough money to leave—just to say you'd left, like Ronnie Sisler had—for that chance to shift up into fifth gear and fly on roads without hairpin turns.

She watched a trucker fiddle with a windsock hanging from the awning and waited for him to go inside so he wouldn't see her climb out of the caboose. She headed back to the shop-and-diner to run the register for them. And Monday passed that way in Cuzzert, West Virginia, with blood running thick and with an ungodly patience.

There had been nothing left for Dotte and Aimee and Crystal but to go back to Glorybound that next day without Cord Lemley. Crystal called Ronnie and asked if he would pick them up, and she heard the sleepy wonderment in his sweet voice. "Yes, we're still here," she said over the phone, "on this side of Jordan." She said it with a sadness not yet coated with anger. She said it into the wall phone in the kitchen where she saw that her daddy had left his leather-bound Bible on top of the toaster.

The people gathered at the Tabernacle like a flock of dazed birds lost on their migration route, having landed in a frozen field of snow. The church meeting was what Aimee and Crystal had always known; they had never seen the world outside of Glorybound on any Sunday morning of their lives. Nobody said much of anything at first. Dotte refused to sit in her usual chair. She stood at the back, still wearing her white dress with the white-rose buttons, looking down at the floor where Art Shrout scuffed his shoes in an irregular rhythm. Aimee sat but looked at no one. She sat beside June Tatum and kept her eyes fixed on the one window in the basement room.

Crystal stared at Elsie Felton's humped back, wondering if Elsie'd been dreaming of the straight neck and shoulders she'd have in Glory. It was Crystal, with her straw hair in a braid loose from being slept on, who led them in a praise chorus of "Hallelujah" and then, at Ashby Welch's raspy request, "Come, Lord, and Tarry Not." Ronnie Sisler strummed as best he could on the guitar that Cord had left in its case in the corner. Nobody stood up or clapped or waved, but everybody joined in, and when Ronnie's sweet tenor voice started *a cappella* with "I'll Be Somewhere List'ning for My Name," Chloe Shrout untied her sheer headscarf that she wore for town, raised it high and moved her lips, almost silently, in the rapid prayers of that tongue only the Spirit could understand.

Crystal abandoned her notebook to her loose corner of carpet and got work at Cool Springs. She called the Cuzzert High School secretary to tell her she would not be back to school that fall.

"What's your reason?" the secretary asked, without trying to dissuade her.

"Honor thy mother," Crystal answered, "if thy father ain't nowhere to be found."

Dotte all but quit sewing and mending for pay, barely mended the girls' clothes. Miriam Louks slipped a fifty dollar bill in Dotte's purse one Sunday; Crystal watched her do it. Miriam cooed at Aimee then and patted her head, "Poor pretty thing with no daddy." Crystal took the fifty when her mom wasn't looking and, after church, went to the bathroom where the handwritten sign was taped to the wall, "Please don't flush tissue down unless you truly must." She tore the bill to pieces and flushed.

Ronnie came around Cool Springs for a while, walked Crystal home at closing, even after he'd started back to school. One time, he was waiting for her outside the shop-and-diner while she closed up. He sang a hymn, quiet, and reached upward on the chorus to tap a set of chimes hanging near the front door. They plinked a sweet, silver sound, so fine next to his voice. She watched him from the doorway, his back to her, his form lean and his hair freshly wetted and combed. She could have sneaked up behind him and hugged him round his waist and buried her face into his denim shirt. She felt color rising in her cheeks.

Ronnie turned then, and his nice, large teeth filled his smile. He said, "Wouldn't sneak up on me now," like he'd read her thoughts. He knew she wouldn't let herself run up behind him and smell him deep.

They walked Manheim Road without grabbing hands. He wore his daddy's belt buckle, a bronze head of a buck. He looked out at the river, and she looked at the tulip poplar tree that stood just past the Methodist church. Its leaves were just starting into gold, a beautiful green-gold that was out of reach in the high limbs.

"I wanna have that leaf," she said. She pointed to the tree up ahead. "That one at the very top."

"Well," he said, "I'll race you to it, Crystal Lemley."

"You will not, Ronnie Sisler," and she took off running. He laughed and hollered out, chasing her to the poplar. She ran on stiff legs that got nimbler the farther she ran. Her lungs burned, and she sped up, hearing Ronnie's breathing close behind her and the sound of the river racing them too. The color in that tree made her feel young—they were two kids in a mountain town outrunning the river, outrunning everything. Ronnie overtook her, his legs longer than hers, and she closed her eyes, half expecting him to catch her up in his arms, but he bounded up into the tree instead, swinging on the lower limbs like he was meant for it, then scrambling up to a high tuft of green gold. His belt buckle shined in the late-day sun as he tugged down a skinny branch and plucked a leaf.

"Ain't the top one," he said, coming down, "but here. Here you are." He held the leaf out to her, dangling it from the stem and grinning. "I'd do anything for you," he said, shy as she drew close. "Your daddy woulda wanted that."

Crystal stopped cold. "My daddy," she said. Like a dog when it has run the length of its chain, she felt the chokehold. "So you just come 'round me for Daddy's sake?"

"No, I didn't mean that."

"We're doing fine on our own," she said. Her pride thickened her voice as her leg muscles stiffened again. "I gotta get home to Aimee." She tucked her hair behind her ear and started walking.

"I didn't mean that," he said, standing like a child with that piece of green-gold at his side.

"It's best you don't walk me no further." She'd gotten close enough to smell him through his denim shirt, yes she had, but she had not wrapped him round.

When she reached home, she breathed even and slow once again. Aimee met her at the screen door and begged her to please let her quit school and find work. Crystal shoved past her, heavy, said fourteen was too young, but the next week Aimee started hanging around Jimmy's Muffler Barn—Aimee had overheard Art Shrout, Jimmy's daddy, talking about the help wanted in the shop with all the trucks coming through to Biggs. She didn't quit school, but she faded from it and started working for Jimmy regular. Crystal let her.

One night in September, Dotte locked herself in her bedroom and didn't come out. Crystal taught Aimee to make biscuits that night, for a supper of biscuits with margarine and salt. When Crystal said grace over the biscuits, she heard Cord's voice in her own, and her mouth tasted ashes. She quit before the *amen* and asked Aimee, "Do you believe he's coming back?"

"No," Aimee said. "'Cause he done took the money Mom kept in her thread box."

"No, I mean Jesus. Do you believe in the Lord's return?"

Aimee stared at her. "I don't know now. I did before. Can't we just eat?"

"See? I think this is a test. God's testing our faith. I mean, God's name don't belong to him who mars it. That's what I been thinking, and we got to call on his name. God's testing us, and you wavering."

"I ain't wavering."

"Two women will be grinding grain, Aimee, one will be taken and the other left. In the twinkling of an eye."

"I said 'I ain't wavering.'"

"Two will be there in the fields, and—"

"I ain't doubting it, Crys!"

"You sound to me like you was doubting."

"Well, I ain't. Alright? It's you who's doubting." Then, softer, "You doubting me—Aimee Jo."

All at once Crystal felt the separateness that had been wedged between them during the time of their daddy's prophecies. She had left Aimee behind, the sheep she was meant to tend, had left her in that ring of split-rail fence alone. Aimee looked hard at the biscuits, hungry, but hungry for more than their flaky crusts could give her. *Two girls will be eating a meal of biscuits in a doublewide,* Crystal thought. *Both left to fend for themselves.*

"I got a idea." Crystal rose from the table and got their daddy's Bible that he'd left on top of the toaster, as if he'd hoped it would catch fire. "You remember that prophet come last spring to preach? The woman-prophet who couldn't go up front 'cause of being a woman, but she preached from our corner rug?"

Aimee nodded.

"You remember when she testified to the power of the Word to give her guidance? Like how she opened her Bible one day and said, 'Speak ye, Lord, and I shall do it.' She pointed eyes-shut to a verse in Mark 8, she said, where Jesus spits on a blind man's eyes and the man sees people like walking trees. Then she went forth and healed a blind woman by spitting in her eyes. You remember?"

"Yeah, I remember. Like how Mom said June could do, I mean read it without seeing. June asked her for a touch from God, even. And she had a nice singing voice."

"Well, I think we should do it too."

"Do what?"

"Let the Lord speak to us, and we do it, according to the Word we get."

"You crazy."

"You just too scared."

"So what if I am; you crazy. What if you get a verse 'bout sacrifice? Or the part 'bout washing in the river—you gonna someways wash in that mucky river? Or the begets: he beget him who begot him who begot him—"

"God's testing you, and you failing, Aimee."

"You ain't God, and you ain't in his mind telling me what he's thinking!"

"I dare you to do it with me."

"You dare me to point to the Bible anyplace?"

"And then do what it says, till the Lord returns or says to quit—else it's all shifting sand."

"If you think you believe strong enough, then I know I do. I ain't no fool. Speak ye, Lord, like my sister says!" She grinned and shouted it, even though they'd been whispering, not wanting to disturb Dotte.

"I ain't joking, Aimee."

"I ain't either."

"I'll go first," Crystal said. She shoved aside the plate of biscuits to make way for the leather-bound Bible. She opened it and shut her eyes and waved her arm wild above her head, coming down with her index finger and reading what she saw by it, in Ecclesiastes 5: "'Be not rash with thy mouth, and let not thine heart be hasty to utter any thing before God: for God is in heaven, and thou upon earth: therefore let thy words be few.'"

They were quiet then.

It might have been a lark, two teen girls playing out a dare to keep desperation at bay. But it was no lark. Crystal felt far from teenage dabbling. She felt helpless, as though her life had already been decided for her. Aimee's black eyes pierced her as her own eyes teared like there was dust in them. It was as though some voice apart from her had read the words, and she had listened from her chair. She had felt her daddy around her, felt swathed in his words, led by his words, like he was still there, waiting for her voice to keep on, to follow behind his in a straight path like in between two rows of tall, rigid corn. She felt her body separating from her voice, like a cat curling away from its own cry, a beautiful cry that had always sung the sweet words of hymns with force and yearning, as though she were rescuing the words from among the snares of the old shape notes on the page. Crystal's voice had always pushed forward. Until now. Her lips still puckered a little from saying the last word, "few." She drew them together and thought of Ronnie, to whom she yet had many things to say.

She closed her mouth on the taste of the salty heat of biscuits, or tears, or both.

"What's that mean, Crys? What're you doing?" Aimee's black eyes teared up too, and she rose up from the table.

"Sis?" she said. "Sis."

But Crystal said nothing, just looked at Aimee with surprise and regretful wonder, and held out the Bible to her. Aimee took it, like a soldier obeying an order.

"I ain't no fool," Aimee whispered. She flipped the thin pages and pointed, eyes closed and wet, to Jeremiah 16, and she read in the same whisper, "'The word of the Lord came also unto me, saying, thou shalt not take thee a wife, neither shalt thou have sons or daughters in this place.'"

Crystal watched as her sister's lips mouthed the words of the verse again, silently, and as her face moved into a series of expressions, twisting and softening and turning blush red. Crystal had watched Aimee's face her whole life, when they'd held hands as little girls at services that stretched so long on Sunday, so long that the girls lay down together on their rag rug in the corner, on the pillow they shared, under the hot blanket of air weaved of the praise and sweat and ache of the worshippers who had coarse voices and coarse lives. She had watched Aimee's face go sleepy and then wake up and crease with laughter. She'd watched Aimee's face for the loveliness in it that her own face lacked. She'd watched it take the shape that a thousand caresses had given it, and she'd seen it take on the darkness that Aimee's own fears had given it. It was a face Crystal loved, and she watched it now as it took in the prophet Jeremiah's brittle *thou shalt not*, gentled it, interpreted and accepted it, registered it as something strange and available, like a ripe piece of fruit, ready for her to just pick it from the vine, because no one but Crystal was looking and no one would take it from her if she picked it. So she did.

Aubrey

....

THE SECOND TIME AUBREY HAD SEEN AIMEE, she'd walked into Cuzzert's one-room community building at the end of his first GED night class. She wore a black halter-top dress, and her shoulders had chapped red in the premature cold of September. Another woman followed her in, carrying a black notebook but no pen, though she might have had one in her shirt pocket and he wouldn't have known because the flannel shirt she wore was huge.

He was explaining what "ethnicity" meant on the intake forms when Aimee sauntered in and pulled out two chairs at a back table, scraping them loudly on the floor. Aubrey lost grip on his sentence. Only three men and one woman had shown up for the class that night. They looked tired from taking the placement test, or from the tedious intake form, or from the dim cement room with nothing but a leftover Christmas wreath on the wall.

"So what do we put then?" asked the man with a thick voice and a crew cut.

Aubrey tasted a familiar metal paste on his gums. He glanced at the man's intake form to remember his name. "Yes, Mr. Walls. What do you put? You can just check 'White' there."

The woman beside Blare Walls raised her hand.

"You don't have to raise your hand, Ms. Felton."

"Call me Agnes, if you please. Not Ms. This GED class's free, right?"

"If it ain't free, the Methodist church'll pay," Blare Walls said.

"It's a free class," said Aubrey. "When you go to Biggs to take the official test, that will cost you forty dollars."

"The Methodist church'll pay that though," Blare said again. The other two men nodded.

"You think with my GED I could do hair?" Agnes asked, raising her hand halfway, then patting her tight black curls. She looked at least sixty, but Aubrey noted forty-six on her intake form. Agnes had slipped a cellophane-wrapped snack cake into Aubrey's hand when she had arrived that night. She'd leaned in and said: "I worked the register at King's Service Station for thirty years, and I'm sick and tired of it." Aubrey had started a poem in his head about this woman lifted out of poverty, a woman who'd never seen the outermost rim of her tiny mountain town, much less the larger world. She would shed her heavy, smoky skin like a spring snake. Or like a chrysalis, sloughing its cocoon.

"Maybe, Agnes." Aubrey said. He pushed his hot sweater sleeves up past his elbows.

"Write any personal goals you have in that last blank," he said, "and that's all for tonight. I'll look over your pretests, and I'll bring textbooks tomorrow night. Tell your friends. We've obviously still got some space." Blare Walls laughed at that from deep in his stomach. Aubrey hadn't looked again at Aimee and the woman in the flannel shirt until then. When he looked back, Aimee waved dramatically like a child, and the other one stared at him and pressed her mouth into a thin line.

"Good night, then," he mumbled. Agnes Felton shook his hand, and he walked to the bathroom in the back corner, a tiny room with dark paneling on the walls, ceiling and floor. Aubrey wondered if it had been added to the cement-block building to replace an outhouse.

He closed the door and looked into the mirror, ran his fingers through his shaggy blond hair to calm the cowlicks. He wished he'd found someone to cut it before tonight. He pulled the collar of his shirt out from underneath the neck of his sweater, straightened it, then tucked it back under. When he came out, everyone was gone but Aimee and the woman in the big shirt, and they stood at the front of the room leafing through his papers.

"Those are intake forms," he said. "You can take one if you'd like to sign up for the class. I'm glad you came." He was talking to them like he would to an old person, or to someone waiting in a doctor's office with an obvious pain that you don't want to directly address, but he couldn't adjust it. His voice felt too far away from his rising heat.

"Here." He reached for two pencils from his box on the table. "The class is free."

"We heard that part," Aimee said, running her fingers along the black strap of her dress.

"I offer morning sessions and also evening," Aubrey said. "Tuesday to Thursday. There's plenty of room. As you can see." He made a sweep with his arm toward the four pushed-back folding chairs, the four placement tests with pencils left on top. His hand caught one of the tests and sent it to the floor at Aimee's feet.

"Aubrey Falls, Blare Walls," Aimee said in a sing-song voice. She bent to pick up the papers, and Aubrey felt his cheeks burn, the metal around his tongue turn sharp and cold.

"Who's your friend, Aimee? Would she like to sign up as well?"

"Blare Walls is dumb as a stump, poor soul. He quit the eighth grade and don't read nothing but the funnies. This here's my sister Crystal. She'd like to sign up for your class."

"Hello, Crystal. I'm Aubrey." He held out his hand, but Crystal didn't take it. "Would you like morning or evening classes?"

"She don't talk," Aimee said.

"Okay." He untucked half his shirt collar from his sweater neck, then retucked it. "I'm pretty quiet myself."

"I mean she don't talk."

"At all?"

"That's right."

"Okay."

"You single? The Apostle Paul says it's best you stay single for the work of the Lord."

"Well—" He tried to smile, then tried desperately to be serious. "Well, I'm a VISTA, so I guess I'm working for the government and not the Lord."

"We all in service either to the Lord or to the Devil. Ain't no in between, even for you, Aubrey Falls."

Aubrey couldn't help but laugh, but he immediately regretted laughing. "I forgot. The prophet."

"You done made up your mind 'bout us, ain't you, Aubrey Falls? You think I'm trash." Crystal reached for an intake form and took Aimee's arm as though to leave. "No, Crys, I come here to say something. Leave me be."

"I don't think you're trash," he said, though he had no idea what he thought. This woman hindered his capacity for thought.

"Bull shee-it," she said, dipping her voice down low. She covered her mouth, like a naughty child, then laughed, first out loud and then just with her eyes of black glass. Her eyes were as hard as her movements were haphazard. He stood back from her, remembering all too well their first encounter. She slipped her changeable voice into a matter-of-fact tone:

"I want to explain Hershel Dunmire. That's what I come for. He wasn't meaning nothing when you come into the Muffler Barn last week. Hershel's sweet on me—the old fella who sits there playing with them rubber bands? He got hit by a semi a few years back, and it jellied up his mind. He's sweet, though, brings me coffee from the Save-a-Lot, holds the dustpan when I sweep the floor, never lays a hand on me. Faithful as a damn guard dog."

Crystal stared at Aubrey as Aimee talked on. He had the bizarre feeling that this silent woman knew him—not that they'd met before, but that she perceived the part of him beneath his speech and actions. She made him feel like a school kid, so much so that he straightened his shoulders. Her stare was as forward and strange as Aimee's swiping the front of his pants the week before.

"He was crossing Route 40 four-wheeling's how it happened," Aimee said. "Sneaking up on skunks and dogs and running them to death. Hershel shot a bobcat once—he claimed, 'It'll get my chickens if I don't get it first,' but he done it out of meanness, really. See how sweet he is now, though? Now the Lord got hold of him? That meanness all bashed out. I think he's lucky, don't you? So don't pay him no mind. You ain't been back 'round to my shop. I wouldn't want Hershel to scare you off." Crystal pulled Aimee's arm again.

"It's okay," was all Aubrey knew to say. He watched Aimee's frantic movements as she spoke. It was like watching a baton twirler in a parade.

"I brought you a cigarette," she said.

Crystal folded the intake form twice, stuck it in her shirt pocket and walked to the door.

"It's okay to fill that out at home, Crystal," Aubrey said. "You can bring it with you next time." He spoke too loudly, and she didn't acknowledge his permission. "Here's one for you, Aimee." He held out a form, even while she twirled a cigarette-baton, a prop for her routine.

She didn't take the form, just danced in close and whispered, "I ain't come for no GED. I come for you. Aw-brey."

She slid the cigarette in between his neat shirt collar and the neck of his sweater, and she followed Crystal out.

Aimee

....

AIMEE'S LINE OF MONDAY WASH hung wet and still, heavy without the play of a breeze. She sat on the back steps to cool herself, lost in her mind for an hour, maybe more. She didn't know how long she sat. Then she stood and walked around the trailer toward the road, following, before she realized it, the path of the silver-rimmed pearl button she'd thrown to the ditch like it was a worthless stone. She followed it to the ditch, and she kept walking, down Route 40 in the direction of town, in her short, backless dress and her Tingley overshoes.

Aimee often walked the road, humming to herself and kicking rocks, thinking of the people driving by and how she looked to them as they passed. They might say, "There she is, the one who walks the road." She wondered if she was someone memorable to them. She chastised herself for vanity but couldn't help the moments of exultation when she heard a car coming from in front or behind. She flew up like a bird and watched herself from above, watched from the windows of the cars and pickups, to see what the drivers saw. Most often the car was one she knew, and she just waved, disappointed. She bowed her head if Bud or Joshie Dixon drove past, hollering something filthy.

But sometimes a stranger came by, someone on his way to Biggs or another place far away from the cluster of things called Cuzzert. Some nice family or a young, quiet man like Aubrey who might offer her a ride. Or a woman with black hair like her own—this woman would be headed somewhere fine, and as she traveled on, she would remember Aimee, the girl who walked the road.

Aimee wanted to be remembered in body because she felt she might catch fire any minute. She felt herself dying, not in the regular way, but deep down. She felt her womb shriveling up, full of hot wind. She bared more and more flesh to the world with a frantic wish to be memorable, not willing that she should be just a handbreadth. The Psalms said that: *Behold, thou hast made my days as a handbreadth*. Miriam Louks squinched her leathery face and quoted it all the time, downplaying her life's importance, though she did it in a way that would make the other churchwomen say, "Oh no, Miriam, you're so important to us; it's us who's made of breaths."

Begging the psalmist's pardon, Aimee refused to believe the handbreadths applied to her. She would die, yes, but she would last in people's memories.

Prophets are remembered.

She missed June Tatum as she walked. One Sunday service, a few months before June died, the church had been praying on holiness as a way of life. Art Shrout, who'd stepped in to do most of the preaching after the Tabernacle had found themselves without a preacher, had given the Word. "Let us all be holy," he said, tugging on the suspenders he wore over his white undershirt, "as the Lord God is holy. And what does that look like in our TV-watching, in our dress, in our drink"—and June had broken out into tongues. The jammering-on, sweat pouring from her, first high-pitched and loud then soft as baby coos, so only Aimee could hear sitting beside her, and softer, down to just her tongue clicking like a hen's. At the end of it, at the Spirit's sighing-out, Aimee had buried her face in June's fleshy arm and cried.

"Why don't I get the tongues?" she had asked June.

June had said to be patient. "We know it from Second Peter, child: one day is with the Lord as a thousand years, and a thousand years as one day. And the Lord's not slack in his promise, no. You'll come into your time." And June's egg-white eyes had rolled around in their own water. They'd almost swished.

It was not for tongues that Aimee waited now. It was for something greater. Something she was meant for. Something having to do with her dark-haired daddy sleeping in a jail cell and declining his bread and meat.

Jimmy might have driven past and asked her why she was not at the shop, but she kept walking, even flailed her arms a little and stretched out her fingers, thinking on how to make a handbreadth broader.

She could hear the Heritage Fair setting up at the grounds ahead. The rides would open Tuesday night. She followed the road to the field that struggled all year to grow patches of grass just to be trampled back to dirt during the four-day fair. She stopped on Route 40 facing the field of unfolded Midway rides and the first tents going up, still just skeletons of poles and wires. It was afternoon by now, hot, and her sweat had dampened the low front of her dress. A truck passed and honked at her, a black pickup she didn't recognize. Probably someone coming in for the livestock auction, since the truck pulled a steel trailer behind it. More strangers than usual came through during the fair. No doubt she made an impression on the driver who honked and yelled something at her, something she didn't quite catch. She imagined what he'd said, and it was something memorable—'You're liable to break my heart,' or, 'You're diamond, girlie.' It could have been like that.

She could be too—pure diamond, pressed hard, sharp enough to cut glass, like Aubrey had told her diamonds could do, pressed for a thousand years from coal blackness. Aubrey had held a rock of coal in his hand once and told her that diamonds are just coal pressed down immeasurably. After he'd said that, she studied the coal bucket by the stove at Glorybound. She never looked at the pieces of coal the same way. Sometimes, in the light, they shone.

The CONROY Coal Company Heritage Fair came right in the dead of dog-day heat. Aimee wished they would wait a month and hold it in the cooler days, when the maple trees and tulip poplars started to turn and the hot ground went crisp under your feet. The fair was sponsored by the CONROY office in Biggs, but the date was set, no doubt, by the head office based out of state, in New York or someplace. That's why the timing was all wrong, Crystal used to tell her, when they sat dying of heat near the donut booth as girls, letting the smell of fried dough melt down onto them. The top dogs in the coal office had first brought in the fair, years and years before, to boost the morale of the miners. And even though none of CONROY's operating strip jobs employed Cuzzert people anymore, the fair still came to that spot. Because of the awful mound of trash to pick up, Crystal had said, like our place is a dumping ground, and folks from Biggs come in and use it as such and then go on home.

Still, the girls had always attended the Heritage Fair dawn to dusk, and past that once someone had strung up lights from tent to tent so the fair could last a few hours longer.

Aimee watched the coronation pavilion go up, a dull, gold tent with no walls. Two thrones sat under it, built of good wood, expensive cedar, hand-built with an outline of a crown on the back of one, to distinguish that throne as the queen's. Reverend Angus of the Methodist church had made them; he'd carved the crown shape with a rotary tool.

The queen and king were seniors from either Cuzzert High or the school in Biggs, most often from Biggs. King Coal contestants had to put on a suit and write a speech about the importance of coal mining and give it in front of the school-teacher judges, but the girls competed in that big pageant held at the VFW between Biggs and Cuzzert on Manheim Road. They gave a speech, too, but had to do a few other things, like dance in an evening gown around the square room.

Queen Coal had been a girl from Biggs every year since Aimee could remember, mainly because of the expensive, evening-gown part. Aimee knew she could have been queen if she'd stayed in school. Her daddy would never have let her run for it, but he was gone. Miriam Louks would have pulled Dotte aside and all but forbidden Aimee entering the pageant on account of immodesty, but Dotte would have allowed it Aimee was sure. And if she would have won that pageant, then Dotte could have made the Queen Coal dress, even though she hadn't touched needle and thread for years. She used to make all the court's dresses, for the runners-up to the queen, the train-bearers, but never for the queen herself. They special-ordered the queen's dress, and that had always hurt Dotte.

The queens from Biggs came to the fair in Cuzzert like they were doing the place a favor. They sat through the coronation, did their waving, and then went home. They never stayed to sign the little girls' notebooks or preside over the auction like they were supposed to. Aimee would have, had she been queen. She would have stayed long past dark, with those lights strung up like fireworks, walking around in a dress so pretty, embroidered flowers on pink satin, pink for the dress she and Crystal had been baptized in.

Aimee didn't even know who'd won queen this year. Usually Dotte found it out from someone with a newspaper and then told her, but Aimee hadn't spoken to her mom before taking to the road. It would be a name that meant nothing to either of them.

From Route 40, she saw the little red cars of the Tilt-A-Whirl, ready to be put on their tracks, and the swings were already up, those swings that hang on chains and go round and fling you sideways, going like a bullet. The crafts and quilts and canned goods sat up in a huge, white tent and, beside that, the biggest tent, with three heavy poles poking up its center, for the livestock auction. A man on a four-wheeler was hauling a box trailer of woodchips inside for the floor of the tent, where the animals would sulk around till they got bought and butchered.

The same tents came back every year, like the junk-sale tent where her daddy had bought her a ceramic bloodhound bank as a little girl and she would slip her change in through the slit on top of the dog's head. Then there were the game tents, the ones with balloons blown up and taped to a board you threw darts at, balloons with a number inside that said whether you had won a stuffed elephant or a key chain from Florida or some such. Another tent with no walls stood near the coronation pavilion; on the tables underneath, the Methodist church served a corned-beef-and-cabbage meal, five dollars a ticket, and the money went to missionaries.

There used to be a freak tent you could pay to go into to see a woman with no head. The sign told you she'd had it cut off in a train wreck but was still alive. Bud Dixon had known as a sixteen-year-old it was a sham, and he'd taken a Biggs girl in there for their viewing time—Janey Close—and had gotten her pregnant. That baby had been a stillborn because of their sin. At least, that's the reason everybody gave. So they'd done away with that tent and replaced it with a fun-house trailer with mirrors that made you fat or skinny.

Aimee crossed the road and scanned the grounds, nudged a clod of dirt loose with the toe of her rubber Tingley overshoe. A few men eyed her, but none came over to talk. She squinted to see what Melanie Angus, the Methodist preacher's wife, was unloading onto a table in the junk-sale tent, and something caught her eye: a new tent, just beyond the junk-sale, off to itself—a big, black tent with no metal poles to speak of. It was jerry-rigged out of black tarps, baler's twine and cut branches like stout, wiener-roasting sticks. She had never seen it at the fair before.

Aimee moved closer, past the Tilt-A-Whirl cars and the men she didn't know driving stakes for the auction tent. She could make out a white, cloth sign, hand-painted and duct-taped to the top front of the tent. It read: "Whosoever Will Worship Center of the True Pentecost" in letters that got smaller at the end so they could all fit on the sign. The words sounded familiar, but she couldn't place them. She saw a red pickup parked beside the tent with a door that didn't match, a black one with a white stripe. Something hung from the rearview mirror—a small plastic cross with flames painted up the side, like flames you'd see on a muscle car or a leather jacket. She stood looking from in front of the junk-sale tables, aware that Melanie Angus, who said nothing to her, was fussing over the items more than she needed to, like she was afraid Aimee would steal one of the crocheted doilies.

Aimee watched, half hidden by the junk-sale tent's flap. The massive black tent had a slit in its hanging front door, just beneath the white sign, and Aimee watched that slit, because she heard someone singing in there. She couldn't make out the tune, but she knew the voice. She watched and listened—all but holding her breath, sweat pouring off her—for a dense minute. Then the slit opened wide in a rush and out walked Ronnie Sisler.

She hadn't seen him in five years. He looked strange, but she knew it was him by his singing voice and his blushed face, his horse teeth, his small ears and his big eyes always about to cry. His arms were bigger round than she remembered, and he'd grown a neck now thick as his mom Arlene's. His light hair hung long and fanned out wide over his shoulders. He pushed it behind his ears and rolled up the sleeves of his collared black shirt, revealing a big tattoo on the inside of his right forearm.

Aimee felt something like joy to see him—and something like loathing. He hadn't sent a word to Crystal in those five years. He kept humming his song—not a hymn, more like a radio song—his voice the same as she remembered it, the same as the day he'd taken up her daddy's guitar from the corner of the Tabernacle and strummed out "I'll Be Somewhere List'ning." Hearing his voice reminded her of Crystal's, how it used to accompany his with that tambourine like a rattling chain binding them together.

She remembered one night, on the eve of Easter, the spring before Jesus was supposed to come back but didn't, Crystal had practiced a sunrise song with Ronnie at the church and hadn't come home till late. Because they'd had to wait for Dotte, Crystal said, doing up the flowers with Miriam, who fretted over such things forever. But Aimee had watched from the bedroom door as her sister's fifteen-year-old body lay down in her blue dress, and as she fondled the string of plastic pearls that Aimee had lent. Crystal never said it outright, but Aimee found a pregnancy-test stick under the bathroom sink on Easter, its negative sign gone red, and the two of them, Crystal and Ronnie—thick as thieves till then—never seemed to touch again. Except for a foot-washing one time, but even then Ronnie had blushed, and Crystal had only looked at her socks in her hands.

Ronnie tied his hair back, and Aimee got a better look at his right arm. What she'd thought was a tattoo looked more like an awful scar, in a thick, winding path. It opened up in dark pink on his pale arm, like someone had sliced it just then, peeled the skin off and it was about to bleed. But it didn't bleed, and he didn't seem to feel it. She remembered what he'd gotten mixed up with down in Charleston, the serpent-handling church, so maybe it was a snake-bite scar.

Ronnie walked stiff to his truck and opened the mismatched door to grab a box from the bench seat. Aimee stood motionless at the junk-sale tent, watching him draw the flat box close to his chest with both arms, like you might carry firewood. The cardboard box had holes in the sides, the same kind of box you get a raft of baby turkeys in through mail order at the Biggs Feed and Supply. He held it up to his face so the holes were at eye level, and he sang a little louder into the holes, shook the box some. She saw that the skin of Ronnie's face had a darkness to it—not like a sun tan but a darkness having to do with what was in that box.

He looked up, as though to judge the time by the sun, and set the box down on a patch of grass away from any shade. Then he went to the bed of the pickup and pulled out a few folding chairs and took them into the tent.

Aimee watched the holes in the sides of the box. At first, she saw nothing, then a movement, quick. A rusted metal color, then ashy white. Then rust and white again, something patterned. Then nothing. Then she saw the flicker of a tongue.

"Shit," she said, and Melanie Angus—Aimee had forgotten she was there—sniffed and walked off.

Ronnie had lowered that box down to the grass with his fingers crooked inside the holes, like there were just baby turkeys in the box after all, just tiny, harmless beaks. But, no—it was a copperhead. That snake could have snapped at Ronnie's fingers if it had cared to.

"I rather be spared that true Pentecost, wouldn't you?" A man with a hammer at his side had come up beside Aimee and spoke to her while he fooled with a candy dish on the table, a hollow glass chicken cut in half. He checked the bottom for the price sticker Melanie had given it.

"Three dollars for a peep in that there fanatical tent, Missy. I can think of something else I'd rather pay to see." He grinned. She didn't know the man. His shirt was too small, and the bottom three buttons were undone down to his undershirt—all smudged with dirt from driving stakes.

Aimee said nothing and looked back at the box on the grass. She remembered the sending service the Tabernacle had held for Ronnie before Arlene had sent him down to auto-mechanic school. They'd cleared out the chairs and gathered around him in the center of the basement. They'd laid hands on him, all over his shoulders and his head of short hair, and on his back which had been narrower then. He'd shivered a little with all those hands touching him. June Tatum had offered the blessing prayer; Aimee recalled some of it.

"You'll go on to fight the good fight," June had prayed with her face tilted upward like always. "Down a windy road and oft-times a lonely one."

"Takes a goddamn nut to punish hisself that way," the man with the hammer said. "How 'bout I get this here hen-chick dish for you? Would you like that?"

"Amen and hallelujah," June had said, and then repeated it again and again. "Son, you got big waves, big waves of glory washing over you now, and be not afraid—they will not get you drowned, for Lord Jesus got hold of you." *Yes, yes,* Art Shrout had said. *Yes, yes,* everyone had said, but Aimee could not remember if she had said the *yes,* too. She remembered her hand on Ronnie's neck and Crystal's over hers. Even at that service, Crystal had not touched his skin.

"I see you got a interest in that business," said the man, stepping close. "Got any interest in me, honey?" He put his hand low down on her back.

"What I got," Aimee said, "is wash on the line." She batted his hand away and walked back toward the road, half dizzy. She walked fast and nearly tripped over her loose Tingleys.

"There'll be fire and fire, glory and glory," she heard June Tatum saying. The words rang out with each strike of metal on metal, a hammer on a tent stake somebody was driving into the ground.

Crystal

....

CRYSTAL LOCKED THE FRONT DOOR of the Cool Springs shop-and-diner at five o'clock. She propped the *Closed* sign in the window with a slab of rough-cut cherry painted with an American flag. At the counter, she sat on one of the orange stools and wrote, in her awkward cursive on the back of a receipt, "Might open late Tuesday morning," and taped it to the window beside the *Closed* sign.

Crystal turned off the lights before she wetted the rag to wipe the counter and the four tables, trying to cool herself in the dimness, to soften herself before the walk home.

There was a knock on the front window. She looked up to see Aubrey's face peering in, cupped by his hands. She waved and went to the door.

"I was just passing by," he said. "Thought you might want a ride home."

Crystal knew he was lying; he'd pulled his Jeep into the lot with a purpose. She let him in, and he walked over to the box fan chirring beside the counter, bent down to put his face by it. He closed his eyes to the fan breeze and stroked the reddish blond stubble that grew patchy on his chin like a teen boy's. Aubrey was shy like a teen boy, too, but he had grown less shy around her.

"It's a hot one, today. A good day for Tom Petty," he said, thumbing toward the radio on the counter. "'American Girl.' That's not your usual gospel."

Crystal flushed, having forgotten the radio. She always listened to the gospel singers on the Biggs Believers Station, but this afternoon when the radio preacher had come on she couldn't bear his wailing, his damning and hooting, not today. She shuffled to the counter and switched the music off.

"Hey, come on. He's a classic, Crys."

She smiled despite herself, with her hand covering her mouth. She took the rag to the back room to run it under the spigot.

"Now this is some real handiwork," Aubrey said to her from the counter. She saw him tapping Loyal Sisler's rockers made from Mountain Dew cans. He got a few rocking at once, all of them crooked, clinking on the counter in a limping chorus. "I've been looking for one of these for my kitchen table at the cabin. Something just like this guy here." He lifted one and read the tag: "'Ten dollars, by Loyal Dye Sisler's hand.' That's a little steep. I don't know." He smiled at her and pulled his wallet from his back pocket. "Too classy to pass up. Ten bucks it is."

Crystal shook her head and refused the money. Loyal would grin bigger than life if she handed him money from a sale the next time he came in with Arlene. She knew Aubrey knew that, and his knowing something that vulnerable—which would have made her angry when he'd first moved to Cuzzert the year before—gave her some relief, now.

"Come on. I have to have it," he said.

She gave in and took the money, set it under a salt shaker by the register.

"I'm much obliged," Aubrey said, and he picked up the rocker, its arms coiled into split-metal curlicues. "It will make the centerpiece of all centerpieces."

Crystal smiled again, covered her mouth then uncovered it and looked Aubrey long in the eye. Her face hardened before she could stop it.

"You didn't come today," he said, moving his gaze to the box fan. "You and Aimee."

She shook her head again, wagged it slow and put her hands in the pockets of her jeans. She walked out the door, forgot about locking up and climbed into Aubrey's Jeep. She rested her head back on the vinyl headrest and let the sun hit her face through the window with a broad, hard stroke. Aubrey followed her, holding the Mountain Dew rocker gently by its seat. When he started the Jeep, the end of the radio song came out of the speakers, and Crystal twisted the knob to *off*. They turned left into town.

"I just thought you'd be there," he said. "Aimee promised." He drove past his cabin and the Methodist church, the cemetery and Paint Davis' bar, where Crystal saw Joshie Dixon standing in the middle of the parking lot looking lost. With their windows rolled down, the river smell reached into the Jeep like fingers on their faces, marked them with the sulfur stink. Crystal wiped her face with her T-shirt sleeve.

"She looked me in the eyes and promised me, Crystal, and the eyes are the windows of the soul. So they say, in a manner of expression. Not that you're going to talk with me about this, of course, but they're the windows of the person. Do you understand? I looked into your sister's eyes for a trace of honesty, and I thought I saw it." He looked at her, that way he often looked at her, like she had answers to questions he didn't even know how to ask.

"I keep thinking I know her," he said. "She told me you two had an understanding. Monday at nine. Your dad really needs you. I mean, I don't know what else to say."

Crystal looked inside her mind for the windows of her sister's soul, those black eyes set in a face she loved and watched. *The curtain's pulled closed,* she thought. *That soul can't show itself.* Crystal looked at Aubrey's thin arms and his hands careful with the steering wheel, his T-shirt with a logo from where he'd gone to school. His eyes were bald open, though his soul was neatly tucked away, not because it needed protection, but because he had no idea how to draw it out. He was from a place where folks were too decent to peer in. He was lonely; she could see it plain, but Aimee's suffering was no kin to his.

And he does not know what happens when people grow up in a place with no laurel bushes and no strong walls to hide nothing, cars whizzing by, and they do their sobbing in the open. They go without privacy so long, they board up their windows after a time.

"Not that you're going to talk to me," Aubrey said again. "Not that you would ever open your mouth to tell me anything at all." He breathed out a sigh and shifted down, preparing to take a left at the road's junction with Route 40. Right then, Crystal saw something on the roadside that pierced her. The face of Jesus, set in deep blackness in a frame, leaning up against the stop sign in front of Jim Louks' house on the corner. She sat up and twisted around to see, jabbing Aubrey's shoulder so fast and hard he almost ran off the road.

"What? What is it, Crys?"

She pulled on his T-shirt sleeve like a kid and pointed back to the stop sign.

"You want me to pull over?"

She nodded *yes,* and he eased the Jeep to the shoulder of the road, beside Jim Louks' mailbox. Crystal got out before Aubrey pulled the brake, and she ran back to the stop sign. In front of it, she slowed, catching herself. She squatted down.

It was what she had thought: a painting of Jesus. In a white, plastic frame of interlacing white roses and thorns. A painting of Jesus' face with a velvety black background, his face floating there, disconnected from a neck or body, like a suspended thing. Beside it sat a tied Family Dollar bag full of trash, a cracked planter still caked with soil at the bottom, a pair of dolls, the ones with eyes that close when you lay them down but these lay down with their eyes open wide. It was Jim Louks' trash pile set out early for trash day tomorrow, Tuesday.

Crystal touched Jesus' head where the crown of green thorns met the skin on his temple. The thorns were painted like new, still quick with life, as though just cut from a bush growing outside the border of the blackness. The skin of Christ's face was a dull gray, with something like rouge on the cheeks. His eyes looked off to the right, past Crystal's, and she found nothing lovely in them, but those green, angry thorns and their stems as strong and willful as tiny arms wound by someone they were fighting against—they were stubborn arms wanting to pop out straight. Crystal rose from her crouch and picked up the painting by its plastic frame.

"Crystal, wait. You can't just take that." Aubrey had followed her to the trash pile and was touching one of the dolls' heads with the toe of his sneaker. "You can't."

She nodded and headed for the Jeep.

"Wait—Crys—this is Jim Louks' trash."

She stopped and hugged the painting to her chest.

"That's probably from his mom. You know Miriam gets that stuff for him at the church bazaars—he's always telling me about it. She got him a porcelain nativity for his birthday, four feet tall. And he's not even religious. He's a halfway reasonable man, which I, for one, value around here."

She turned and walked toward the Jeep again.

"Okay, sorry. I know Miriam's part of your church. Jim should be more sensitive about throwing it out in broad daylight. But, come on, look at it." He reached for the painting.

She hugged it tighter, the shrill, green thorns muted into the airbrushed purple and gold on her shirt. She locked her hands behind its cardboard backing.

"This is unbelievable. It looks like—I don't know—some rock album cover. You're smarter than this." Aubrey dropped his eyes when she glared at him.

She could picture the spot on the wall at the Tabernacle. She wanted to hang it between the window and the board of numbers—but first to show Aimee and their mom, because they would see what she saw. She knew the painting was trash. If Miriam Louks hadn't gotten it from a bazaar table, then she'd bought it for Jim at the dollar store. Crystal's old anger flickered up toward Aubrey, toward his boyish face never once misted over with that dark shade, a shade that kept some self from the mind, like a mystery, the way the Spirit hovered over the waters, in a mist, and used to come over her just before she opened her mouth to pray in an unknown tongue, and used to come over Ronnie, too. He'd shout and reach his hands high, past the light that came in the window, reaching for glory and sound and mercy. She missed Ronnie so much, and she felt sorry for Aubrey. She held the painting away from herself and looked at it. The green thorns in a sweet round of mean life, hacked from a bush and coiled and piled there on the gray ghost of his head. The Man of Sorrows, framed in plastic and set out to be laughed at where Route 40 met Manheim Road. She was taking it.

She carried the painting to the Jeep and climbed in. Aubrey said nothing when he followed her and pulled the Jeep onto Route 40. He wouldn't even look at her or at the warped cardboard backing that she faced toward his driver seat. They both watched the road and the fencerow and, when it came up for a stretch, the Heritage Fair, all the tents raised now toward the hot sky.

Aimee

....

THE BUSTED RUBBERMAID LAUNDRY BASKET caved in on itself when Aimee picked it up by its handles. She had to carry it in front of her to the clothesline like a big bowl. Split in two places, it stuck out its sharp edges when sitting on the ground. She reached up to the line to scratch at the oil stains that had dried on her Muffler Barn shirt, and the basket edge caught her leg. A mean cut. She bent down to ease the scrape with spit on her fingers, just a pink mark with blood rushing up to the surface but not breaking through, yet, and she felt her stomach knot itself again.

Her mint-green dress, when she bent, showed the back of her upper thighs toward the Dixons' kitchen window. Even though the blinds were up and she knew Joshie and Bud were taking turns at the window, she stayed that way, bent in half, even when she heard somebody pull up to the front of the double-wide. Not until she heard Aubrey's voice travel through the front windows and come out, calling her name through the mesh of the back screen porch, did she straighten her body and take the stained shirt from the line. She dropped it onto the stiff dry towels already in the basket.

She heard the front door open and shut, turned to face the back porch where she figured Aubrey would come out looking for her with his sweet, savior face on. That's what she called it: his savior face—his little-boy eyes and little-boy face hair and his swooping down out of the sky on a plane from Chicago to help the poor folks in Cuzzert. Even those like her daddy who didn't deserve the help. She was angry, and, despite it, she ached to see Aubrey.

But it was Crystal who came to the screen of the porch, holding a big piece of cardboard to her chest. She waved, and Aimee waved, too. Ronnie's come back, Aimee needed to tell her, and she saw again the box fit for baby turkeys but filled with a snake getting mad in the sun's heat.

"I thought I'd see you there, today," Aubrey said, coming around the back corner of the doublewide.

"Hoo! You scared me. Couldn't see you for my wash hanging."

"Aimee, where were you?"

"Couldn't come, 'cause it's wash day."

"I'm asking you directly."

"Well, I'm a telling you—directly. And mind you keep quiet, Aubrey Falls. Mom's inside, and she don't need to know nothing 'bout all this." Aimee stepped toward him through the hole between two long-sleeved shirts still hanging.

"I'm sorry," he said soft, "but I waited for you all day."

He really was the gentlest man she'd known, and she could not bear it. She said, just as soft, in a tease, "You wanna come inside? You know, be sweet? Or you chicken-shit?" She giggled, but Aubrey didn't. The sadder his mouth looked, the more she had to giggle and sway.

"Please don't," he said. "What happened to your leg?" The blood had broken through, and a line bled down onto the bone of her foot, in between two toes. She made no move to wipe it, and Aubrey took a dried washrag from the line. Before he could hand it to her, she spit on her fingers again, wiped the creek of blood and wiped her fingers on her dress, did it again and once more, till the scrape stung under her pressing but no longer bled. The blood messed her mint dress in a cluster of fingerprints, and she was sorry for it.

"Monday's wash day," she said, and she took the rag from him, dropped it into the basket. "I got appointed today to do the wash—and, buddy, you do the wash while you can, 'fore the drought dries up the well. I got myself appointed, and you just call a strike of lightning down if I'm wrong."

She clapped once, hard, and raised her hands above her head, felt her dress hem slide up. "This here's what I'm meant for today. It was not my appointed time to go see Daddy, not my ap-*point*-ed day. A fire lit under me, and it told me, 'Woman—you get your wash on the line!'" She pointed to the screen porch, to Crystal, though Crystal no longer stood there. "And she knows, and Mom knows; seems like the only one who don't know is you, Aw-brey. There's things you don't know. Got to get you saved, mister." She whooped and bowed down in a rush to ease the ache in her abdomen. "Then you'll know 'bout God's appointment." She grinned and felt a salt-sting in her mouth like her gums were bleeding, then she knew she was crying. "You don't know nothing 'bout being saved, sweet man, and here you go trying to save people."

Aubrey hadn't moved. He still held the two clothespins that had fixed the washrag to the line. He backed away from her, like he always did when she acted like this, as though he were afraid, and she was sorry. His savior face blurred through her crying, and her stomach hurt. Her leg stung, and some bird flapped wild inside her with sharp splintered wings and sharper cries, calling out such that she stilled herself and looked down, touching the blood smear on her dress.

"We tried to go," she said.

"Then what happened?"

"I was all dressed and ready." She felt the bareness of her skin now, remembered how she had tossed her mom's old blouse and long skirt to the floor that morning and had not yet returned them.

"I walk into that room every week," said Aubrey. "Your dad is the first thing I smell. He doesn't shower. Some of the other men won't come to the class anymore because of him. When he came the first time in the spring, he had thick black hair, like yours." Aubrey dropped a clothespin to touch her hair, but she backed off. "Now it's thinned out, and most of it's gray. He's starving himself to death, Aimee."

"You done told me all that."

"They keep him alive with fluids, but just the mandated amount. It's like he's dying of old age, but it's because he's punishing himself—"

"We all purified someways, like silver in the fire, seventy times burned in the furnace."

"That's a backward kind of punishment." He spoke so quiet she could hardly hear.

"Aubrey out saving the world, all us backward folks. You saving men who you don't know what they done." She turned her dark eyes on him.

"I know what he did, and I told you what he did—a hit-and-run, a crime that deserves a penalty, but the woman lived. I looked into it, and she didn't die from the accident. They think your dad even kept her from dying. Maybe he saved her life, Aimee."

"Hoo," she whistled low.

"I know he left you. I'm sorry." Aubrey looked around like he suddenly realized he was out of place. "You have every right to be angry."

"Damn right I do—ten years ago he left, and you come up to me last week, out of the blue, telling me, 'You got yourself a convict daddy,' and it's me and Crys have to tend to his no-good self, when he up and left us with nothing!"

"He was half crazy then."

"No, he was always crazy."

"But he's so sorry. I read you what he wrote last Monday—"

She held up her hand: No more. Aubrey went quiet. She looked to the ground, saw her leg beading up blood again. She touched it and left the blood on her fingertips. Aubrey squatted to the basket for the rag, softened it into folds and touched it to her leg.

"Don't you try nothing, Aubrey." She said it without feeling, like an over-rehearsed line. "I'm a virgin prophet, and I got work for me. God got work for me."

Aubrey stood. "Nobody can touch you, can they." He looked embarrassed. "I'm tired of not touching you."

"God got work for me."

"What work is that? Maybe God's work is keeping your dad from dying like a pious fool."

"I said it ain't yet our appointed time." And she walked past him, up the back steps to the screen-porch. She passed into the living room, where Dotte sat in her nightgown watching TV and holding a lit cigarette she wasn't smoking. Aimee wondered if she'd heard them. Her mom's black cardigan draped her shoulders and front like widow's clothes. Aimee leaned on the doorframe and watched her mom till she heard the Jeep pull out.

Dotte turned on her thick neck toward Aimee. "That Aubrey?" she asked.

"No, Mom."

"What you get on your dress, Aimee girl?"

Near dark, Crystal still hammered on the lattice over the front door, forcing the wood back into its crisscross pattern, but it broke off in blue chips. Aimee watched through the screen door and lit the Pall Mall she'd taken from Dotte's pack on the coffee table.

"Just leave it, Crys," she said. She had walked down the hallway through the kitchen and felt on her face the humid heat of soup and baked biscuits. Crystal quit hammering, but she bent to gather the chips and splinters from the dirt. Aimee saw that her sister had changed back into the filthy blouse she'd worn that morning, saw again the missing button and a new small tear in the sleeve. Saw the way nothing in Crystal resembled their daddy except her large hands.

"I said leave it be. Let it bust up, dammit, let it all go to hell." She had meant to say something kinder.

Crystal dropped the wood chips, and Aimee came out the screen door to sit on the top, cinder-block step. She put her feet up on the bottom one, looked at the silhouette of the big rocks by Route 40, their red ring of phony Indian paintings born again out of the dusk each time headlights passed. She looked until Joshie Dixon went by on foot, kicking gravel.

"You slick up your fuckhole for me?" Joshie yelled, curling his flannel shirt-sleeves down over his hands. He kept walking, though, and moved quicker when Crystal turned toward him.

"They was just ragging cramps today, Crys. Found blood on my slip when we got home. Don't seem fair, all my baby eggs. If I ain't meant to get a child, I might as well quit the bleeding. It's not worth the damn cramps."

Crystal pulled Aimee up from the steps and opened the screen door, disappeared inside, her bare feet slapping the linoleum. She returned holding a picture and gave it to Aimee.

A white-framed painting of Jesus, all a deep blackness but his face. A thin gray face. "Well," Aimee whispered. He looked like he was dying slow, and the thorns were what would kill him in the end—so alive they'd grow over his face and over his body which you couldn't see in the painting. They'd wrap round him, fierce and pretty, and he'd become a brier bush himself. She handed the painting back to Crystal and nodded.

"It'll look fine there on the wall," she said, knowing Crystal would hang it out at Glorybound. Aimee sank down on the steps, propping the door open with her body. A few moths got inside to circle the stove light.

She put her elbows on her knees, laced her fingers together. The harsh valley of her back sweated in a heat that even the shade of night could not relieve. Crystal propped the painting on the floor in the doorway, disappeared again like a specter and came back with a cool, wet rag for Aimee's leg. It felt like a kiss. The smallest touch, all that the day had room for, now. Crystal let out a barely perceptible sigh.

"It's Charlene Marie Sparr got queen this year," Dotte said, sudden, from the doorway behind them. "Gets a dress from Stephanie's Bridal Shop."

"That right, Mom?" Aimee said.

"Girls, we got moths coming in."

Aimee turned to look at her mom. Her cardigan sagged open, and, without a belt around it, it fell from her large front and looked kid-size. Dotte bent down and picked up the painting of Christ in the flowery, white frame. She held it in both her hands and angled herself to look at it in the stove light coming from behind.

Aimee turned back to Crystal's face so full of calm and full of power and full of hush.

"If you want," Aimee said, "I'll find a button for your blouse."

Crystal nodded.

"There's something else, Crys." Aimee whispered now. "I seen Ronnie Sisler today." She could see, by the stove light, and by the quick passing of another car's headlights, that Crystal's lips parted with an intake of breath, as though a word were about to come through.

Cord

....

May 26, 1999

Write about something you did that made you proud.

God casts down the prideful and raises up the meek. I write these papers in glory to God, I can not then write about me being proud which I should not be in Gods eyes. Like you do not mind my cursive writing, please do not mind if I change the ending word to—Made Somebody Pleased. We live to please the Lord Jesus and we are not to have the pleasing ourself, but I believe there is times when pleasing somebody is same as pleasing Him.

I remember one time I was real small, maybe age of 5 and Mama still lived. She said to me—Honey, like she called me, I need for you to get me water. We was at our place in Roane and at that time we was on water from a plastic tank, cause the mine company done spoilt ours. They done left tanks all over this state, maybe you never seen one or knew what it was. The tanks is white or yellow and have code numbers painted on them, and the white hoses go in the house in the basement if the people have a basement, or else in a front window, sometime I seen it that way. I know they put them in this town too, and you could see one.

Anyways my Mama sent me for water to boil our beans and to drink. I seen in her black eyes that she was sick and tired of that tank water. They was new bluelake beans of her sisters, Aunt Gails, with no spot nor blight, and she wanted good waters. My Daddy was not around like most days, and she give me a 5 gallon bucket to haul it. It was almost big as me so she said—Just fill it half up. It was evening and the sun was near down and she said one more thing to me—When you watch the light go that is the best time to get the water. I always remember that. I think looking back now she meant for that to keep me from trouble, cause I had to go to the pump at the Baptist church, which we was not members of that church body so it was like I stoled it. She wanted me to go when nobody could see, but looking back, I know our waters was stoled from us and it was not sin to take from the Baptist pump. It may be for fact that you can not steal water at all, God done made water gush from a rock and it is all of it free, to His glory.

   I waited next the church till the light done went entire, then I snuck to the pump. It was high off the ground, the handle part, I could not hardly reach but when I did I yanked it and crashed it loud again the base. I forgot to be secret about it. I brung it up above my head and down to crash, over and over till the water come out. If you never seen a pump like it, it come out in a little bowl in front for to sip, but you lift the spout on the side of it and it goes in your bucket then and not the bowl in front. It is hard to say it right. I got wet from it, cause the water falls a long way to the bucket, but it was hot even in darkness so I did not pay it much mind. I filled it just half up like she said and I pushed the spout back in, water come out the front then. A small stream of it like you see in fountains, I stood tall as I could and I drank from it. You aint never tasted water like that I bet. It was cool and I could tell it was clean, cause it come from so deep. I hauled the bucket back home, I had to stop many a time to catch my breath, it was that heavy even half full. It was dark and the lights was up in the house so I could see clear in the screendoor to Mama at the stove. I went to the back door of the house to bring it in like a surprise, when I come in that kitchen Buddy she was pleased. That pump is still there I bet, that is an hours drive south in Roane where I am talking about. It is so close here, and I can not help but think of that water now to taste it. You can be so close home and not get there. I think of that, cause the black man next to where I stay here is flushing his commode all the time, even if he does not use it, like he thinks the water is dirty itself. Then it come up like a sound in my sink after he done flushed, I think I must be drinking that black mans sewage. But that is my stroke of bitterness, it is all turned Wormwood, it is mine to bear it. To Him be glory.

Aubrey

....

THE UNBEARABLE HEAT WOKE AUBREY early on Tuesday morning. He threw off his bed sheet to cool his body, naked except for his underwear. In his dorm room in college, he had never slept without a T-shirt and loose pants, nor even the year after, in the neat apartment he'd kept above the bookstore in Chicago. But it was so hot in Cuzzert—or "close," as people said here and the word made sense—the heat drew close enough to suffocate you. The thick, wet air began crawling up from the Donnie Manse River in early June, swollen with the spring rain and creek silt. It set in everywhere, so that, by now, in early August, it reached for him from the cabin walls themselves and from his mattress on the floor.

Yet the air in that place no longer suffocated Aubrey. Instead, it peeled his clothes from him and laid him bare to the smell of the cabin's rot, to the hush of the mountains hemming him in and to the salt of potatoes and biscuits that wafted from the other houses along Manheim Road. Here in Cuzzert, for the first time in his life, he felt like he was beginning to shed his padding. He was beginning to touch the world. But after almost a year in this town in the middle of nowhere he was still just beginning. He usually ate alone and always slept alone, and among his students and neighbors—even when visiting the Lemleys—he remained an outsider.

He thought about Aimee's cut leg, her blood beading up, and let his mind linger there. He let his eyes wander around in the defects of the ceiling.

The cabin was an original, like something straight out of Thoreau. A parsonage built in the 1920s for the preacher of the four Methodist churches in and around Cuzzert. All the churches on the charge were closed now, except for the one next door to his cabin. The existing Methodist preacher, Reverend

W. D. Angus, bowtied and round, lived with his wife, Melanie, in the newer, brick parsonage and rented out the cabin. The church building dated back to the twenties, too, but had undergone some renovations: a vinyl-sided addition and a marquee announcing, for the past few weeks, *Come on in, our church is prayer conditioned.* The only apparent renovations in the cabin were a toilet curtained off in the corner of the bedroom, a stand-alone sink in the kitchen side of the main room and shelf liner in the two cupboards—contact paper with butterflies on it.

When Aubrey had been preparing to leave Illinois, Jim Louks, the only VISTA contact in Cuzzert, had warned him by letter that the cabin had no shower. Aubrey had assumed that meant only a bathtub with no showerhead, but it meant there was nothing at all. When he had arrived, he'd found a gray tub leaning against the cabin beside the front door. Handwritten underneath its label, *Biggs Feed & Supply*, was "Cattle Water Tub (can also be used as a dyeing vat or for fish breeding)." On his second night, Aubrey had put the tub in his bedroom to stand in while he sponge-bathed awkwardly, pinning his Loyola sweatshirt over the bare window.

A wood stove heated the cabin in winter, its flue not quite flush with the hole in the ceiling, black soot all around it. "You got to hold your mouth right to get it to take," Reverend Angus had said when he'd demonstrated how to bank the fire. The kitchen table, occupied now with Loyal Sisler's crooked, pop-can rocker, sat under a single-bulb light with a pull cord. There was one bedroom in the back left corner of the cabin. Inside it was another pull-cord light and the floor mattress with no box spring.

When Aubrey had moved there in the fall of 1998, he'd felt like he'd gone back in time and off the map. He'd inhaled the cabin's smell of urine, sulfur and wood smoke so deeply he'd almost gagged.

Aubrey got up from the mattress and pulled on his jeans. He walked to the kitchen sink and splashed his face, then pulled a pan from the cupboard and boiled water for two eggs. His eyes traced the trail of blue ink on the loose-leaf paper taped to the wall above the sink, a handwritten copy of Robert Frost's poem "The Road Not Taken," still creased from being carried in his back pocket since his senior seminar on American poetry at Loyola. The day he'd left Chicago, he had read the poem a few times in the airport to ease his disappointment. His top VISTA placement choices had been New York City and San Diego, but he had received a one-year assignment to Cuzzert. It was certainly "the road less traveled by."

Aubrey had applied to VISTA's service program for an unremarkable reason: his life had come to a halt, and he needed a change. One night, he had stayed late at the bookstore, waiting out a downpour with his pen hovering above a blank page in his journal. His attraction to working at the bookstore after college had been, of course, proximity to books, which he'd hoped would inspire his writing, but he was beginning to hate the smell of new books, with the photos of their authors smiling out at him about their success, seeming to tell him to just go into medicine like his dad, which was his mother's wish. That night, he'd picked up an announcement for another poetry contest he knew he would not enter. He collected such announcements in the back of his journal, like baseball cards.

As his pen hovered, a young guy barged into the store, drenched from the rain yet grinning like a fool. He had a bushy beard, despite his youth, and long, curly hair that rebelled against his ball cap.

"Hey," the guy said, heaving his wet backpack onto the counter. "Can I leave a stack of brochures?"

"Sorry, no solicitors." Aubrey scooted his journal away from the dripping pack. Homemade patches hung from safety-pins attached to its pockets.

"It's a good cause though, kid. Here." He fanned out a set of brochures on the counter: Peace Corps, Jesuit Volunteers, VISTAs.

"I don't think so. Kid," Aubrey said.

"Hey, I have to run—didn't lock my bike. Info meeting's at 121 Howard tomorrow night. You should come out." He picked up his heavy pack and put his arms through the straps.

"You can't just leave these here," Aubrey said.

"Tomorrow night at seven."

"Sorry, I'm busy." Aubrey spoke loudly and wished he hadn't. He wished that he biked in the city and that he could grow a beard instead of just pathetic scruff.

"Oh, I see." The guy glanced at Aubrey's blank journal page. "You look real busy." He opened the door and said, "Careful, man. You're going to wake up astonished one day at how old you look." He thumbed toward the street. "My bike. I'll see you. Seven tomorrow." He bounded out the door with his pack and rode off in the rain. Through the window, Aubrey watched him snake between cars at the traffic light, with no helmet or bike light. Aubrey wiped a smudge from the window, irritated, and studied his reflection. A high hairline like his dad's. He wondered if he'd go bald.

On the counter, the faces beamed from the brochures like the faces of the authors on the backs of their bestsellers. He took a VISTA brochure and stuck it beside the poetry contest announcement at the back of his journal.

Old man in a padded suit. That was the metaphor he came up with. He was an old man in a padded suit, impervious to intrusion. He started to write that in his journal. No, a *soul* in a padded suit, he revised. He didn't believe in the soul, but if he had, it would have smothered under all this padding. He wrote that, then scratched it out. *Soul encased in glass.*

He pulled the brochure from the back of his journal and opened it.

He didn't attend the informational meeting, but he called the number on the back of the brochure the following day.

Now, Aubrey took his boiled eggs in a bowl to the writing desk that sat at the back of the cabin's main room. He kept his typed poems, still in need of revision, in the desk drawer with the checks his mom had sent. The checks remained uncashed, folded into the medical-school applications. She had highlighted the deadlines, all of them now passed.

Besides the Frost poem, nothing hung on the cabin walls except for a piece of embroidered cloth that someone had framed in plastic gold and hung above the desk before he'd moved in. *Fear knocked on the door*, it read. *Faith answered. No one was there.* It annoyed him, but he'd left it hanging because he had nothing else to hang. Directly underneath it on his desk, he had set out his Thoreau reader and two poetry anthologies.

He pushed his books aside, along with his reading glasses and the small stack of papers, so he wouldn't get eggshell on them. Out the window, he saw that the sky looked dark and swollen enough to rain soon, though he'd learned to doubt such appearances during this summer of drought. The gray would likely change to a bone-white.

He watched Melanie Angus march down her daily path to the vinyl-sided section of the church building. At the door, she set down her mop and bucket to get her key and to make sure her neat bun of purple-gray hair was still fastened. His window was open, and the clink of the handle falling to the side of the metal bucket came into the cabin like a spoon clinking his bowl, along with the sound of her grunt as she lifted the bucket of heavy, hot water from the parsonage.

On the cabin's outer wall, just beneath that window, Reverend Angus had nailed a marker to show how high the floodwaters had risen when the Donnie Manse had flooded in 1985. When Aubrey had first moved in, he would hear voices outside his window, people pointing to the marker and talking about it, a pretense for coming to check out the stranger from the city, even though he wasn't from the city, originally. He was from a suburb of Chicago, from a housing development where he'd grown up quiet and careful and where people would never come to point and would never let their voices carry intrusively through someone else's window screen.

He got some shell in his bite of egg white, a grit in his teeth like sand, and he spit it toward the bowl. He missed and hit the top paper in a stack of writing responses from the Cuzzert Correctional Facility. The stack was Cord Lemley's, every paper he'd written since he'd first come to the class in May, all bundled with a rubber band that bowed them into an open curve.

The very top page was blank, except for Cord's identification number and Monday's date, August 4, 1999, in the upper right-hand corner. And, flush to the left-hand side, the prompt that Aubrey had printed at the high school library, which had the only computers in town except for the one in Jim Louks' house.

At the end of Monday's thirty-minute writing period, Cord had turned in that blank page bound with all the writings that Aubrey had handed back, complete with his own margin notes in red ink. In the last few weeks, Cord's starvation had broken down his logic, and his final writings had read more like a dream sequence.

"Better that a seed of wheat go into the ground and die," Cord had said, raspy with hunger, as he had handed Aubrey the stack. "Let it be record."

Aubrey wiped his eggshell spit from the paper, feeling the spit disrespectful. He had accepted the papers from Cord without a word. Aimee and Crystal had not come, and Aubrey had been greatly affected by that, to his own surprise. Why did this father-daughter reunion matter so much to him? He felt, of course, some basic humanistic responsibility for the life of this man, but he knew that his concern had mostly to do with Aimee, with his desire to help heal a hurt that was sure to be deep in her. And—when he was honest with himself—he knew he hoped his attempts would convince Aimee to let him get close to her.

There was more to it than that, though. He realized he had come to care somewhat deeply for Cord. Aubrey was strangely drawn to this charismatic man who addressed candid notes to him at the end of the writing exercises, without embarrassment or reserve. Aubrey felt that, in this stack of papers, Cord had handed him his last will and testament. Maybe that was indeed what had happened. Aubrey planned to reread all of them.

He'd watched Cord closely during the rest of Monday's class. Aubrey had said nothing about the daughters' planned visit, but Cord had seemed to know, anyway. He held his thinning body slack, let it sigh down into his chair with resignation, and left his pen—usually racing with fury across the page—lying still on the table. The two correctional officers stood on either side of him; he was on close watch, seen as unstable. His face was as gray as his shirt and pants and shoes; even his eyes had dulled. They were once as black as Aimee's, black like coal, and just as pressured into a wild dark light.

Cord held something in his left hand, and Aubrey spent much of the class trying to figure out what was in that fist. At one point, Cord loosened his fingers: he held a button there in his palm, cupping it, and Aubrey saw then that Cord was missing a button on his shirt. He just held it, as though he weren't even sure whether he was supposed to put it back on or not, as though waiting for someone to tell him or to sew it for him.

A man of force and motion, but a man—Aubrey suspected—always taken care of by women, hand and foot. And then that impure mix of indignation and deference, a bow of the head toward the floor, an instinctive self-abasement, but at its center, pride as sound as stone. Crystal had inherited that character, and Aubrey felt like a fool for not realizing who Cord was till a week ago when the gray man finally wrote his name, "Cord Paul Lemley," and his legacy, "I been dead to my girls 10 years."

This shy pride pervaded Cuzzert's people. In the face of it, Aubrey always expected them to catch themselves, to catch their own pious axioms and slurred diphthongs, to see that they were a cliché of themselves, but no one ever did. And, more than that, it was as though they all rubbed up against their own dying, without protection. Just the cruel fact of death, its grating texture inflicted on the landscape itself, on the over-timbered forests and the mountains nearly razed from relentless mining. The raw sense of mortality in Cuzzert filled him like an intoxicating wine.

Aubrey's main duty as a VISTA was to teach General Education Development classes in town, mostly to unemployed miners.

His first week, he'd had a meeting in the one-room community building with the Economic Development Council of Cuzzert. He walked into the building in his best dress clothes, and found Jim Louks waiting for him.

"Welcome, on behalf of the Council," Jim said, laughing as Aubrey shook his doughy hand. Jim Louks *was* the Economic Development Council, "the founder, the chair, the whole roster of board members." It was Jim who had applied for a VISTA worker.

"Half the men in this town are living on welfare checks," Jim said, stroking his generous stomach, "and the other half are living on pride and the sweat of their wives. CONROY's strip jobs all switched to machine awhile back and knocked the miners out of the race. We've got sixty-five percent of folks who can't get a leg up. *Sixty-five* percent. They got no high school diploma, son. And that's where you come in." He winked and punched Aubrey lightly on the shoulder. Jim wanted fliers out right away and classes started in a couple of weeks. He wanted to offer something at the prison, too, just a reading and writing class, though this had not been mentioned in Aubrey's job description.

"It's medium-security, on the small side, just eight-hundred beds. It moved in here in '94, and we ought not to leave it go to the devil. There's a lot of blacks there, from up in New Jersey and New York." He couldn't go in himself; he taught history, English, and biology at Cuzzert High, and he coached the River Lions' ball teams, so he had no time.

"We brought the facility in," Jim said, "for an economy boost. Well, it backfired. Most people in Cuzzert don't qualify for the jobs, and if they do they're too timid to go near the place. The warden and corrections officers got shipped in, transferred from prisons out of state. The other jobs got shipped right out, to folks over in Biggs. There's been no growth of commerce like they promised." He laughed. "I'd say we got a few tipping back down at Paint Davis' bar, but we'll lose even the booze revenue once they fund the four-lane highway. It'll cut us right out of the deal." His face was red with agitation, but he kept his grin. He pulled at his tie, then studied it, as though noticing its paisleys for the first time.

The only other people going into that facility, Jim told him, were Biggs women giving church—a whole bunch of American Baptists on a blue bus. They came in because Reverend Angus believed in an eye for an eye—too respectable to concern himself with convict souls, and the only other church in Cuzzert was too half-witted to arrange services at the prison, the Glory-bound Holy-Roller Tabernacle, which met, he was embarrassed to say, in his own mother's basement.

Jim Louks himself was not a church man, but it was his firm belief that even convicts needed some education. "We'll give them something," he said, "even if they did leave us high and dry—and that's where you come in." He winked again, slapped Aubrey's back. "You're a green wood, son. Fresh in from the

Middle West. It'll take a little while for your fire to catch here, but this'll be a good year for you, a real good year."

After the meeting, Aubrey had walked the length of Manheim Road, from the westward-edge switchback curve to the east end where a sign stood in the yard of a house with its purple siding peeling in places and a huge satellite dish in the grass. He read on the sign, *Cuzzert Unincorporated, Population 335.*

A boy came out of the purple house in a dirty, Disney-World T-shirt, holding a spoon and wiping his mouth as though he'd been in the middle of a bowl of soup.

"That was 'fore the prison come in," the boy said, scratching his freckled face. "We never done no recount yet. But I bet it's up 'bout twice that with the jailbirds. Some people mighta died," he added, "and brung the number down, but nobody else here going no place, 'cept for my brother Ronnie who done left already. You got a face like him."

Aubrey said nothing. He thought about the brief handout he'd received during his three-day VISTA training in Pittsburgh. *Sociology of Appalachia,* it said at the top. It gave the summary of two kinds of poor: The stationary poor, which was Appalachian poor—heads of household erratically employed, functionally illiterate, fatalistic, houses in squalor, children will be poor the rest of their lives; and the upwardly mobile poor—heads of household hard-working farmers and laborers, living by standards of middle class, houses in good repair, children clean and taught respect and encouraged to move out of the ranks of the poor.

"Loyal Sisler," the kid said, "and who the hell are you?" Loyal walked back into the house without waiting for Aubrey's name or his muffled "Nice to meet you."

Aubrey turned back to look down Manheim Road, paved a long while ago and studded with potholes. The Muffler Barn stood a little ways from Loyal Sisler's house, the Save-a-Lot next, the community building, Family Dollar, then the cement-block building with the KENO sign out front. Jim Louks had pointed it out as the bar operated by Paint Davis.

"You go in there," Jim had said, either as a warning or a recommendation, "and you won't come out till morning."

Next came the Methodist church marquee, his tiny cabin, the sunken-in houses beyond. All of it simple, like a grove of trees huddled together at the base of the coal-stripped mountains that threatened to shove it all into the river.

A year-long VISTA assignment felt, then, like an eternity. It was a town at a standstill, not exactly the place to get his life jump-started. Like a ghost town, he could joke, or lament, in a letter to his mom, but he knew he wouldn't send her any letter. He would start several in his journal but would never find the right words to finish them.

The eggs left Aubrey's mouth pasty. He got up to set the percolator on the hotplate for coffee. Class would start at nine at the community building, so he had time. He put the bowl in the sink, the pieces of shell neatly mounded in the center, a neatness that Aimee had made fun of when he'd first gone for supper at the Lemleys' the previous fall. They had served him boiled potatoes and boiled eggs, and he'd peeled his egg perfect. That's what Aimee had said: "Don't you just peel it perfect."

She had invited him to supper the third time he'd seen her, a couple of weeks after his first GED class when she'd given him a cigarette that he'd never smoked but kept in the case with his reading glasses. In such a small town, he had been sure she would show up again, but she hadn't. He had avoided the Muffler Barn, but he'd pictured her a few times in her black, halter-top dress standing at the door of his cabin.

That third time he'd seen Aimee she'd been walking down Route 40. He was driving home from his class at the prison, driving the Jeep he'd bought used from Jim Louks' cousin in Biggs. He slowed the Jeep and rolled down the window on the passenger side. The cold air of early fall hit him hard, yet Aimee wore a short-sleeved blouse with a low-scooped back and a white skirt hitting mid-thigh. She hugged herself as she walked but dropped her arms when Aubrey pulled up beside her.

"Well. Where you been?" she said, leaning in through the window.

"I was out at the correctional facility. I teach a class there on Mondays."

"No, I mean where you *been*? You ain't come 'round to see me."

"I know. Sorry. You're not working at the auto shop today?"

"No, Jimmy's closed up to take his aunt to hospital in Biggs. He takes her for dialysis once a month. I seen your Jeep go past my place awhile ago. I live a little ways from here on 40. Crystal got the truck today, so I just took me a little walk and wondered if you'd be by again. I get my mom's cigarettes at King's Service Station. Cheapest place. She don't need none today, though." Aimee pulled out of the window and looked down at the road.

Aubrey was silent, pummeled by her stream of words. Then, embarrassed, he realized she was waiting for him to offer her a ride. "Would you like a ride?" he asked.

Aimee grinned a natural grin. He saw that her lips cracked a little in the cold, a pink lipstick breaking up into cracks of lighter pink. She opened the door, and, before she got in, she slapped her hand on the seat and pointed at him. Her grin went strange.

"You gonna behave, Aw-brey?"

He just watched her lips and didn't say anything, though he felt like he should apologize for watching her lips, but they were just part of her mouth, so he said nothing as she got in. He turned up the heat and drove on.

"Why doesn't your sister talk?" His question surprised him, but he had to say something to keep from watching Aimee tug her skirt down to cover more of her legs.

"Same reason I don't lay down with no man."

"Why's that?"

"We done took our vows."

"So you're like—nuns."

"We gonna be women-prophets, like I done told you already."

"Then you'll tell the future." A shy smile teased Aubrey's face, but Aimee continued solemnly, settling her hands on her thighs.

"Could be. A prophet's meant for something, so she walks the straight and narrow. Could be meant to prophesy what's coming or to heal people or something else. I don't know what I'm meant for, just yet. Been nine years since Crys got her Word from 'Clesiastes, and I got mine from the Prophet Jeremiah who was to take no wife. He was a seer of pain."

"Whose pain?"

"His own. And everybody's. He seen evils, and he wrote 'em down. I know it 'cause I done read his Word through many a time with Crys. She reads it silent, and I read it out loud to her and Mom, and he said in Chapter Two that my people done two evils: They forsook the fountain of living waters—that's the Lord— and they hewed them out cisterns, broken cisterns that can hold no water." The way she said *hewed*, it coiled around him, moved in close to his skin, mingled with the currents of heat blowing from the vents. He said nothing in response.

"You ain't listening to a damn thing I say," she whined.

"Yes, I am," he said quickly. "Broken cisterns. That's a beautiful image, actually. I don't read the Bible much."

"Well, ain't you a case for hell, Aubrey Falls."

"Possibly."

"A body suffers something fierce when you take a vow. A person suffers like Jesus."

He had no response for that either.

She tapped her hands on her legs randomly, without rhythm. She said, "That night in the community building, you told me you was a VISTA. What's a VISTA-man?"

"Volunteer in Service to America."

"Like the army."

"Different kind of service."

"Still gets you a badge though. Helping us poor folk, all us trashy girls."

"Please don't."

She stilled her hands for a beat. "That there's the Cuzzert Pike," and she pointed down a gravel road, "the turnoff for my church, Glorybound Holiness Tabernacle. People who come out there, we get 'em prayed up."

Aubrey remembered Jim Louks' words: holy-roller church. He wondered if everyone there was as wild as Aimee.

"Did you always wanna be a teacher?" she asked.

"I was supposed to be a doctor like my dad."

"Why ain't you one, then?"

"You and your sister never came back to my class. Why is that?"

She grinned once more, almost naturally but not quite. "I done told you, I don't need no diploma. I come there that night for you." She said the last part quietly and looked out the window. "Where do you think them people's gonna work when they through with your class? Ain't nothing for 'em here. They'll have to move on out to Biggs or someplace."

"Is that such a bad thing?"

"They got ties here. You fooling with their life."

"They only come if they want to."

"Well," she said, letting her voice linger. She tapped her bare legs again. "What's them prison men like? You teaching them GED too? Is there really lotsa blacks in there? That's what people say. A black kid come to our school one time. Crys said to me—back when she was talking—'Black same as white in God's eyes, Aimee, neither Jew nor Gentile.' But people didn't treat him good. I don't know too many others."

"A lot of the men seem really young," he said. That morning, one man in the class had put his head down on the table like a little boy. Nobody had seemed to notice but Aubrey. The man was huge, and he'd put his arm over his head. He had a tattoo up his forearm of a heart tangled in thorns, flames engulfing it, a banner flying on the skin below: *Never Forgotten* in black script. Aubrey had walked over to put a hand on the man's shoulder, but before he could, the man had looked up and said, "Fuck off," and then started writing with his hands shaking. Aubrey's hands had shaken, too, for the rest of the class. But he didn't tell Aimee any of that.

"And a lot of them like to write," he said to her. "I teach basic reading and writing, but they don't usually like anything I bring for them to read. They like to tell their own stories."

"What type things they write on?"

"I have a list of prompts from my training. I got it from a guy who teaches writing in Pittsburgh. He's a VISTA too. He runs a place called the Safehouse."

"What's a safe house?"

"It's a place for runaways and people in the city who need a safe place."

Aimee turned toward him with her back against the door. Her skirt shimmied farther up her thighs, but she made no move to pull the hem down. Her naturalness faded into someplace deep inside, and it left an actress face, a face ready for another performance. "And what do *you* write? In there?" She nodded toward his journal on the Jeep's console between them. "I bet you write poems in there."

"No." Aubrey felt his face get red.

"I bet you write poems, Aubrey Falls. You need to write one for me. For Aimee Jo Lemley. I got my grandma's name, from Mom's side, and lots of things could rhyme with that. I'd like it to rhyme. Crys is Crystal Lee Ann; she got herself two damn names, named for both Daddy's sisters, one Lisa and one Annabelle, but Daddy called 'em Lee and Ann for short and give them names to Crys. You need to write a poem for me so you don't forget me—dear Aimee Jo." Her words aimed at a surface, like rain striking tin, and didn't seem meant for him, but he loved to hear her voice, anyway. He hadn't written anything since he'd come to Cuzzert, just notes and impressions, but he reread the typed poems in his drawer now and then. They were wooden and contrived. His voice was flat as a freight train crossing Illinois. Aimee's voice bounded and ricocheted, curved and languished and then spouted forth again.

"Who do you talk with if your sister never speaks?" he asked, interrupting her. Aimee jerked her words to a halt. "I mean, you said it's been nine years. That's crazy. How can you stand that? Or maybe you have somebody else."

"It ain't crazy."

"I just mean, well . . ."

"It ain't crazy. 'Cause how else we gonna stand firm? You think it was easy for Jeremiah—seeing all that damn pain? You think it's all s'posed to be easy, coming here from the city, and you a VISTA, and you this, and you that. Well, there's gonna come a battle and a bloodbath, buddy, and I'll be a standing my ground."

Aubrey said nothing. He sat there and watched her turn forward again and get her hands going, rapping the dashboard. She looked at him, half in pain, half wild. She laughed a little, but her laughter was soft and burnt. She sank her body down into the seat. He had no way to defend himself or to defend her, and he sensed she needed defending.

"Crystal and me work out just fine," she said quietly. "She don't need to talk." Aimee looked down at her knees. Red around the knee cap and dry. "And I don't need nobody else. I can tell her things. I can tell Crys anything, and, boy, can she keep a secret. You could say she's my safe house." She smiled at that, toward her knees not toward Aubrey. "Needs to start dressing like a woman, though. She wears them damn blocky shirts and you can't wrestle a dress on her besides Sunday. I'm always telling her that." Then she looked at him. "You wanna come for supper, Aubrey?"

"Supper?"

"You eat, don't you? Shore you do—and you can drop me right there, turn left there. It's just me and Crys and Mom, and I'll get Mom to the bath 'fore you come—and it's this here one on the left, with the blue front. You come tomorrow night for supper. 'Bout six, okay? I thank you for the ride."

Aubrey looked at the trailer through the window past Aimee. The front siding was dented in near the steps, like the side of a truck that's been side-swiped. She looked at him expectantly, and he hesitated. This was crazy. He said, "I don't think your sister likes me very much."

"She likes you fine," Aimee said. She moved her face further into his line of vision, swung her black hair around to frame her cheek. "We like you fine. You come for supper." She reached as though to touch him, but she tapped the journal on the console instead. "Don't you forget my poem now."

She opened the door and got out. Before she shut it, she leaned back in. "Hey, Aubrey?" saying his name as if it were a question.

"Yeah, okay," he answered. "I'll come. Tomorrow evening."

"Hey, Aubrey. I ain't trash." Her cracked pink lips pressed together as she held herself there for a moment, blocking Aubrey's view of the doublewide.

"I know," he said.

Crystal

....

Ride a passenger train.

It was written in pencil in the crooked cursive of Aimee's twelve-year-old hand.

The next line on the page: *Go see the ocean,* in Crystal's more somber letters, the slow, careful writing she'd done at fourteen. Back and forth it went, from one penciled line to the next, their list of things to do before the rapture of the saints, before Jesus caught them up for glory and the Overjordan.

Aimee: *Save enough money in my bloodhound bank to buy June a dress.*

Crystal: *Find Janey Close and pray her through.*

Aimee: *Take a boat down the Donnie Manse.*

Crystal: *Write a song with Ronnie.*

Aimee: *Have a baby girl, name her Jenni.*

Crystal: *Have a baby girl, name her Naomi.*

Aimee: *Make Jenni and Naomi a treehouse (they will be close cousins).*

Crystal: *Buy N and J locket necklaces with the face of the Lord inside.*

The list was in Crystal's black notebook that she'd taken out from under the corner of carpet in her bedroom. It was Tuesday, near noon. She had seen the cross of sixteen-penny nails there too, beneath the notebook, the cross wound with copper wire. She touched it and thought about what Aimee had told her the night before, about seeing Ronnie. So he was alive, after five years without so much as a postcard, and it was true he handled snakes and charged three dollars to folks sitting in folding chairs, eager to see him get bit.

She had left the cross in its place and carried the notebook to her bed.

It still had a few blank pages, and she planned to write Aimee a note. She hadn't written much since she'd gone silent; she didn't need the noise of words on paper to ease the silence. She didn't want her silence eased.

Now she held a pen but wasn't sure how to begin. What she wanted to say was that she would go see their daddy on her own. *To spare you pain* was the phrase she wanted to use. She would go with Aubrey, and Aimee wouldn't have to. She could go next time.

They had slept late, or had lain there, sleepless, waiting for the other one to get up first. The night before, Aimee had taken Crystal's blouse with the missing button and promised to fix it in the morning, then they could go. That's when they would be ready—good and ready, Aimee had said—and she had insisted Crystal have all her buttons if she planned to wear that old blouse again.

But now, close to noon, Aimee was still at work on the blouse, having disappeared into the back room that used to be Cord's study but was now filled with junk and all his clothes and all Dotte's old sewing things.

Crystal had climbed slow out of a dream when she had waked that morning, a dream of blackbirds so real they had called to her, their eyes crusted with clay-dirt. They'd been slick and cold and circling. She had gulped in the air stirring from their flapping wings, then found that it was just the wind blowing through her open window, its screen duct-taped but loose.

It had begun to rain, in the real drought-ridden world of Tuesday in Painted Rocks. One of the dream-birds looked as though it somehow felt the wet rain on its face, then it faded from her mind.

Her breath was short. She gulped the wet air and the sadness and the doubt of the small, one-window room, of the Tuesday itself, and did not murmur it away. She did not shake it loose with any utterance, like a hand on an apron shaking loose a house spider. Not even a hum, a prayer, or a whisper to her sister through the thin particle board, louder and louder till Aimee would hear.

Crystal lay there thinking of her daddy, who had lain once in the patchy hayfield strewn with old popcorn cups and Midway ticket stubs, the day of that electrical storm: a pile of black clothes in the field, that dark bird circling but she had not known which kind; it had been too high.

Would he be old, now? she thought.

He would.

She felt ancient at twenty-six.

She sat up into the weird light coming through beneath the timid rain and the hot clouds still assembling. It was a piercing light, and it made her sight blank, like a bright light does. But her silence in that moment seemed the opposite of blankness.

One time at Glorybound, Cord had preached from the Sermon on the Mount: blessed are the pure in heart, for they shall see God, those are the ones who see God. And everyone in that place had tried to see, eyes closed—Crystal's, too—to see God in the Tabernacle. They'd taken it to be a test of their purity. Cord had whispered loud for them to look and look, peer deep down for God; he'd put his hands to the sides of his head like blinders on a horse, but he evidently could not see, because, then, amid the humming and the low wailing of Chloe Shrout and the oldest Felton daughter who'd just moved home to care for her mother, amid the looking and looking, he'd broken like a hypnotized man from a trance and asked for a hymn. He'd muttered something about how even Moses got God's back and not his face.

"God, spare us the pain of the vision of thy face of fire," he'd prayed then, as Ronnie started in lightly with the acoustic guitar. Cord had seemed to pray it in anger.

To be pure in heart. It had kept her captive as a teenager. Washing her body in the tub at night, she would pray, "My soul, too, Lord Jesus. My soul, too." But her silence now was not concerned with purity, though it may have begun that way. The first year of it had been the worst, because she could not wipe herself clean with words. Then that nagging ended; there had been a letting-go. After ten years, her silence had become soiled, filthy like her blouse, unable to fend off what was thrown at it. It soaked everything in, even this rain starting on the roof like a tentative typing machine.

The rain would bring some relief from the heat, and she loved hearing it come. It might release them, let something loose that they could not loose themselves. She rose with the sure purpose of going to the prison that afternoon.

Crystal dressed and sat back down on the bed to write the note to Aimee. She leafed through the notebook, through her years of recording her daddy's sign-reading, and found again this list she had made with Aimee before Cord had left, even before the lightning had struck as the cruelest sign. They had written it together, out on the back screen-porch, knees drawn up, air coming in under their skirts to cool the parts of them that were dark and wet.

Save a soul, in Crystal's solemn hand. Then, in the same hand: *Ride a motorcycle.* She smiled at that.

Drive all the way to California, Aimee had written, *in a car with no roof.*

Help Mom read better, with a lopsided star drawn after it, which meant they both shared that one.

And Crystal remembered how they had sat thinking, then, not sure what other dreams they had. Or, for her part, sure of the dreams but not sure which ones to share with Aimee, for the girls let each other have private dreams now and then. Aimee had turned her face from Crystal, her jawline like a chiseled, marble edge, her sheet of black hair like the kind of drape they must use in museums for marble things. Aimee's dreams seemed to scatter through the million tiny holes of the porch's screen, and Crystal watched them go out, invisible among the deer flies butting the screen mesh.

"Can I tell you something, Crys?" Aimee's soft-butter voice had surprised her. They'd been making their list in quiet for the most part, giggles here and there.

"What?" Crystal said.

Aimee set her pencil in the folds of her yellow dress where her torso met her legs, and she hugged her knees to herself. She said, "I'm not shore I'll get to go."

"Go where? To California?"

"No. To heaven and the Overjordan. When the rapture comes."

"'Course you're going. You believed in your heart and confessed with your mouth."

"But how do you know? I ain't never got the gift of tongues, yet."

"But you got healed that time from the stomach flu. That's sign enough, Aimee. You're saved and dunk-baptized. Jesus don't lose no sheep. You just need to pray."

"I been praying." Aimee studied the yellow fabric of the dress that covered her knees, seemed to stare through the threads. "But what if there's things to keep me from it? From heaven?" She started to cry without noise. Crystal started crying then, too, mostly for Aimee but also for herself and for the dense, hot thoughts of Ronnie Sisler that she thought in bed while she smelled the new particle-board partition between her and Aimee's rooms. Crystal looked down, in her notebook, at the roofless car that would go all the way to California. She had sometimes thought in secret that Aimee was the chosen one and she was not—as though it were God's favor that made a girl pretty, made her a gift. She felt guilty for that thought now.

"Well, I just won't go without you," Crystal said. "And if we get separated in that time, when the rapture comes or the tribulations, we'll need a place to meet. We'll meet at the cemetery, at the tall pretty cross where Janey's baby is buried. You know the one. The one the flood didn't touch."

"Yeah, I know the one." Aimee looked back at her knees.

"That's where we'll meet. Let's promise." And she set out her fist on her lap until Aimee tapped it. Fist on fist, like they'd seen the Dixon boys do to seal a pact.

"Now let's make our own private lists," Crystal went on. "Here's paper for you." She ripped a sheet from her notebook, because she knew Aimee didn't keep a notebook of her own. Aimee's thoughts just skipped and fell without record.

"I don't have nowhere to keep it."

"Use this." Crystal picked up her pencil sharpener from the porch floor. It was plastic, the shape of a tiny, two-inch Bible, with *He Lives* in blue letters on the top. She swiveled out the middle, the sharpener part, and emptied their pencil shavings. "You can fold up your paper small and hide it in here." The gesture helped ease her guilty feeling.

Aimee took it and pulled out the middle part a few times. She stood up, no longer crying. Then, thoughtfully, she squatted back down beside Crystal. "Don't forget me," she said, "when you get taken up." She pointed to the notebook page in Crystal's hands, a few inches beneath their resolve to help Dotte read better, with its penciled star. "Write it there in your book, to not forget me."

"I done said we'd meet at the baby's cross."

"Just write it."

Crystal felt Aimee's breath on her cheek as she spoke, squatting there in her long, yellow dress, insistent. So she wrote, in slow cursive, *Do not forget dear Aimee Jo Lemley.*

Aimee had stood then, walked into the trailer with her pencil, her blank sheet of paper and the Bible pencil sharpener.

Crystal had stayed on the porch. She had meant to write a private list, how she wanted to write a book, one day, and also to marry Ronnie Sisler, but she had written nothing.

Now, almost noon, Crystal looked over the old list and down the yellowed page to the last thing she'd written in her fourteen-year-old hand—that admonition to remember her sister. And she decided again to write nothing.

She would just go, without leaving a note, because what does it really mean to spare someone pain? It was not in her power to do that. The words made no sense to her. *Pain falls wherever it wants,* she thought, *like so many drops of rain. Ain't nobody spared that. Can't no soul go without.*

Inside her, another letting go: she pictured herself moving out underneath the drizzle, then the downpour, on Route 40, on foot, the warm rain like a second baptism. She was not going to the Overjordan today, holding hands with her sister among the saints, in all manner of light; she was going to the Cuzzert Correctional Facility for Men to see if her daddy had grown old. She would go on foot, and she would leave Aimee behind.

Crystal walked the linoleum toward the kitchen, wearing the same jeans and *Jesus Saves* T-shirt. She left her hair loose, falling in thin locks down her back like sparse clumps of grass. She could feel a slight ripple in it where her ponytail had gathered the day before.

"It might amount to something." Dotte startled her from the kitchen table, looking out the screen door. Crystal hadn't expected to see her mom, though this was the usual time Dotte came out of her room for her cold coffee and cheese. Crystal had lost a sense of the rhythms of the household.

"It might amount to something," Dotte repeated. Crystal knew she meant the rain. She looked at her mom and saw her own pale hair and poorly ordered teeth.

"You keep dry," Dotte went on. "It's good you're going in to work."

Crystal nodded. It would in fact be good to go to work, even though she didn't plan to. She thought briefly of Balaam, and she hoped he found the grassy patch in back of the shop-and-diner and left the potted junipers alone.

"You know where Aimee went?" Dotte asked. "Jimmy called, asked is she coming in. 'I thought she was there,' I said to him." Crystal shook her head no. She didn't remember hearing the phone ring. Aimee must have been too quiet for Dotte to hear, still in the back room that was most often shut up unto itself.

"Well," her mom said. She shifted her heavy body in her chair, pulled her black sweater together so the front parts almost touched. Her nightgown underneath looked like sallow skin but for the three greenish-silver snap buttons unfastened at the top.

The girls had kept Cord's whereabouts hidden. Did Dotte somehow know anyway? Had he sent her word in secret these past ten years? Crystal knew of only one parcel that came within the first year he was gone, but Dotte had opened it in her bedroom with the door closed.

She squinted at her mom, tried to see inside her. If you had to be pure in heart to see God, what did it take to see inside another person?

She squinted to see Dotte as the young woman who would come to the tub where Crystal bathed her little-girl body. She would come in to wash Crystal's hair. Another baptism. Dotte would fill a big plastic Pepsi cup and pour water over Crystal's forehead. Crystal would tip her head back and sing in a low register with her vocal cords pinched so her singing would come out frail.

She squinted to see the figure of her mom before it had grown so wide, back when her hands had been quick, trim and careful. Her mind had always been simple, but her hands had been fastidious. Crystal remembered a favorite housedress her mom had sewn for herself, how it zipped up the back, red with white flowers all over. She remembered Dotte hating the doublewide but laying clean rag rugs and washing them every Monday, and keeping her sewing things tidy in the living room.

After Cord had left, Dotte's hands had stilled. She had traveled someplace inside herself where nobody could see. Away from her flesh, her body a condemned sack. Set on the kitchen chair to get big. She sat yellowing inside loose skin.

"Keep dry," Dotte said again, but Crystal was already out the screen door. She walked quick past the white truck and let it sit, heading toward town on foot again. It was too much, all the years swelling up their trailer with stale life, all the voices she heard and soaked in: Arlene at Cool Springs going on about the stolen money; Aimee jittery over Ronnie and the snakes; Aubrey with the helpless way he loved her sister; Aimee digging through buttons right then, looking for one to put on a blouse fit for a ghost; Dotte saying when Crystal was small, "We do like he says, now. You got to allow for him—he's God's hands and feet—he's a minister of the Word." Crystal gathered in the voices and memories, gathered them like the rain gauge she saw now on the fencepost, measuring rainfall. Only Crystal measured everybody's pain.

And that cross of sixteen-penny nails, coiled round with copper wire and lying restless under her carpet. Ronnie was alive. Up ahead at the fairgrounds, he was in a black tent with a writhing snake, and she would pass him by on her way into town. She could not stop. She could not speak to him, to anyone. She meant to seek out her daddy and see if he had grown old and grown sore where that lightning had left the bruise in the shape of a fern.

She broke into a run, and the rain came hard.

Cord

....

#96309

June 2, 1999

Do you believe a man is worth more than his worst deed?

Now that there is a good question, cause it depends on which kind of man you mean. But the fact of you asking is a sign unto itself. It proves true what I am going to lay out here. For this first part—I opened the Word this morning like I do every day before the breakfast meal. It is dark when I do it, but there is some lights that stay on all night, I can read by them. I come to the man David in the second book of Prophet Samuel, Chapter 11 and 12—I can not tell if you read the Word or not Boy but you need it, I know my testimony is spoilt, I still say it. What happened was David laid down with another mans wife and got a son. That man was Uriah the Hittite, and David had that man killed in battle so he himself could marry Bathsheba, that was the womans name. It was a evil thing, cause he took a poor mans lamb, that lamb being Bathsheba, so God done struck Davids son to die. David fasted 7 days. He ate no food and took no drink for them days to try and save his boy. But God told him to rise after 7 days—Your son is dead—they said to him, and he rose up to eat a meal. So even if David done this evil deed, and even if his son got struck, the fact of him rising up to eat puts David worth more than that bad deed of killing.

I got a second part to this one. You got a man worthy like David who God done anointed with oil for king, then you got a man like me. And it is harder to tell with me. I kneeled at my cot here to pray after reading David and Bathsheba, and it entered into me like a sting that it is 40 days since the Judge knocked the hammer on me. If *you know the Word you know 40 days be always a marker for the Temptation and the Desert. So I prayed on that at my cot. I put my hands on my legs before me and God showed me my fingers were too fat like somebody filled them up with lard. I looked at my fingers and I could tell they was swole up fat with my own sin. I took that for sign that I would go into fast like David done when he took the poor mans lamb. Confirm it O Lord—I said like we always say when we open the Word and lay our finger down for a calling. I shut my eyes and put my finger to a page that opened to me. I read thus in the Lamentations—He putteth his mouth in the dust. So I knew it to be confirmed that I would not eat.*

I can say I feel the hunger come even now, it is bitter. But I must make my body my slave. I will fast like David up till God tells me to rise even though my boy is dead—the boy I do not have that bled out, I would have called him Amos. But I mean by that probly the woman runner that I hit with my truck on the highway. When I hit that runner it was the Lords summon for my sin. I stopped and got out to look, she was laying facedown in a ditch of water, and I got scared, and fear turns man evil, I drove off. But in the court they told me she was face up when they found her and I could not figure that, except that the Lord turned her over and she did not drown for she ought not pay for my sin. But neither ought that boy of Davids had to pay. Well Gods ways aint my ways.

I do not know now if the woman runner is living, she was laid up still in hospital when I come here. But before that deed, I had many a year of darkness and felt forsook by God. I done other things in this life Buddy. Hitting that woman might not be my worst deed even. I will stay down in my fast till God sees fit that I rise up and eat. He will send Word at that time. It might take more than 7 days to get my supper. That is why I say it is harder to tell with me.

So let this be record here of my fast. I took breakfast this morning for my last meal. I had a slice of ham that we never get to eat here and white eggs. I tasted it long, cause it was my last and it tasted good. I see that as Gods hand on my last meal. Even in a fasting time I will keep coming here to do these papers. To God be glory.

Aubrey

....

"WHAT DO YOU MEAN, it don't make no sense, Mr. Falls?" Arlene Sisler's huge chest shook above the tabletop she leaned on. She wore a *Relay for Life* T-shirt, its dates for the relay faded to nineteen-eighty-something. The pink and purple silhouettes of women jogging for breast cancer cracked from the strain on the small shirt.

Aubrey sat with Arlene at the table in the community building during Tuesday's class. The morning was barely over; it was twenty minutes after twelve, and they would break at 12:30 for lunch.

"It makes perfect sense, son." Arlene swung between a mock formality and an overly familiar contempt whenever she spoke to him.

He fidgeted in the metal chair. He had drunk his black coffee at his cabin and had put off coming to class until the last minute, thinking maybe Aimee would drive up and say something sensible and real. She would assure him he was not a meddling fool and that he need not give up on her and run back to the Midwest just yet.

He had walked to class in the rain, which had somehow heightened the isolation he was long used to. The world had been moving, but only outside of himself. His legs had moved, and the rain had drizzled on his bare arms, but inside: still and stale as a freezer, a tomb, a shut-down mine shaft. He had listed and revised the metaphors and tried not to think of Aimee naked, that gentle fire of a thought that always seared and soothed him at once. Funny that this morning's chapter in the literature book would be about figurative language.

Arlene's loose-leaf page lay on the table before him. He wiped some sweat from the bridge of his nose, nudged his reading glasses up and tried to make sense of her peculiar sentences. He sat like this often in class. People were patient and wanted little instruction, mainly wanted to hear his questions so they could translate, as though from a foreign tongue, what it meant to write, "I'll show you what hog ate the cabbage," or what the advantages are to a pole bean over a bush bean and when you pick them so they don't need to be strung but still have some flavor, and what a little bacon can do if you put up beans with a pressure canner. They were tickled when he taught them proper capitalization and spelling; they were much more interested in spelling than in controlling the ideas in their sprawling paragraphs. To convince himself he was really doing something, he would write questions in the margins of the papers in red ink. When he handed back papers, the students answered his questions right away: "Well, that there's the way it happened." Often what they wrote were letters to family members who had either moved away or died, so, if his red ink questioned their logic or their sentence order, they said, "Uncle Pete will know what I mean, don't you worry."

At the table with an agitated Arlene, Aubrey pointed to the Langston Hughes poem they had discussed that morning from the textbook. They used the high school's old books from the eighties, barely intact—some, like this one, without covers. He'd begun a page in his journal one night about how the books embodied Cuzzert's stoppage of time, the way the people here were stuck while the rest of the world moved on. He had lifted his pen when he'd realized how Cuzzert's situation was much like his own and had felt his insides freeze up.

"See in these first lines, Ms. Sisler, how the comparisons work?" He read from it: "'What happens to a dream deferred? Does it dry up like a raisin in the sun? Or fester like a sore—and then run?'"

Arlene puffed air from her lips and made a hooting sound. She crossed her arms over the pitiful, pink-and-purple women on her shirt. Aubrey knew he was insulting her. She was a smart woman, the most regular class attendee. She suspected he had no idea how to teach, and she was right, but she came to class as though to prove his incompetence. She came as faithfully as a pious girl to Sunday school.

"I read the goddamn poem," she said. "That there Langston explains one thing using another. I know it. And that's how I explain this here truck with a quilt pieced out. Maybe you ain't never seen a patchwork quilt—it don't match, but it gets its being the only one of its kind from the mix-up pattern of the squares, like I say there." At that, she flicked the loose-leaf, and Aubrey kept it from falling to the floor.

"But that is nothing like how a truck actually looks," Aubrey said to her.

"That's 'cause you ain't seen my boy Ronnie's truck, like you ain't seen a quilt pieced."

Aubrey felt his blood rise. "How would you describe your son's truck?"

"The truck doors don't match, like the quilt squares. He got a red truck, one door's green, one's black, so it don't look like no other kind of truck. One of a kind. My mama made quilts, that's how I know, pieced from dresses and rags and such, and not a one of 'em's the same. Like the truck, see? Want me to draw you a pitcher?"

"No. That's fine. It's just that you didn't explain it well in your writing."

"Well, I just explained it, ain't I? My mama made lots of things, quilts and things. I don't make nothing, but my boy Loyal, he's creative. Got no sense, but makes good with his hands."

Aubrey took her mention of Loyal as his chance to look like less of an idiot. "Yes," he said. "I bought one of those rockers that he made out of a Mountain Dew can."

"No shit? From Cool Springs? That's fine, Mr. Falls. It's a fine item. You want a restful time-ticker, you just set it rocking, 'cept you have to keep it going or else the time stops. But my other boy Ronnie, he's a lost cause, and a sight frail too. Cries when the cat dies, like that. Sad. He lives too close to the bone. And not a drop of goddamn loyalty since his daddy died—turned all my money over to holy rollers, and now he come back for more. I been telling everyone." She stood up from the table and addressed the other three members of the class. "It's the truck my boy Ronnie got from Shrout's, the one he took to Charleston when I sent him down to auto-diesel school. I tried to do right by him, to get him outta that goddamn nuthouse church, and away from the damn Keno games and the boozing at my brother's beer joint—else he'd end up like you, Joshie." Joshie Dixon, picking at the acne on his face, hung his head in mock guilt, then looked up at Arlene and grinned.

"Damn fool kid," she said. Then, to Aubrey, "You go to church?"

"Me? No. I did go to a Catholic university."

"Well, I don't mean Catholic. I mean a fool Christian church. I saved Ronnie from it, then my boy got mixed up with a new one in Charleston and now he's a handling snakes like a crazy man, drinking poison—you know they only drink it if there's enough there to kill 'em—now tell me if that sounds Christian. Bunch of no-account men's what the church is. And weepy women. And nutcases. And you know it, Miss Chloe." She spoke to Chloe Shrout, a waif of a woman, without looking at her.

Arlene put her hands down on the table in front of Aubrey and leaned the weight of her bulk on them. "Some folks been saying my boy's aiming to do that nonsense up here at the Heritage Fair, but I'll be damned if I'm there to see it. He got some money don't belong to him, hear? So if you see my boy's pickup you holler. The one with doors that don't match, like a pieced quilt."

Chloe Shrout looked up toward Arlene and smiled. "Hallelujah," Chloe said.

"See?" Arlene kept her eyes on Aubrey. "Pack of crazies." She took her paper from the table and went back to her big purse on the chair.

Aubrey watched Arlene as though watching a tidal wave recede. *Too close to the bone.* He repeated the phrase in his head. He knew a few things about Ronnie Sisler from Aimee, that he'd sung in her church at one time and that he and Crystal had been sweethearts. Too close to the bone. All your nerve endings exposed, all the sensation coming without mercy to the poor white of the bone. For all the padding Aubrey had shed from himself in Cuzzert, he couldn't say he lived with closeness to the bone, and he suddenly felt a surprising, unwelcome stab of envy.

Aubrey swallowed back the taste in his mouth, the dregs of his cowboy coffee from that morning. He'd drunk it while watching the rain start. How weird the rain had seemed on the hot ground. He'd half expected to hear the earth hiss like his mom's iron when she would spray water on it to test its heat. He had wanted to feel the rain, had wished it would have rained the day before because then Aimee would not have hung up her laundry, whether appointed to or not, and would not have cut her leg. But then he wouldn't have touched her leg, and he didn't want to undo that part.

He was tired and said nothing as everyone packed up for lunch.

When Arlene had first come to class the previous fall, in mid-October, he'd felt an unlikely affinity between them, if only because she could comment on the others in the room, as one looking in from outside. She was an outsider, like him, though of a different variety.

She was quick and clever, despite her disheveled look. She had walked in and thrown a knowing look toward the class in the community building. Without a word of greeting, she'd given a nod to each person in the room and offered Aubrey her commentary as fact.

"Chloe Shrout's a space cadet for the Lord," she said. "Praise Jesus for dementia."

He glanced at Chloe and smiled despite himself. The woman came to each class kerchiefed and sunny, had a fourth-grade education and had signed up so she could learn how to write down her visions of God. Chloe had told him once, "I hear the young folks say God's dead, but, son, he ain't dead. He weren't even sick when I talked with him this morning." Then, after a long pause, "God looks a little like a train conductor. And we best board his train, son, for his train's headed for glory." Chloe Shrout went to the same church as Aimee and Crystal. She gave him a quarter every class. Didn't say a word, just folded it into his palm.

Then Arlene nodded at Gary Wayne Hayes, an out-of-work miner in the class. "Gary Wayne's the kind of welfare case that wears it like a medal," she said, not quietly. "A guy on welfare's like a cow in pasture that sits in its own shit, and most folks got sense enough to stay sitting, but Gary Wayne's the cow that stands up and struts around so everybody sees he got shit on his ass." The man did sit listless and sedate, self-satisfied. He came to the class, Aubrey thought, to have a new place to loiter. He was the man who bought chewing tobacco from Aimee at the Muffler Barn, every first of the month, on credit. Tobacco juice stained his teeth and caked in the corners of his mouth.

"And that there," Arlene said, nodding to the third and last member of the class, "is the foul-mouthed Joshie Dixon, court-ordered to be in here, I'd guess, after three DUIs, and he goes straight to my brother Paint's to booze up after class. Tapping his foot like he's gotta take a piss or get in some girl's pants 'fore noon."

Arlene looked squarely at Aubrey. "And then there's me. I don't give a damn 'bout a GED. I want to read my horoscopes, and I think I done got cheated by the jailhouse people out of my rightful money for my farm. I think the gas company's a cheating me too, so I want to do figures better. My husband's been dead long enough for me to know what's what. If you make me pay for this here class it'd be like robbing me blind. I'm a single mother, and I'm bigger than you, so how's 'bout I join up?"

Something loosened in Aubrey, and though he meant to tell her it was a free class anyway, he just started to laugh. He laughed out loud, improperly. He could finally recognize the people in the room—the people of Cuzzert—as a cast of characters, and for the first time could view them without despair.

Arlene had grinned but hadn't laughed. She'd shaken Aubrey's hand firmly. On that mid-October day, she hadn't exactly been a comfort to him, but it had felt good to let his guard down and laugh.

Now he watched Arlene rummage through her big purse, probably for money for a bag of chips from the Save-a-Lot across the street. Chloe Shrout shuffled up to him and gave him her quarter, warm from its long clasp in her hand.

"Thanks, Mrs. Shrout," he mumbled. The room was soon empty, and he rubbed the quarter between his thumb and fingers. "Space cadet for the Lord," he whispered.

He remembered Arlene's first day in his class even more starkly because it had been the same day he had gone to Aimee Lemley's for supper, his first time inside her home. He remembered gathering his things in a hurry after that class, rushing to his Jeep parked in front of the community building just off Manheim Road. He'd sat there, feeling alien in the cold driver seat as his skin had broken out into wakeful gooseflesh. He'd headed for the Route 40 junction, picturing Aimee in her doorway.

He'd rolled the window down a crack to feel the whip of wind and let himself quote Thoreau out loud: "October is the month for painted leaves." He'd never seen anything like these roads swallowed up and thick with color, the sugar maples, the golden poplars, everything burning at once.

At the trailer park, Aubrey had parked beside a white pickup with rust spreading like bruises above its tires. A green Pontiac rattled past him and stopped in the dip of dirt by the trailer behind Aimee's. The boy who got out looked like an older version of Joshie Dixon, and Aubrey assumed it was Bud, five years older, the brother Joshie had written about. Aubrey saw a doghouse jutting out beside the parked Pontiac. A sign on its front read, *Beware of Pit Bull with AIDS*. A scrawny husky chained to a stake by the doghouse lifted its head to Bud Dixon as he walked past without a nod to Aubrey.

Aubrey could see just the end of the Dixons' trailer. *Liberty*, like the model of a car, stamped on the roof flashing. He scanned the other trailers, all with the same *Liberty* in a faded brand and with the same dirt-packed parking spots. They were like boxes, and each had a wide strip of white-painted aluminum wrapping its base like a table skirt. Where the skirt had peeled away, he could see cinder blocks stacked as supports under the corners. He thought he saw newspaper covering the windows of a trailer in the back.

Aubrey rushed toward the Lemleys' door, made anxious by the thought of Joshie catching him there, or of the husky snapping its chain. He stood on the front steps, the blue lattice a garish frame around him. He didn't knock. The lattice formed a cage. This was crazy. He was about to leave, but Aimee swung the door open.

"Well, if it ain't Aubrey Falls. You showed up." She spread her lipstick-caked lips into a wide grin. "You'll see what I told you, Mom," she called out to a mother he couldn't see. "Skinny as a rail! You best come in and get yourself something to eat." The blue eye shadow Aimee had smeared clear up to her eyebrows stung him like the blue of the lattice. She wore tight jeans and a loose tank top with thin straps. It had a rose printed on the front, with tiny sequins sewn on the petals like raindrops.

She pulled Aubrey in by the arm, then slipped her hands into her back pockets as though she didn't quite know where to put them. "I'll go get Mom," she said. "She's watching her show." The rose and sequins disappeared down the hallway.

Aubrey stood on the thin rug by the door, with his coat on. The windows had shone at him when he'd pulled up, but, inside, the trailer was almost dark. When his eyes adjusted, he noted all the sources of light: the dim overhead globe just a dark disk of dead flies; the weak bulb above the gas stove; and the gas stove itself. A blue flame licked the pot that Crystal was tending.

Crystal didn't acknowledge him. She was still, not stirring whatever was cooking in the pot. She seemed to guard it, maybe keeping it from boiling over. She wore a man's white T-shirt that hung heavily on her. The shirt had been clothespinned on a laundry line and not ironed afterward—he could see the slight puckers where the pins had pinched the shoulders.

In the blue light, she looked lit up, like a Japanese lantern, and he saw only her luminous profile. Her lips were blue, and she was thin, but her hands at her sides were large. He could see the dark outline of a bra; one strap had slipped off her shoulder underneath the shirt and made her look childlike. She glowed and didn't really stop glowing when she backed away from the stove, moving the pan to a small, wire rack on the table. She returned to the stove, where the blue flame still danced, shapelessly, upward.

Then, Crystal reached out her hand and put it over the flame, as though contemplating setting her hand on fire. Aubrey felt a sudden fear but couldn't bring himself to speak or move. She was so pale, like paper that would catch fire easily. So still it unsettled him, like a person who's calm on a ship in a storm when everyone else is wailing, as though she knew something he didn't. As though she could put her hand in that flame and it wouldn't burn, or else it would burn and she'd bear it. And, burning, she could drench the dark kitchen with light, and Aimee and their mother would come in and they'd all just watch, even her mother, even her sister, even him—this was crazy. *He* was crazy. It was as if the fire would have come from inside her, the most natural thing in the world. And then he would put his hand in, too, natural as could be. How would it feel to burn over a blue gas flame?

"Hello, Aubrey," said a voice he'd never heard, a slow voice, but it jarred him.

At the entrance to the hallway, Aimee stood behind her mom like a puppeteer, urging her to keep speaking. The big woman wore a housecoat and, underneath, a bulky, orange dress like a poncho. She pointed to him. "Are you cold? Your coat is on. I'm Dotte, Dorothy really. Dorothy Jean."

"Nice to meet you," he said, but he eyed the stove. Crystal hadn't put her hand in the flame. She had brought her other hand up and held both there, rubbing them. He could see, then, that she was warming herself, and he felt foolish. He did not find Crystal pretty, at least not in the way he found Aimee pretty, but he felt strangely moved by the warming of this spectral woman's hands.

"And good to see you again, Crystal," he said.

She looked at him for the first time.

"She don't talk," Dotte said, for his information and without apology.

"I know."

Crystal nodded at him, then. She grabbed a folded dishtowel from the table, opened the oven door and reached with the towel to pull out an iron skillet, a cracked mound of brown-gold bread. The smell of it washed over Aubrey. Since he had come to Cuzzert, he had not been invited inside anybody's home. He could feel the smell warm his skin, up under his coat, a smell that he'd caught at times when he'd walked past the houses near his cabin.

"See? Skinny as a rail and ready for Crys' cooking," Aimee said. She didn't take Aubrey's coat, just went to the table and sat, patted the chair beside her. When Aubrey still didn't move, she scooted the chair toward him with a small scrape on the linoleum floor. "You gonna sit or what?"

Crystal cut the cornbread like a pie. She opened a metal cupboard for plates; the rusted door fit over it like a lid that pushes onto a cookie tin, metal on metal. She served a triangle of cornbread on each plate, Aubrey's plate last. The rest of the food they served themselves: boiled eggs still in the shell; boiled potatoes; soupy brown beans that Aimee and Dotte poured over their cornbread and then smothered in ketchup; and a second bread, flaky biscuits with the puncture of fork holes on top.

Aubrey's hands felt like wood when he took a biscuit from the plate Aimee passed him. Nervous, he studied his biscuit closely as he spread the salted butter that melted and ran off like slow rainwater. He spread a lump of red Flavorite jelly and was about to take a bite when he noticed their heads were bowed, eyes closed. He bowed his head then, but nobody spoke. He saw that Aimee held Crystal's hand under the table, in a loose grip of a few fingers. Aimee's other hand traced the seam on the side of her jeans near his chair. He might have taken her hand, but her face shot up before he could.

"Amen," Aimee said, and Dotte echoed. "Crystal's turn to say grace," Aimee explained. "Be glad it weren't Mom's. All your food woulda got cold." She laughed at that. "You get your ketchup? And if it were Daddy, you'd be liable to fall asleep in your pinto beans 'fore he quit."

"Mind," Dotte said.

"Mind what?" Aimee shoved a bite of potato into her mouth and chewed as though it were harder than it was.

"Mind." Dotte tugged at the neck of her orange dress. "He could walk through that door and hear you mock."

"Shore could, Mom. Any day now. Get yourself some ketchup, Aubrey Falls."

Aubrey took the ketchup but didn't want it, just squirted some off to the side of his mushy beans. Aimee had told him in the Muffler Barn that her father had died, but maybe that had been a crude joke. He studied Crystal, as though her face would tell him what was true. He looked for a trace of her blue glow. She didn't look up.

He took a bite of the cornbread soggy with beans, bit into a rock of baking soda that hadn't been mixed in and a rock of brown sugar. He thought of how raw everything was, so ridiculously raw that it hurt. He knocked an egg on his plate and peeled it carefully, set each piece of shell into a mound in the bowl.

"Don't you just peel it perfect?" Aimee said loudly. Then, more shyly, "Real sweet." She went quiet, almost reverent. Everyone was quiet for awhile except for Dotte who was full of intermittent notes, like a big teddy bear you press on the tummy and each time you press it says a different thing.

"That there hanging—Miriam embroidered that," Dotte said, pointing with her fork at the framed hanging of what he assumed was a psalm. *I will lift up mine eyes unto the hills, from whence cometh my help.* She did not explain who Miriam was, but Aubrey suspected Dotte meant Jim's mother, Miriam Louks, who went to their church.

"She give it to me for my birthday.

"Crystal's got a job working the register. Aimee does phones at Jimmy's. They're good girls.

"Had Crystal when I was fifteen. Made them curtains there," pointing with her fork to the window. The curtains hung without a sash. They were a light color, but they looked blue, and Aubrey saw that the stove burner was still on, casting color and heat.

"Your face calls up Ronnie Sisler, yessir.

"Your coat got a rip at the elbow. I'll sew it if you want."

"Aw, Crys," Aimee chimed, "Mom's getting her fingers back with a man around. Ain't sewed a stitch for nine years, and when a fine man come 'round, she's up and sewing."

"Mind," Dotte said to Aimee again, not as a reprimand, but more like filler. "I could do a easy slipstitch. My husband's out on mission," she said, as though explaining why no man was around.

"On mission, my ass," Aimee muttered.

"Mind, Aimee girl."

"Mom, you go ahead and wait for Daddy to walk through that door." A fire flared up in Aimee, as he'd seen before. "He had us all set up for the coming-back of the Lord, Aubrey Falls. Had it all worked out, and it was horseshit, and he took off. He couldn't prophesy a song on the radio, like I did that once—you member, Crys?—I said that song'd come on, the Patsy Cline one, and we was sitting in the Family Dollar parking lot in the truck, me and Crys, and it come on. I said what June Tatum told me—even in the worldly forms God shows hisself. I prophesied it, and it come on the radio next. You know it, Crys."

"Mind," Dotte said again, but Aubrey got the sense Aimee's mom permitted just about anything. Aimee looked at Aubrey with a silly grin. He couldn't help but think her face clownish with that makeup, her caked lips. Pretty, nonetheless.

Aubrey looked at Crystal again for a clue to their father, but she reached for the pan of beans and dished herself a spoonful, with great care not to drip on the table, as though not only mute but also deaf.

"Tell Mom 'bout Chicago, Aubrey. We heard you was from Chicago." Aimee's words dashed out at him before he could get his mental bearings. He was interested in Dotte's husband. He hadn't noticed his coat had torn, and he felt for the elbow's tear under the table.

"Chicago?" he said. "It's like a big cement anthill." He had written that one time.

"You're funny," Aimee said.

"I mean—I'm not from Chicago really. I'm from North Heights, an hour out of the city. I always thought it was ironic they called it 'Heights,' it's so flat there. It's a development. All the houses look pretty much the same, except for the color of the garage doors." He was nervous, alien, he bored himself. He looked toward the hallway that was still dark.

"Your people go to church anyplace?" Dotte asked.

"I went to a Catholic university."

Dotte was silent.

"And my mother goes to a Presbyterian sewing group," he added. "She makes those pillow packets, the ones with old-fashioned storefronts on them. Things like that."

"Oh." Dotte stared at him blankly.

He hadn't gone on a tour of the trailer, confined to the kitchen by that narrow hallway kept dark. The kitchen's scuffed, yellow linoleum came up in low, jagged peaks in places. He did not imagine a labyrinth of rooms—he imagined this same room copied a few times, a toilet someplace. Aimee slept somewhere back there, but it was far away. He felt his face get hot, and he withdrew inside himself. He couldn't help it. It was as though he were not real in the dim trailer but still sitting in that house with no trees around it and with the red garage door. He tried to imagine his mom in the Lemleys' kitchen. She had patted his leg—under compulsion, he'd thought—before he'd left for West Virginia. She had said, "It's good you're going to help those people for a year, but come back and apply to medical schools. It would make your father so proud." And she'd smelled like fabric softener and that metallic soap in the carpets. In this doublewide trailer, in which time did not seem to exist, a year-long term suddenly felt like a very short amount of time.

Aimee jabbed his leg and brought him out of himself. He looked at her old fingernail polish chipping off.

"You hear, Aubrey Falls? I say you oughta tell Mom 'bout you being a VISTA teacher."

He grabbed Aimee's hand under the table, at first to stop her jabs, then he held it. She let him.

"Arlene Sisler came to my class today," he blurted.

"Married my cousin Hiram," Dotte said, nodding. "God rest him."

"She's really something," he said.

Dotte shook her head. "Hiram died in the mines. She needs the Lord."

"She's smarter than most people. It's like she's not afraid of anything. And I don't feel sorry for her." He didn't know why he said it, but he realized it was true—he didn't pity her like he found himself pitying the others. He also understood, glancing at Crystal, that she did not need his pity either. He looked at Aimee and said, "I don't pity her at all."

Crystal stood. She glowed again for a moment, when the light from the blue flame struck her. She took the bowl that had one more hunk of boiled potato in it. With her own fork, she stabbed the potato and put it on Aubrey's plate. He recognized it as kindness, but he didn't know where it had come from.

"Thank you," he said, and she nodded once.

Aubrey let go of Aimee's hand and ate the potato quickly. "Speaking of class," he said. "I have one to get to tonight, starts at seven-thirty." He got up from the table abruptly. "Thank you for the meal."

"Do as you like. Come any time," Dotte said. "I can do a slipstitch for you."

There were two triangles of cornbread left. Crystal went to a drawer and cut foil, wrapped a piece of the cornbread and gave it to Aubrey.

"Thank you," he said, not sure what else to say.

Aimee stood up but stayed planted on the linoleum.

"Good night, then," he said, his arms shaking slightly, as though they'd carried something heavy for a long while. He opened the door to the cold and closed it behind him. He slipped the cornbread, still warm, into his coat pocket and walked around the white pickup to his Jeep. Then the door opened, and Aimee came out in her tank top and jeans. The sequins sparkled in the moonlight, though he saw no moon.

"Folks think they got her pegged—Crystal, I mean." She went around the pickup, too, stood in front of Aubrey and set her hand on the white hood with a thump. She looked cold with no coat. Her face had softened again. "Told you she likes you—gave you the last potato and that there bread. People ain't too kind to Arlene Sisler, but Crys is. It's good you said that. Arlene's got a boy Crystal was sweet on once."

Aimee hugged herself and made a gap in her tank top. He saw the same silver camisole that she'd worn the first time he'd met her and had tried to buy cigarettes. "Nobody knows," she said. "They think they know. I've heard them take bets on what'll make Crys talk. Like they know what she wants."

"What does she want?" he asked.

"You think my place is trashy, so you going quick."

"No. I'm glad I came." He meant it, though the thought of his mother standing in that kitchen had given him a dismal feeling.

"Crys's smart as a whip. Strong as a ox too, and sharp as a damn tack." Aimee rubbed her arms, and he offered his coat, but she wouldn't take it. "It's hard, you know, taking care of Mom the way she is. She ain't always been so big."

"I thought you said your dad was dead." He felt shy about saying it, but he needed to speak pointedly.

"He should be. Got struck by lightning, shoulda killed him." She said it bitterly, but the bitterness did not come naturally to her. "We don't know where he is. Ain't seen hide nor hair for nine years." She worried loose one of the sequins near the bottom of her tank top. Aubrey could tell she was trying to think of something to tease him about.

"You best watch," she said, "holding my hand like you done in there."

"Oh yeah?" He surprised himself, took her hand from where it picked her shirt. He thought of the few people he'd been touched by in his life, people like his mother; they'd been so careful to be light and uncommitted that he would barely notice when they withdrew. Then he stopped thinking of them. Aimee's hand felt heavy. It latched, gripped. She pulled, without moderation or modesty, such that his body just followed, till he stood close enough to her face to see a spot over her left eye that she'd missed with the eye-shadow brush.

"You got a poem for me like I asked you for? A poem to remember Aimee by?"

"I don't plan to forget her."

"You a case for hell, Aubrey Falls," she whispered.

"Possibly."

"But don't you worry none. I'll get you saved."

She kissed him with her mouth still open from speech. A heavy press, brief, then she backed away. She hugged herself again and hurried to the trailer door, that lattice gone black in the darkness. He wanted her to go inside and stand by the gas flame to warm herself, and he wanted to go with her. *Like a moth to flame,* he thought.

Yes, a year felt very short indeed.

He felt for the bread wrapped in foil in his coat pocket. He got in the Jeep and drove back to town.

It was the fourth time he had seen Aimee. After that, he had quit keeping count. After that, she had never kissed him again.

By now the rain was pouring down, and Aubrey heard someone at the community building door. He suspected it was Arlene or someone deciding to eat lunch inside instead of under the awning of the Save-a-Lot.

He removed his reading glasses, closed the coverless book on the Hughes poem and stood up to find his own lunch. Crystal came through the door. She was soaked, her hair a gray sheet slicked to her head. The day was hot, but she shivered, and she breathed hard, as though she'd run there.

"Is she okay?" he asked, meaning Aimee, even though he should have been more concerned about Crystal as she stood soggy as a dog in the doorway, jeans caked with mud from the knee down.

Crystal nodded quickly, *yes,* so Aimee was fine. Those eyes bore into him, speaking her mind for her, and he knew.

"You want to go? To see him? Is that it?"

She nodded again, pointed downward with her index finger, as if to say, *right now.*

"You want to go to the prison," he said again, not as a question.

She shivered, but she had that calm, that strange core that steadied him. Something you'd find at the center of an old tree.

His class was not over for the day. He wasn't even sure he could get them into the prison at that hour. She pointed downward again, then pulled her hair behind her ear as though to listen better. She held her other hand in a fist.

"Then we'll go," he said.

Aimee

....

AIMEE LAY ON THE FLOOR of Cord's old study. She felt the noontime of Tuesday swell the room and swell her fingers as she fooled with the ribbon belt of her red dress. The morning had lifted and left only the rain that fell, lazy at first and then with force. The one window in the room opened toward the Dixons' and let in the steady sound of rain on metal. She lay with her head on her rag pillow in a lake of spilled buttons, letting her memories loose like restless spirits in that room.

Back when Cord had used the study for Bible-reading and prayer, Aimee had not been allowed to come in. His desk was mounded now with Dotte's sewing things: scraps of fabric wadded in Family Dollar bags; pieces of gingham pinned to sleeve- or collar-pattern paper, never joined into a shirt; spools of ribbon, coffee cans of thread, and yarn rewound into balls; a pincushion Dotte had made from fiberfill and tropical-flower fabric—she loved the flowered prints—flowers like red trumpets, now grayed with dust, on the soft disk poked through with straight pins. The electric Singer machine sat on the floor. It had a slide-off case that was partly open, as though someone had meant to take it off and sew something but had been interrupted.

The summer after Aimee had turned twelve, she came to the doorway once and asked if she could come in, because her daddy had a box fan and she wanted to cool by it. "Not till you straighten up," he said, and she stood taller, straighter, but he said, "I mean not till you quit acting filthy, strutting around," and he slapped her behind as she turned to go. "Get yourself a sweater on," he called after her. "That dress cuts too low," even though it was July and she was sweating and the dress was already so snug to her neck that she'd slipped the topmost hook from its eye.

She knew very young that she was bad. That she was a temptress who, if she didn't watch, could bring men to do things they did not want to do, as though she had an evil spirit lurking inside her smooth skin. Her breasts had grown before Crystal's had, and she'd gotten her period first. It had come on a Sunday, after the morning's service; she rolled out of the cab of the delivery truck, after her mom and Crystal got out, and Cord was the one who saw the blood on the back of her dress. She was thirteen.

"That there's the mark of Eve's curse," Cord told her. "You got it early 'cause you got the bent of a harlot. Now go clean yourself and pray."

She felt that if you opened her up, her sin would be like tar stuck to the very sockets of her bones. Something sweet Aubrey Falls did not understand.

Aimee had come into the study late on Tuesday morning, brought Crystal's blouse, with that slight poof of its sleeves, and shut the door. She needed to find a small, white button to match those on the thin blouse. Crystal would be in her room, she knew, waiting to go to the prison. Waiting for her blouse. They would visit their daddy in one of those places with glass between them, like on TV, and they'd talk on a phone through the glass, unable to touch.

Before Cord had left them, he had stopped talking to Aimee altogether. He'd say to Crystal, "Tell your sister to clear the table," and so on, as though Aimee weren't right there in the room. He barely spoke her name, but he watched her move, watched her skin when a small part of it showed. Then, to Crystal, "Tell your sister to get a sweater."

At the prison, he would choose to speak to Crystal through that wall phone, and what a shock when his Crystal would say nothing back. He'd say things Aimee wouldn't hear, and he'd look at her, his youngest girl, his spitting image—black hair, coal-black eyes—but he would not hear a thing about these last ten years of living: about their call to be women-prophets; about Aubrey who told them of their daddy's prison papers; about their mom slipping back behind the thick flesh of herself; about Ronnie and what she had just seen in his box fit for baby birds; about Hershel and how she took care of him at the shop and spread mustard on his sandwiches when he said, like a kid, "Can you put me some?" Her daddy would not hear a thing, not from Crystal's lips, not unless he talked to her—to Aimee Jo—not unless he said her name.

She would go when she was good and ready.

Aimee knew right where the buttons were: inside a cookie tin in Dotte's hard blue suitcase, still packed from the night, ten years before, when they'd watched the TV turn to a cold snow that showed no sign of the Lord's coming back. Aimee pulled the suitcase loose, out from under a stack of McCall's dress patterns with their tissue paper, cut up and used once and then folded so carefully back into their packages. She unlatched the suitcase, and out poured the musty smell of waiting, like that of sweaters pulled from a box after summer.

A couple weeks after Cord had left, when Dotte would lie on her bed for days as one sick, Aimee and Crystal sneaked into the study and opened the suitcase that their mom refused—or forgot—to unpack. Maybe Dotte thought she should stay ready, in case Jesus came back any day from then on. A suitcase packed for the Overjordan, for the kingdom and the glory. Inside it, the girls found the cut-out pattern of the lacy, pink dress they'd both been baptized in—dunked in the Donnie Manse—and swatches of the deep-purple velveteen and the paler taffeta that Dotte had made the Heritage Fair dresses from that year, along with a few feet of white yarn with flecks of silver through it—not even enough to crochet a hair ribbon—doubled over and tied in a bow, and the huge tin of collected buttons.

"What, she planning dressmaking for angels?" Aimee had joked to Crystal in private. But this was not a toolset for a seamstress at work; it was a set of vestiges, as though their mom planned to take up new work in glory and wanted simply to remember these labors of her hands.

"She's got one foot outta this world," Crystal had said—this was just before she laid her finger down in Ecclesiastes and sealed in her tongue. "She's never breathing easy here now."

Now, from the bottom of the suitcase, Aimee took up the Currier-and-Ives cookie tin with ice skaters on its lid. She shook the heavy tin to hear the buttons rumble like the pocket change in her bloodhound bank. She'd stolen a few of the pretty, bone-colored ones the day she and Crystal had first sneaked a look into the suitcase, but Crystal had made her put them back. After that, Aimee would open the tin only to get a button to replace one that had been lost, as a matter of course. Since Dotte's hands had stalled out, the basic sewing tasks had fallen to Aimee.

She pried off the stubborn, tin lid, and it popped open, sending the ice skaters flying. The tin fell to the floor and spilled the buttons everywhere, with the sound of glass breaking.

"Shh," she whispered, "My." They were dress and coat buttons, metal and plastic and wood. "My." Mostly random, and the random ones were somehow desolate, lost from their purpose, but some were in sets, still unused and fastened with thread onto cardboard squares, five of one likeness, and these hadn't met up with their purpose yet, with the sheer silk or rayon they would bring together to cover a body's front, enough buttons so there would be no gaps, no puckers.

Fake, pearl buttons an ashy pewter, with four circles radiating out from its center, red plastic and pink, tiny pink for a doll's jumper. A copper one, from a pair of jeans, and she picked it up and kissed it. They were to her like coins for a love-offering, or like pebbles on a roadside. Like they were something else. Everything like something else, other than what it was. All these buttons, chipped and fooled with, color worried off of some by nervous fingers, in a tin too big for even thousands of them.

Aimee picked a tiny white one with two holes for thread, for Crystal's ratty blouse.

She went for a spool of white thread in the coffee can. Behind it on the desk, she saw her small canvas bag with an *A* embroidered on it, empty and rolled up like a newspaper ready to swat a wasp. She and Crystal had packed a bag for Christ's coming, too. In her canvas bag, Aimee had packed her rag pillow and nothing else but a necklace that Miriam had given her, plastic pearls that got big in the front, like marbles, and then smaller toward the clasp, till they were small as seeds. She couldn't bear the possibility of leaving the pearls behind, or the pillow. She had said to Crystal—watching her pack her favorite books, her black-cover notebook, her pencils, an extra pair of shoes—that she didn't think she needed much, because she expected to be suited up by Jesus. But really, she just didn't think she would be going, because she was not fit for the Overjordan.

Crystal had done things in the dark with Ronnie Sisler, but they'd paid their debt for it: they'd parted ways and had never again stood close but to sing. So Crystal was fit, wiped clean. Aimee didn't know how to pay her debt, because her sin was the tar kind, stuck to bone.

She and Crystal had unpacked their bags after the Glorybound service the morning after Christ had refused to show up, the sad service when Ronnie had trembled like a leaf in rain as he'd picked up their daddy's guitar. Aimee had lost the pearls in time, but the rag pillow had stayed with her. It had made its way into Dotte's piles of sewing things, eventually, into a bag with loose zippers and pages of sewing tips torn from *Better Homes & Gardens*.

She picked out a thread spool, then found the bag with the zippers and the torn-out pages. She pulled her pillow from the bag, sat on the floor, and lay her head down on it, a soft, lumpy island in that lake of buttons.

It was a child pillow, and she used to take it to Glorybound on Sundays. Dotte had made it from white bed sheets with big yellow flowers on them that had faded, so it looked like dark white overtop purer white. It had a seam down the center like an open book—one half for Crystal's head, the other half for Aimee's. Dotte had stuffed it with knots of other ragged sheets, and, when the threads came loose at the pillow's corners, Aimee tied them with kitchen twist-ties, so it looked like it had four dog ears.

When the service got too long and too hot, she and Crystal would lay their heads on the pillow on the basement corner's rag rug. The girls shared the pillow and traced each other's white peach faces and did not lose sight of each other. They fought the sleepiness and stayed fixed, read each other's thoughts while the church people swayed and wailed and begged down blessings. The girls made a refuge of that pillow, until Crystal got older and sat up with their daddy and prayed out loud in a way that made Aimee know God heard.

The first time their daddy told Crystal she was too big to lie in the corner on the pillow, after she'd gotten her own Bible and notebook to carry to service, Aimee felt the bigness of that pillow all her own. She lay her head down, and the lumps felt mean, and she cried that first time without her older sister who had been chosen instead of her. She slept with the pillow that night, too, facing the particle-board wall that newly separated their rooms. She sucked on the four dog ears, and they turned a darker white in time.

Even after Aimee turned thirteen, she went by herself with the pillow, retreated to the corner when the service stretched past noon. She was careful, when she bled once a month, not to lie down too long and let the blood spill over the edge of her pad onto her dress. And sometimes, when she wasn't bleeding, she lay there and touched her body in secret, her breasts rounding so she could cup them. She traced her bra outline, fussed with its bow at the center of her chest where she could feel it through her cotton dress. And afterward, she prayed and touched nothing and listened to the voices of the faithful that shouted out above her in a wonder of crossfires.

Once, she listened close to her daddy's preaching, with the flimsy pillow curled up around her face and covering her ears. It muffled his voice, and she pretended the muffled voice was meant just for her. Though she knew that to be untrue, since he had all but quit speaking to her by then, she pulled the pillow from her ears and sat straight up on the rug, taking his words into herself.

"'I am that I am,' God says here in his Word, the great I AM—there ain't no questioning, brother, there ain't no doubting, sister—'I am that I am,'" and her daddy's words were hot as they struck her, his voice bringing her blood to her face, she could feel it like a magnet drawing hot steel.

"It's the great I *AM* sent you here today and got you up outta bed and washed you clean for worship." He stomped some, set his Bible on his chair and rolled up his long sleeves in a flurry of white.

"Yes, it's the great I AM sent me here to speak his truth. I AM hath sent me unto you, we can say that with the man Moses—amen—that we be the hands and feet of God, the mouth and the tongue of the Almighty, can I hear you say it? Can I hear you say, 'It's the I AM sent me'? He sent me here today, alright now, and we feel it, 'I am that I am,' ain't no question, ain't no question." He looked back toward Aimee, in her corner, though she knew it was dim and he probably couldn't see her. She looked in his black eyes and saw herself there. He was handsome and dark and the sweat pasted his shirt to his chest. He kept saying it, "I am that I am," in a low, crooning chant, and the words wrapped her. She kept hearing them, even after he quit, even after Dotte's shaky voice went up somewhere into a chorus of *hallelujahs* and everyone followed her up that long stairway of sound. *I am that I am;* it hemmed Aimee in close, the way she felt in their long-chute hallway in Painted Rocks, or in the slim pass beside the washing machine on the back screen-porch, when she walked by her daddy and his eyes fell to her face in a hot hail of shame and he told her to get a sweater.

"He is that he is," she heard herself whisper on the rag rug, keeping back from the staircase of praise everybody else was climbing, even her sister Crystal in her low-shine voice. Her daddy was not to be questioned, for her black-tar sin stuck to her bones, and he loomed so that he could surely see it.

Cord closed his eyes after the singers descended to their folding chairs, and he started to pray the closing. She couldn't close her eyes in prayer. She stared wide-eyed at the basement ceiling and at the painting of Jesus with bloodsweat coming down his head. She stared upwards like June Tatum always did. She searched for her daddy's words as they flew up, wondered—did they ever make it out of that room to the ears of God?

After that day, she no longer took her thin pillow to the service, never went to the rag rug in the corner again, but sat up with Dotte behind Cord and Crystal. The pillow was dirty to her, mussed and shadowy from being on the floor. It had those knots of torn sheets stuffed inside, but her secrets, too, so when she packed her canvas bag for her chance to cross to the Overjordan, she packed the pillow that held her secrets. And after that, she didn't pick up the pillow again.

Except one time, years later, when she was twenty-years old. The day June Tatum died, and they mourned her at the wake right there in the basement church. Aimee didn't take the pillow to lie on it, but thought she might give it to June where she lay in the pine box, because, when the pillow had been new and fresh, Aimee would put it in June's hands after worship so she could feel how soft it was. Aimee took the pillow and a sack of half the money in her bloodhound bank, because she'd always meant to buy June a dress with it but never had. She went up to June's large body and touched her face that somebody had shaved smooth. Chloe Shrout sang "Near the Cross" with no accompaniment. Crystal stood beside Aimee and may have wanted to unseal her voice and sing, but she didn't.

"In the cross, in the cross," Chloe sang in her wavery voice, "be my glory ever, till my raptured soul shall find rest beyond the river."

Aimee placed the sack of coins beside June's body in the box but clutched her pillow to her chest. She'd fooled herself: she hadn't brought the dog-ear pillow for June but for herself, so she could mourn in secret, into its dark, white flowers.

Now Aimee lifted her head from the pillow on the floor of the study and pulled her body up from among the scattered buttons. She felt the heat of her monthly blood and wanted to take care that it not spill and trickle onto her red dress, even red on red. She took the needle from the spool and threaded it. She knotted the end of the thread and sewed the tiny white button to Crystal's blouse.

Dotte

....

DOTTE SUCKED A GROUND OF COFFEE from between her teeth. She had swallowed a mouthful of cold grounds when she'd finished her cup at the table. Aimee walked down the hallway toward her in a flash of red, carrying a long rag, in that tank-top dress with the three ribbons for a belt that Aimee tied in a knot instead of a bow. The extra ribbon strands flew as she walked.

"Where's Crystal, Mom?"

"I thought you was gone already. I didn't hear you in the house."

"Where'd she go?"

"She done went to work. In the rain. I told her it'd amount to something." The rain was coming down in a hard slant, so there was wind now.

"She go in the truck?"

"No, it's out there. You need your work shirt? Jimmy called to know if you was coming in."

"I'm headed to work, Mom." Aimee took the truck key from the nail on the wall beside the framed embroidery Miriam had done. She held Crystal's blouse and not a rag like Dotte had thought at first.

"You got Crys a button then?"

"Yeah, I'll drop her shirt at Cool Springs. She look fixed up when she left? Like dressed nice?"

"Not special. Had her hair down, I think that looks nice. She'll be needing a change of clothes. From being in the rain."

"Shore will. What, she crazy walking out in this?" She kissed Dotte on her uncombed hair, then took a cigarette from the pack on the table. "You 'bout out. I'll get you some Pall Malls from King's." She went out the screen door and let it slam. The ruffle of her dress-skirt swished above her knees.

In that dress she was probably headed to the fair and not to work, but Dotte didn't call out after her; she just let Aimee get in the truck and go. She allowed it. She had never been strict enough, because Cord had been so strict it hurt. The daddy was to be the head of the household, and only God was head of him. Brother Noose had explained that when he'd married them.

"From the head cometh the water and the bread and the blood and the command," Brother Noose had said, like a poem Dotte didn't quite understand. The wife was to be subject to him, as to the Lord. And Brother Noose had said that the man sanctified his house like Christ did the church, with the washing of water by the Word.

It was the same out at the Tabernacle. Brother Noose was the head, and when he died, Cord was the head, so that he could take the church to glory, not having spot or wrinkle. Cord quoted that from the Word with his eyes closed: So that it should be holy and without blemish. Only the men ought to lead, but the women could lead in singing and could prophesy. Cord told her that women-prophets were good, because the church was too stiff without the hearts of women. The women were the ones who swayed with praise and danced and let themselves get slain in the Spirit. That's why Dotte let her girls go on believing they were called as women-prophets. With him gone, their family had no head, and she guessed—like a chicken butchered—a family without a head ran around crazy. But he would be back. She knew that.

She stayed in her chair at the kitchen table and thought on her girls.

They were hurting. But life set down in this world was not meant for healing. No, it was meant to learn the ways of their salvation. So she allowed the girls to learn the ways. She let them do things, and she held her tongue. They did not know she knew everything that she knew.

Once, years ago in the winter, she followed Aimee out behind the back trailer that nobody lived in anymore. Out back, where there was a stand of hickory trees and some brush that people threw trash in. Aimee had a black garbage bag full of something, but it wasn't full of trash. Crystal was at work, even though Dotte had asked her not to go out in the truck, because Route 40 was almost drifted shut with snow.

There was a metal barrel back there, and the Dixon boys burned things in it sometimes. Aimee opened that garbage bag and took out her dresses, the ones Dotte had made: Dress after dress, with long sleeves and long skirts; the hook-and-eye Dotte had sewn so careful, the buttons and zippers; the tiny, pink dress they were both baptized in at the river; the small, little-girl dresses that didn't fit anymore, but the bigger ones too; even the white one Dotte had sewn for her girl's passing into glory—those sleeves had silk at the cuffs.

Aimee put all the dresses in the barrel and took a crumpled up newspaper from the bottom of the bag. She lit it with a lighter and dropped it in. It was winter, and the red flame went up and cut the white of the snow. Dotte watched her from behind the trailer nobody lived in anymore.

She watched Aimee burn all her hand-sewn dresses, except for the one or two she would keep wearing on Sundays. All the other days, she started to wear store-bought dresses that Dotte didn't care for.

Aimee wouldn't know her mom could be there to see the fire, because, at that time, Dotte didn't come out of her room some days. Those were bad days, bad like when she'd miscarried a child, between having her girls, and had not left the room for a month. She had still pieced out simple blouses on the bed when the pain didn't keep her from it.

Dotte had made each of those dresses with her own hands, but she said nothing to Aimee. That day, behind the back trailer, Aimee was hurting. Crazy like a chicken with its head gone, watching the fire till it was all ashes. Dotte knew because she stood and watched, too.

Cord

....

#96309

June 9, 1999

Write about your fears. What scares you most?

One thing only, that is the wrath of God Almighty.

I was not going to put more on this paper but there is more to it. It used to be I would say my Daddy scared me more than anything. My worst scare was over his 1955 Pontiac Star Chief. It was red with a white top and two white stripes down the hood, I mean something pretty. I loved it up one side and down the other like a young boy does when he got his mind set on the worldly goods. You do not see cars like that one now. But it was old and beat up and it had rust up the fenders, he did not wash it or tend it like he ought, cause he was a drunk. When I was 14 I wanted to drive that car so bad. A evil entered me one day when he was gone drunk into town, my sisters done went to Uncle Jacks and Aunt Gails. He must of walked I thought to myself, cause his key was on the spike nail inside our house in Roane. I am tired now so I will not say it all, but what I did was take his car out on the road and run it into a mailbox. Buddy I tell you I was scared. I run like a rabbit, I did not tell nobody, I just went back to the house and waited. What scared me was my waiting for him, cause he was not a man above whipping his boy, and I done bent the hood up again that mailbox where the white stripes went. I waited clear till dark fell. My sisters stayed on with Aunt Gail like they did many a night. Of course here he come up the road walking where I knowed he seen the hood smashed up and he knowed who done it too. I was 14 and it was one year before I got saved by God, so the evil was in me big time. He was mean drunk and cursing at me but he stayed outside and told me to come out there where he stood. But I waited and after a time I went out, he said—Did you steal my baby?—that is what he called that Pontiac, and I striked him with my open hand. I always had these big hands and he fell to the dirt and I run all 5 miles to Uncle Jacks. After that night he did not come round me and my sisters much. Soon I took up living in sin with my girl at her aunts. It was evil pride made me strike but I honest did not fear him again.

Before that time the thing scared me most was Mama dying, which she done. My worst fear at that time came to pass, I do not think that is something for a young boy to bear, but Gods ways aint mine. I waited with Mama the day she died, I had aim to die with her. I waked up one morning, I remember it was summer and the brier bush had our house in like a wreath, thorn vines growed in through the window and under the wall since the floor was dirt (part of it was, some boards laid overtop but the dirt come up and we did not sweep it, cause Mama could not get up to do it). With that dirt it was like we lived in a garden, I remember I thought it was not all bad. I waked up like I done said, then I went to Mamas bed and maybe it was God telling me but I knew she would die that day. I sat down and said to her—I will die with you. She was a bleeder, that is all I know, she had pain something fierce. I took a pitcher of water and gave her some all day long as I waited. I was not afraid to die, I even had notion that it would be nice to die in that wreath of briers, they could just grow up over us quiet like they was arms holding us. But I was afraid of Mamas dying without me. It took me time to know when she past, cause her eyes stayed open. That scared me. I remember I could not move my hands right when it happened, like they done died but not the rest of me. But after while I took her sewing scissors and cut back the brier bush that come in the window. I do not know why I done that. I was empty inside for many long days.

But at this time it is just the Lord God I fear in His wrath. So I punish myself, I suffer the loss that I be saved—yet so as by fire—as it says in the Word. It is 7 days since I took up my fast, I have yet no sign for me to rise up and eat. I take in water only, one day I took the juice they give at breakfast, but I heaved that up into the commode so that was evil again God. I am waiting now and it is like all my fear is a waiting for something, like for wrath or my Daddys whipping me or my Mamas dying. I see that now, like it falls upon you and aint chosen. Things is clear when you do not feed the flesh but live in your Spirit.

(This here is a long paper, and I am tired which testifies to the power of the Lord. Glory to Him. You done wrote on my last paper about that woman runner—that she *is living and could be it was me that put her face out the ditch before I drove off, could be I just forgot I done it and not God. Boy it is clear you got no faith, just a educated mind that keeps you from it. It was the Lord Hisself and not me who done the saving. I know that. You best believe. Glory to Him.)*

Crystal

....

CRYSTAL RODE IN THE JEEP BESIDE AUBREY, leaching rainwater from her jeans onto the seat. Her clothes chafed, and her hair hung in tangled strings. She wanted it braided but couldn't do it herself. Aimee always braided it, when it was still wet from a shower, for Sundays. Crystal combed her fingers through and looked in the rearview. No, it would look like knotted baler's twine if she braided it, and it would fall out in no time at all. She needed Aimee.

Aubrey had canceled the rest of his class and walked her to his cabin in silence to get the Jeep. He walked quick, and Arlene Sisler watched from across the street by the Save-a-Lot, gave a half wave and took a bite of something from a tinfoil wrapper. Crystal waited for him outside the cabin in the rain, wet all the same. W. D. Angus lumbered out front of the Methodist church with an umbrella and his pail of black marquee letters. He changed the sign to announce the corned-beef-and-cabbage meal the church would serve at the Heritage Fair, using an *S* for a 5 to give the ticket price.

Aubrey stayed quiet as they drove past the cemetery with headstones black in the rain, even the tall cross marker; past Paint Davis' bar, its cement-block walls gone just as black and bitter. They rolled their windows down halfway, despite the rain, and the smell burst in: the smell of quick mud washing the road and loosening the roots of the ditch flowers; and the sulfurous smell of the disturbed waters of the Donnie Manse.

Then, without warning, the downpour petered to a drizzle. It was letting up too soon, a sure sign of drought—a fierce spurt, just enough to make the ground thirsty. Crystal breathed in the slacking rain and tried desperately to keep hold of its power.

Aubrey turned left at the Route 40 junction. "I'm at the prison strictly on

Mondays," he said. "I don't know if I can get us in. But I'll try. I'll talk with Jesse Nedrow—at least that's who works the gate on Mondays—but I don't pull much weight there."

Crystal nodded.

A white, plastic sign soon came into view, up ahead on the right: *The 52nd Annual CONROY Coal Company Heritage Fair,* printed in dark blue letters. The sign was new and its white crisp. As they drove past the fairgrounds, Aubrey didn't slow, but he said, "It opens tonight, I heard. My first Coal Heritage Fair. It's a shame it had to rain on the grand opening."

Crystal looked hard through the tents. When she had run past earlier, she'd kept her eyes to the road, hadn't dared look through the rides and booths for that tent, black as night in the very back, Aimee had said. She hadn't dared search for Ronnie, but she searched now.

Everything that was meant to look new for the fair looked haggard and wasted, except for the sign that bore the company's bright name. The front ticket booth looked like a porta-john with a big-lipped woman trapped inside. She counted tickets and change behind the slide-up window. The stand beside it reminded Crystal of the shelves of trinkets at Cool Springs, cheap and flashy—a rack of Indian chief headdresses with neon-colored feathers stood out under the drizzle, unprotected. The rain had turned all the tents to a dirty mud-green. She saw Hershel Dunmire without a cap on. He was leaning like a tired dog, waiting beside the funnel-cake counter for the first batch, for a handout.

She looked instinctively to the tree line at the left edge of the grounds, the spot where she had found the blue kite on the pile of rocks the night after her daddy had been struck by lightning in that place. The Sno-cone Hut stood there now, a big wooden Sno-cone propped up beside it, ice-shavings painted red, and a hole cut out where kids could put their faces for a picture. In such a clutter of tents and rides spinning for their test run, she couldn't find Ronnie's tent in the back, and she felt relief and sadness both.

The tents gave way to the lax, barbwire fence and the skinny trees that would line the road the rest of the way to the prison, except when they passed Painted Rocks. Aubrey slowed the Jeep in front of the huddle of trailers. They all looked dented in by the rain. He didn't pull in, and he didn't say anything about Aimee not coming with her. He trusted Crystal, and she was thankful that he kept driving.

The white pickup was gone, though. She reached to touch her hair.

Crystal let the black tent rise up in her mind, imagined its wet hanging doors, heavy as iron, and inside, Ronnie sitting in the blackness with the hiss of snakes all around. She imagined his hands reaching for the box of serpents, but she could not see him take them up, like she knew his church people had done and *he* had done. He was swallowed up in there, and she remembered the night the two of them had practiced their Easter song at Glorybound, "Low in the Grave He Lay," in unison through the verses and harmonizing on the refrain. They'd planned to sing it for the sunrise service, the service she loved because it was held just before dawn, in the morning darkness that was all at once shot through with sunlight. The service would start in just a few hours, since their practicing had gone late into the night, but they practiced again and again to make it as glorious as the rising-up of Jesus from the grave.

They'd had to wait for Dotte to drive them home. She'd gone upstairs with Miriam to arrange the silk flowers Miriam had found in Biggs, so they waited for Dotte and worked at the blend of Ronnie's tenor and Crystal's low voice going hoarse. She'd worn a new, blue dress that Dotte had made her for Easter. She did not think she was pretty, but she thought the blue itself was pretty, and so she allowed herself to borrow the prettiness, like she'd also borrowed Aimee's string of fake pearls.

Ronnie had been fourteen, still slick from the day of his baptism in the river when he'd cried out for his dead daddy. Crystal was a year older. The two globe lights that lit the basement church hung like lanterns. The thick night outside—along the graveled ruts of Cuzzert Pike and around the trees pinned with the empty husks of locusts that had clung there since the beginning of time—that night swallowed them as they sang. It pressed them together for comfort. She stood closer and closer to his faint guitar strumming, closer to his sweat-stink and to his voice as it cracked on the second "he arose" in the refrain. He turned and kissed her, and they left the guitar on the green carpet floor. In the corner of the basement, they held each other tight, for that dark was heavy upon them. The black night where the odor of death, of the crucifixion, would hang till sunrise—it was liable to cave in on them before the sun could break through. So he touched her, and she pulled him into her, up under her blue dress skirt, close as blood and bone, before the night could crush them.

In the Jeep beside Aubrey, Crystal could feel the low tones of the Easter hymn inside her, now, like a moan, deep beneath her silence as they neared the turnoff onto Cuzzert Pike. The stalks of dull goldenrod, laden with the drizzling rain, bent low over the pike's gravel and made the road look forlorn.

They hit the seam of smooth, black pavement, and the prison sign, *15 Miles,* rose up colorless from the ditch. In the mirror, she watched the blank steel backside of the sign and felt the urge to get Aubrey to turn around in the lot of King's Service Station, as Aimee had done on Monday when the burden of seeing their daddy had been too heavy to bear. The Jeep rounded the bend, and Aubrey slowed and turned in, as if he'd read her thoughts. Then she saw what drew him.

The white pickup was parked off the road, just before the trees opened to King's parking lot. Aimee sat on the lowered tailgate in a red dress. She held a newspaper over her head with one hand and waved them down with the other, kicking her legs like a child. The old tailgate bent under even her slight weight. As they pulled in behind her, Crystal saw a few packs of Pall Malls rubber-banded in her sister's lap. Aimee set the cigarettes on the truck bed and hopped off.

Aubrey rolled his window the rest of the way down, and Aimee filled it with her face and the soggy *Biggs Weekly Register* open to the front page story about the fair.

"A pity Queen Charlene's hair's getting mussed," she said, as though she'd practiced it. "Better hers than mine." But Aimee's black hair was unbrushed and matted. She'd been sitting there long enough to let the rain, no more than a mist now, seal her red tank-top dress to her body, like a second skin. Aubrey looked into the dash.

Before he could speak, Aimee rolled up the paper and threw it behind his seat, onto his books and empty Styrofoam coffee cups. "I was going to ask can I hitch a ride," she said, "but seeing's how you just got these bucket seats, we'll be needing the truck. Got a nice wide bench for the three of us." She leaned down to look Crystal in the eyes. "You forget me? You looking to leave old Aimee Jo behind? You all ain't going no place without me."

She stepped back from the window and looked at the truck's tailgate. "I said to myself, 'Well, it's a hair past one, they'll be here 'fore two.' And here you come outta the curve like you was keeping your appointment. Right like I thought, and you even give me time to get Mom some Pall Malls. No cash in my pocketbook for a carton, but Agnes signed me three packs on credit, even binded 'em up for me. Yessir. Ain't going no place without me." She said the last part nervous and drew one arm across her belly, as though to cover it and to cover the three ribbons of her belt. It was always a gesture like this that drove Crystal to fly at the world and fend off every force from her sister. And it was a gesture like this that kept Crystal pinned to her seat, that proved there was pain she could not spare Aimee from.

Aubrey got out and shut the Jeep door, leaned his elbow back in through the window, like he needed the support. He was so timid with Aimee, as much a child as she. No doubt he felt as guilty as Crystal for heading to the prison without her.

"You okay?" Aubrey said quiet. "That cut on your leg looks better."

Aimee looked down at her leg. "Come on, sweet Aubrey Falls. You can sit in the middle." She sprang from her gentled state and went for the Pall Malls on the truck bed. She slammed the tailgate shut, skipped around to the cab and came back with Crystal's blouse.

"Crys, I brung you this. I fixed it," and she unfolded the blouse to point to the fifth button down. "Just like I said I would. Change outta that damn tee, there behind the Jeep, in these here woods. Come on. Only one 'round to see is Agnes, and she's thick into *The Star* magazine."

Crystal got out and took the blouse.

"Shit, I shoulda brung you some slacks, too," Aimee said.

Crystal wondered, did Aimee have a change of clothes for herself? And Aimee, as though answering her thoughts, untied the knotted three-ribbon belt from her waist and tied it again, in a bow this time, saying, with her showy movements, *yes,* this is just what she planned to wear.

Aubrey looked away as Crystal slipped out of the wet T-shirt behind the cover of the Jeep and put on the weightless blouse. She pulled her hair back from her face into a low ponytail, but she had no hair tie, so she let it fall back to her shoulders.

They got into the truck, Aubrey in the middle, and as Aimee pulled onto Route 40, Agnes Felton stepped out of the station to smoke. She waved and then put her hand to her face, and Aimee waved back, said, "I told her you'd be by. She said to me, 'Hoo! Better get to my homework papers then'—I shouldn't a tattled on her for reading *The Star.* She don't believe what's in there—don't think that for a minute. She just got a lot of time to pass. She give herself a home permanent last night, little more black hair dye. Looks nice, I told her."

Aimee spoke with an edge, but her voice did not carry the same sense of hazard that it had when she'd refused to drive this same stretch of road the day before. This time her words hurled her forth. "So—it ain't no big deal," she said, one hand on the steering wheel, one lying on her right thigh close to Aubrey. "I mean, we'll go, we'll say to Daddy, 'Eat some food, you damn fool,' and then we'll come home, and we'll leave him in peace. We'll say we're doing fine here without you, we got work, we got food, we got plenty, and Mom's just fine, she's taken up dancing now you're gone—Crys, couldn't you see her taking up dancing? Dancing like an angel once Daddy done shook the dirt off his feet. He shook the dirt off and shook us loose, and we need to start acting like it."

Words hurling her toward a cliff, like she would either jump and take flight or fall to her death, and she suddenly needed to know which it would be. She was ready.

"Aubrey, you heard what they gonna do here?" She pointed aimlessly toward the road ahead. "I heard Jimmy Shrout talking with your buddy Louks in the shop last week, and don't you know the damn prison people gonna put a four-laner in here. They want it more direct to Biggs. All the folks working out there's from Biggs anyhow—and nobody else in the jailhouse going for no drive—but that road's gonna cut out all the business-doing with Cuzzert. Won't be selling no soft-serve cone to no prison guard at the diner, Crys."

"Well," Aubrey's voice stumbled into the breath Aimee took, "a highway's been planned, but they can't afford it yet. They might not—"

"Cuzzert, Cuzzert, like custard, like a custard pie, piece of pie, piece-of-shit home of the River Lions—you know that's the high school mascot here? A river lion. Kids from Biggs call us river rats—home of the river rats and the Coal Heritage Fair—that's what we got to call our own, that and sweet Glorybound Tabernacle where June Tatum rests—in peace, praise be—in the ground right by Miss Miriam's sticks of rhubarb. We do got that, and we do got ourselves a convict daddy. Yessir. And we gonna tell him what's what."

Something had rubbed her raw and hurled her in this way—maybe the great sheets of brief rain, maybe the ghosts she'd wrestled with in their daddy's old study—but her readiness only made Crystal go weak. As though Aimee's sudden resolve had drained Crystal's dry. Aubrey grabbed Aimee's limp hand, looking nervous that she'd withdraw it, but she didn't.

"I'd sing 'cause this radio's busted," she said, "but you know I can't carry a tune in a bucket. Crys here's the songbird. You never heard nothing like her, Aubrey Falls."

Crystal felt the heat from Aubrey's body beside her. She rolled down the cab window as Aimee spoke. No more rain. Aubrey looked at Aimee's bare legs, then looked at the dash and laced his fingers through hers that he held. Crystal rubbed her long fingers across the heel of her own hand hanging just over the cab door.

She watched the sad trees fly past. Nearly a year before, in the fall, the sugar maples and the tulip poplars had borne their leaves, like aching gold bodies, heavy and light at once. How fiery the colors had blazed, right when Aubrey had arrived, as though the trees had wanted to show this boy from Illinois their very best. On these trees they passed now, the early-turning leaves curled like burnt cardboard, more brown than gold. They would not be turning bright, because this rain was coming too late, such that it seemed cruel—it just beat the leaves from their branches. As the white pickup passed by, the leaves fell, soundless and pitiable.

All the trees bent, almost before her eyes. When Aubrey had first come, when she'd seen him in the community building aiming to teach her things, he had seemed to her like a straight rod, bent for no one. She'd thought then about the people of Cuzzert: they go without refuge and they go without work; they're all pale birches in a storm, all of them. The welfare men who melted through the door of Cool Springs and stuck firm to the orange stools, the only thing they knew the day could make good on was its heat and the food they got for cheap at her shop-and-diner. So in they came, wide around at the belt but bending forward all the same, poking the mustards and ketchups and waiting for something to happen.

But Aubrey stood straight, unyielding. She always did believe he meant kindness, but she expected him to leave, because Cuzzert was a place that folded people in half. A place people left. Then he'd come to their doublewide for supper that first time. So cold a night, she remembered, and she'd been pleased with how her offering of cornbread had turned out. She'd seen a change in Aimee then. From the front window, she'd watched Aimee kiss this man beside the rusted hood of the pickup. And when she came back inside to find Crystal at the window, their mom having gone back to the TV, Aimee said, "Just a kiss, and nothing more, Crys. I ain't gonna do it again." And Crystal had wanted to say it was okay to do it again, for she felt the binding strain of their vows. But she made no sign of that to Aimee because the truth of it was, this man looked so much like her Ronnie, and she longed for the press of someone's lips on her own but did not have it.

Crystal watched the two of them all fall and winter, burning, moving like bright fish, side by side, the invisible force of water keeping them a ways apart. Aubrey came for supper now and then; Aimee helped make the biscuits, the pork loin when they had it from the Shrouts. Crystal watched through winter and then through spring, when it broke out with a lambing at the Feltons' farm far up Cuzzert Pike, and now she watched in this heat of summer that devoured them. She watched, and she heard: that tender confusion in Aubrey's voice; those stories he told about the trains elevated high in Chicago where he said he rode alone even in a crowd of people; the bedsprings whining when her sister lay down and rose again, and when she herself lay down alone and rose up, and their mom, too, rising late, morning by morning.

It was Aimee who bent him, who made him almost the same as they were: a skinny birch tree in a windstorm, helpless before it.

"Turn here," Aubrey said. A road forked right from Route 40. The land along this road had been timbered without mercy. The trees were sparse and naked here, a thin veiling for the black stand of buildings Crystal could see far up ahead in the distance. She wanted badly to show these trees mercy.

Aimee gave a low, shaky whistle. "Prison Road, it's called. Least you know damn well where you are."

Crystal had nearly forgotten where they were headed and why. She had not been thinking of her daddy, and she aimed to think of him now. But the thought that came, of a sudden, like a vision in her mind, did not call up mercy in her, as though she could feel the crude power of the saws and the blades that had slashed these trees, and it scared her. An image of her daddy came up, a cruel and familiar one: the image of a snake fat with a rat in his belly, gleaming in the sun with glut.

She had received this very picture in her mind years before, out of nowhere, the first time the Spirit had come upon her at Glorybound and her tongue had gone loose with no gate. She had heard her own voice, at a tremulous pitch, "halama halama," over and over. At once, she'd pictured the sun beside her, felt warmed by it, though she stood beside her metal folding chair in the basement church with green carpet. She felt so sure right then of the green carpet as grass underfoot, felt the hereness of the ground, its firm sod underneath her. But they had told her she would feel flight when she got the tongues; she would sense the Overjordan like an unearthly wind. Instead, she felt the intense realness of the room itself, even the bodies, except that they all stood on natural ground—not inside cement walls or on worn carpet or among metal chairs but out in the sun, on a green hillside that smelled of the richest soil, as though a river had run over it for centuries.

And out of nowhere, she'd received an image of her daddy in the grass on that hillside, a snake too fat with his food and sleeping like death. The picture shook her from the Spirit's hold. She heard "halama" as though in the distance, in her whispering voice, and then from the mouth of Chloe Shrout where she sat three seats away. Cord looked into Crystal's face from up front, like he knew it. She couldn't shake the picture of him. And it came up a few times after that, even after he got struck by the lightning bolt that had to have been

had sat with the girl on the back steps—Crystal had watched from the road, dawdling while Dotte finished at the Save-a-Lot. Melanie sat close enough to braid Janey's hair, and she did, as Janey patted the belly that filled her lap on the steps, her knees drawn up. It was Melanie who would buy the stone cross to mark the grave. A few years later, after Crystal had lain with Ronnie on the eve of Easter, at the age of fifteen, she prayed for Janey Close every night, because she knew it could have been her with the baby born dead.

On the stump, Crystal had to calm her thoughts altogether. She stilled the creek water's movement. She let Janey's face fade from her mind, let the girl's braid become her own.

"Aubrey," Aimee said, "can you fetch me the rubber band binding those cigarettes? I'll be needing a hair tie."

Dotte

....

THE GIRL'S FACE HAD NO LIGHT IN IT. That's what Dotte kept thinking about Charlene Marie Sparr. The girl sat scratching her neck on the throne seat under the coronation pavilion on the edge of the fair closest to the road.

But Dotte said to Louisa, the oldest Felton girl, standing beside her, "My, she's a beauty." And she meant that. She kept in mind that beauty is no sin in itself. Miss Sparr had beauty but not light. Dotte thought on that awhile, during the small speech delivered by the pageant chair, the Biggs high school teacher in a lavender pantsuit.

"Charlene Marie Sparr," the teacher announced, "daughter of Richard Sparr and the late Maude Sparr." Dotte mouthed the words along with the pageant chair who spoke soft and breathy into a microphone.

Jim Louks took the metal crowns from a wood crate on the ground. As the General Chairman of the Fair, Jim was appointed to crown the king and queen. Charlene stood for the crowning with her king, a Biggs boy with a face like a skinny beagle dog's. When they stood, Dotte saw the pretty crown outline that W. D. Angus had carved into the back of Charlene's throne. Dotte felt proud of the job Reverend Angus had done, especially as the pout went deeper on Miss Charlene's face.

Dotte had walked to the grounds in her Sunday dress, one that Miriam had bought secondhand for her in Biggs, with elastic at the neck. It was an extra-large, and still Dotte had asked Aimee to let out the waist. She wore her skirt belt with it, so the flowered fabric bunched. Dotte dabbed a handkerchief to her sweating neck where her pale, wet hair stuck to her flesh. She had come to see the coronation of Queen Coal on Tuesday at 4 pm.

The rain had laid a thick layer of heat over everything and had turned the fairgrounds to mud before the drizzle tapered off to nothing. The mud must have offended Charlene Sparr when she stood from her throne. She held her dress hem high above the ground, and Dotte saw the girl's shoes, like slippers. They'd been dyed too careless, just a shade off color from the dress.

The dress was a deep green chiffon with corded edging like icing squirted along a wedding cake's corners. Such a green amid all that droughted brown.

It was clear to Dotte why the girl had won queen. With that pooched-out face in rouge and lipstick, like a face in a painting. That bust she could be proud of but not embarrassed by, a waist King Coal could wrap his spidery hand around and almost touch thumb to finger. It was clear, all except for the girl not having any light. That made Charlene seem not to be meant for it.

The crown went on her head, looking dull but still silver. At the moment when the girl should have let a smile break out, Charlene Sparr cast an ugly, dead look out to the small crowd assembled before her along Route 40. Dotte saw a man in front of the pavilion fussing with a camera. The queen's daddy, Richard Sparr, she guessed. Yes, that had to be him fussing, in that light blue suit jacket too heavy for the heat. She wondered how long his Maude had been dead. Dotte could not see the shape of his wife beside him, so he must have been long used to the absence.

Jim Louks rubbed his belly and took the microphone for his speech. His big voice came through the amplifier that he didn't need since it was such a small, standing crowd. Much smaller than usual—shallow, with only four rows. Jim's voice offended Miss Charlene, too. The corner posts under the gold tarp roof had soaked the mud upward, like a napkin soaks up spilled coffee. Wherever the tarp had been stored over the year, it had grown mildew stains in layers like roses, almost pretty. Tiny rosettes peeking down at Jim Louks' head where he stood with the microphone as the General Chairman of the Heritage Fair. He picked out two flimsy pieces of cardboard from the crate that had held the crowns. He presented King and Queen Coal with the hundred-dollar scholarship checks from CONROY. He put his left arm around Charlene Sparr's shoulders when he gave her the check. Dotte hated to see the sweaty shirt at his armpit against the puff sleeve on Charlene's shoulder, that cording thick and perfect there in its ridge.

"I'll bet that breaks 'em up," Louisa Felton said to Dotte. "The coal company's awful stingy with their scholarship money."

Charlene took her check and sat back down, bored and scowling. She did not get to speak when she accepted her check from CONROY. Like a doll, really, and Dotte pitied her some. Jim didn't invite the king to speak, either, but the boy took the microphone and said, "I thank you, and I'm headed to Bucknell to study forestry. I thank you."

Dotte admired the line of sequins that veed at the girl's flat belly. That line disappeared down into the fluff of her skirt when she sat. It echoed the V of the neck that dipped down too low but looked nice anyway. The sequins stood out all the more since they were spare. Maybe Charlene Sparr was off to college too.

What does she do or think now in the wet scrub grass, Dotte wondered.

"Her daddy works for CONROY, in a office," Louisa said low. "That prob'ly had something to do with her getting queen."

"Don't you be sour on her, Louisa," Dotte said.

This Charlene Marie in the wet grass, in a green dress, looked like she was kin to grass, or to what the grass dreamt of being, without the brown rust-out of drought. Envy was the only green on Louisa Felton, poor soul, so Dotte mentioned her pretty, pink nails and asked if they were real.

Louisa held her nails out in front of herself in a fan. "Oh, they're true. Just did this manicure myself, too. 'Cupcake' it's called."

A small rabbit, too skinny, showed up at Charlene's slippered feet. It came so close, like the girl was charmed or touched, anointed. Charlene noticed it, and she looked like she wanted to touch the rabbit but held her pose. *Touch the rabbit,* Dotte thought, not sure why. *Touch it.* It was a hungry little thing. Its whole body breathed like one frail lung under a thin hide. If the queen would touch it, maybe it would calm, as though beauty was for that purpose, that calming. And Dotte thought she saw a flicker of a light in Charlene's face, looking down at that rabbit, like she was about to touch it before it could scamper off. She might have, too, if the king hadn't hissed it away. The rabbit went on, tent to tent—Dotte watched—to hide in the trash piles swelling on the fairgrounds.

A crow flew down and perched on the microphone's amplifier. It stayed there, silent and respectful, till Jim Louks shooed it off.

"A rabbit and a crow tending her court," Louisa said, coarse. And then, "Where your girls, Dotte?"

Dotte looked away from the path of the skittish rabbit to Louisa's face. Where were her girls? Jimmy had called a last time before Dotte had left the house. She saw Aimee in her mind in the red dress, Crystal in the blouse with a new button. She knew neither was at work. She was smart enough to know that.

"They'll be here 'fore long," Dotte said, surprised by her own words. She scanned the small crowd assembled for the coronation. She looked for them, saw Hershel Dunmire without his cap on, staring hungry at Queen Charlene. Saw some high school girls from Cuzzert with their mamas, all of them standing up straight and wearing clothes too fine for the occasion. She saw Chloe Shrout nodding in time to a melody in her own head, and Dotte waved. But she didn't see Aimee or Crystal.

Louisa picked at the bottom of the horse decal on her T-shirt. She was thirty-eight, the oldest of seven Felton girls. She must have taken off her shift at the Family Dollar for the coronation. There would be no customers anyhow, because most folks would want to see the crowning. Louisa had come home a few years before, from Columbus, Ohio, where she had been living with a boy in sin. He worked on the power lines, tree-trimming, and he had a bad accident. Had his leg amputated. Dotte wasn't sure whether it was more shameful that Louisa had lived with a boy unmarried, or that she'd left him to fend for himself after the accident. But Louisa had the excuse of her sick mom, Elsie Felton. At Glorybound, they took Louisa back into the fold. Art Shrout said Elsie's sickness was her girl's salvation; the Lord works that way. Three of Louisa's sisters were dead, and the other three had left town in their teens to be a singing group. Dotte guessed they'd gone farther than Columbus, since they'd never come back.

"How's your mama?" Dotte asked.

Louisa's jaw jutted out some. Her lower teeth bit overtop of her upper ones. She reminded Dotte of a bulldog, but Louisa really did have the prettiest painted fingernails. Dotte watched them close every time she checked out at the Family Dollar.

"She's doing alright. Losing weight like a house afire. She got the oxygen tubes all night now."

Dotte nodded.

"Did you know 'bout Ronnie coming up here, Dotte?" Louisa whispered.

"Ronnie?"

"That's right, Ronnie Sisler. See how this crowd's so slight? That's 'cause people's getting good seats to see Ronnie handle."

"Ronnie come up here to handle serpents?"

"And soon. I hear some time 'round five tonight, in a tent back of the junk sale." Louisa never quit picking at her horse decal.

"Mercy," Dotte whispered. She looked at Charlene Marie Sparr, as though to see whether or not the girl knew about Ronnie, too. Charlene adjusted her bra strap under her puff sleeve. She was still without light, and she would be gone in a few minutes, not sticking around to reign like a queen should. She'd leave before five, and she'd want no business with a boy holding snakes in the name of Jesus.

Dotte felt her dress pocket for her thinned-out cigarette pack. Ronnie was just like her Aimee and Crystal, poor chickens with their heads cut. She looked around wild for her girls—then she heard the cough sound of the white pickup.

Dotte looked behind her to Route 40, where the pickup pulled off. It parked in the line of cars all slanting down toward the ditch. They were liable to fall into it, in a line like a parade, and it would be the only parade. They used to have a parade of floats pulled by tractors. Queen Coal would sit on hay bales, with her two little court-girls at her feet and the runners-up beside her in the dresses Dotte made, and Queen Coal waving. The king would drive himself in a new pickup behind, shy behind his queen. You could hardly see the new suit he wore.

Dotte saw Aimee first, in the flash of red dress and ribbon. Crystal came around the truck bed. In the blouse, like Dotte had thought, with her yellow hair braided back. Then Aubrey Falls, trailing Crystal and looking dazed.

"Mercy," Dotte said again.

Jim Louks had thanked everyone, and the small crowd was clapping. Charlene smiled for the first time, maybe because she was happy it was over.

"I swear her daddy done rigged it," Louisa said.

"Now don't you be sour on her," Dotte said again. She kept fixed on her Aimee's legs striding across the road with that skirt ruffle swishing above her knees.

Cord

....

June 16, 1999

If you could raise someone from the dead, who would it be?

Only God can raise up the dead. But if I could I would ask for God to raise up a man died over 20 years ago. The man will be raised on the Last Day praise God, but if he come up out the ground today then he could preach here in this place to get some men saved. What they calling church here is dry stiffneck. By that I mean it aint got the Spirit. The man I mean I will not name, cause of keeping myself hid along with all the people you could find me out by. He was The Tent Preacher humped over, he was the earthen vessel God done used to save me as a boy of 15. He married me and my girl but that was not all of it. He took me in like a new Daddy. He was the Daddy I did not have even with Uncle Jack who done good by me. But The T. P.—I will write it short—he was Spirit Filled. He waved his hands in praise like a woman, that aint my Uncle Jacks way at all Buddy. Uncle Jack striked a man for doing that in church one time, he was that way. But The T. P. danced and waved in his preaching. He helped me read and write like I do here. He got me Holy Spirit Trained. I would feel a heap of shame to have him see me in here for my sin. He would help me get right with the Lord before I fly from this world. You could say I seen me some pain and it is not my fault for being here but he seen his fair share too. He was humped over like I done wrote, he had short breath. He died when his lungs give out, but he never strayed from the Narrow Way so I got no excuse.

The T. P. would lift up Jesus in these meetings here. They got stiffneck religion that aint faith. There is a difference Boy. When you Holy Spirit Trained you know the ways of praising. I went to meeting here by way of the guard, cause he seen me slip my meal to a other man and not eat. He asked me straight and I said straight—I been on fast 14 days. He said to me—You eat or they will pump liquid food in you to make you eat. I said—Then they going again God. I said—God watching over my Soul to preserve it but this here tent is closing up. I will let God deal with that guard, cause he mocked and said to me—That tent do not close up lest we close it. He carried on foul, he made sure I set in church meeting the next day to get prayed up with Jesus—that is how he said it like a joke. He set me down in the Easter service and he said—You pray it up and eat after. They lied to say it was Easter Time but I did not know, I got no sense of time here. The date at the top of this paper only. It could be Christmas by feeling, but that I feel it is hot.

They all black men in the church meeting but a few. I got nothing again them, like here in this class it is you and me and the other 2 whites. One goes by name of Rick but I do not know the others name, them 2 was also in church. When we sit for meals I see we are half of us white the other half black, but in the church it is us 3 whites only and then blacks. I been to a black mans church one time and it was Spirit Filled. There is the dancing and the cymbals so I knowed them black men was all itching to praise Jesus. But we got dry stiffneck service here Buddy. The preacher is in a suit like a vain peacock. There aint nobody dancing or getting saved here. I say The T. P. would give us real church if he was alive. That is why I would pray him raised up. I end in Glory.

(Boy you said on my paper if the woman runner lives then I might get out of here in 10 but I aim to die here. Let this be record. I do not expect you to understand it like the guards do not either in their hard of heart. I done learnt not to share visions with the hard of heart even when I mean to warn, for my visions get mixed and I sometimes need a ear to hear and sort. But I see this to be clear confirmed. I will not rise to eat. I dream it in this time of Temptation and the Desert that come before the Cross, Buddy, there aint no going back. They going again God if they pump liquid food in me. I said that to the guard and I said—No pumping in me lest it is the deadly injection. He told me they do not have a death row here even, if they did you do not get it for hitting a woman and she still living. And he said—We own your body in here. But nobody owns this here tent beside the Lord God, I been bought with that price of blood. Let this be record.)

Aubrey

....

"THREE DOLLARS," a young girl hollered in a high-pitched whine. "Gimme three dollars to hear the word and see the signs following."

The girl stood at the opening of the large, black tent at the back of the fairgrounds. The entrance was a mere slit down the middle of a black tarp, with one side tied back with rope. She held a plastic ice-cream bucket and had cut a hole in its lid so people could shove in their cash. Aubrey thought she was dressed oddly, in a long-sleeved, boxy dress that looked like a school uniform, as though she were ready for a school picture.

Aubrey stood a few feet away from Dotte Lemley, who ate fries from a paper bag. Louisa Felton, standing beside her, had bought them to share. He stood a few feet apart from Aimee and Crystal, too, watching. The crowd disappeared inside the tent, but more and more people hovered outside it, hoping that some room would open up.

"Ain't no way I'm going in, Aimee," Louisa said, keeping her eyes on Aubrey and smoothing down the front of her T-shirt with a horse on it. She'd dripped a spot of ketchup on the mane. "But I could prob'ly get you all in." She pointed to the girl with the ice-cream bucket. "That there's my baby-niece Jenny taking money. I can ask her. I don't want to go in, but I'll ask for you." She looked at Aubrey till she quit speaking. Then she looked down, bashfully. Louisa had been in his night class until spring had ended. She'd written rhyming love poems for his classes, and he had felt relieved when she'd quit coming.

The words painted on the sign taped to the tent had smeared together in the rain. *True Pentecost,* painted small and carefully at the bottom of the sign, was all that was legible. The tent looked too big for its supports, as if it might collapse at any moment. It was just a set of tarps taped together, and the rain had made the tape peel and the tarps gape open in places. It might all slip apart, but no one seemed to fear that.

Aubrey, Crystal and Aimee had pulled up to the fair at the end of the coronation ceremony, and Dotte had met them at the ditch by Route 40, tugging at the collar of her dress.

"I knew you'd be here 'fore long," Dotte had said to them, and they'd answered with silence. She barely looked at them, barely had time to look at them, for everyone in the small crowd moved slowly and purposefully through the booths and tents, toward the back of the fair, where a larger crowd was assembling. A gradual push of people, everyone's face looking formal.

"Got your cigarettes, Mom," Aimee said. "In the truck."

"You said you was going into work." Dotte did not sound betrayed, just shook her head. "Jimmy's liable to cut you off, Aimee girl." But she moved with them, guiding them. As heavy as she was, she seemed light to Aubrey, somehow carried along by the flow of people, as though in a dream: Dotte Lemley as a big, sluggish dream, ready for French fries and for whatever spectacle that tent held.

"Do you know about the handling?" Louisa asked Aubrey as they passed the Tilt-O-Whirl with no one riding. She tried to pull in her under bite when she talked to him. "It's 'bout five now, so everybody's going." He said nothing.

"Welcome to the CONROY Coal Company Heritage Fair," Aimee whispered to him from the other side. Her lips caught his ear. "Ain't got *nothing* like this in Chicago, Aubrey Falls."

They gathered on the drying mud and grass of the fairgrounds. There weren't hundreds of people, but it was a real crowd, and it was rare to see that in Cuzzert. Nothing in town ever drew a crowd except the Methodist church, for the potluck meals held there on Sunday nights.

They passed Melanie and W. D. Angus, who tried to usher people under their canopy for the five-dollar corned-beef-and-cabbage meal. Their money box sat waiting on one of the empty tables set with salt and pepper, ketchup, pint jars with zinnias. The Anguses watched Aubrey keenly as he passed with the Lemleys and Louisa; they knew where he was headed. He could tell they disapproved—off to see the snake-handler that had the crowd all stirred up. They thought better of him, and they didn't think much of the Lemleys, he knew. He nodded to Melanie, and she sniffed and plucked a browned zinnia from one of the jars on the table beside her.

They passed the squirrel cages, still and unmanned. Aubrey saw Gary Wayne in what had to be the livestock auction tent. He poked a stick at a heavy sow just inside the tent's opening, as if to keep the animal awake. He spit the juice from his plug of tobacco into a pile of woodchips. At the neighboring tent, full of garage sale junk, a young boy that looked just like Gary Wayne fondled a leather wallet with the imprint of a bull's head on it. The boy had a wad in his cheek bigger than Gary Wayne's. *Must be his son,* Aubrey thought. He felt the hot hand of kinship reach for him then. He felt that all these people he knew, like Loyal Sisler there at a game booth, throwing a dart at a balloon and looking into Aubrey's face with a lazy recognition, were pulling him into their swollen, stale-smelling motion. And he did not fight it.

A cool, feathery hand touched his forearm. It was Chloe Shrout in her pink headscarf patting him, nodding, then letting him pass, bidding him go.

Aubrey felt a thrill he had no name or explanation for—no words at all. He reached the black tent with the others standing outside and suddenly felt eager to see this Ronnie Sisler whose people he was coming to know. He wanted to see Ronnie handle snakes inside this shelter of flimsy tarps.

Aubrey looked around him with heightened awareness. Somebody had strung old Christmas tree lights from tent to tent, big clownish bulbs, and they were already lit though night had not yet fallen. And under the red glare of one bulb, Aimee stood by Louisa and kept touching the bone of her own wrist, circling and tapping it with her fingers. He had noticed her doing the same thing when she'd first seen the crowned queen under the canopy beside Route 40, a skinny girl in a poofy green dress, about to get into a car. The girl had worn a gaudy gold bracelet, and Aimee had seen it and started worrying her bare wrist as they'd walked. He didn't reach for it. He loved it as it was, bare, under the bulbs lit stupidly in the muted daylight. He saw that she quit touching her wrist when Hershel Dunmire came up to her and offered her a half-empty bag of Twizzler candies. Then Hershel clasped his hands together, stuck his fingers into the rubber bands around his own wrist, and started nodding. Aimee held the candies and kissed Hershel on the cheek. Aubrey hated the old man, then, before he realized it—hated him like a too-familiar touch.

Hershel looked at Aubrey, wanting a soda, wanting something. Wry, Aubrey thought, *A man thinking always of his stomach,* all flesh, as though he were unaware of how old he was. He never had to think on more than flesh. Aubrey tried to give Hershel a dollar, so he would leave, but Hershel shook his head no, no, and stood by Aimee as she talked with Louisa about how to get seats in that tent. Aubrey was surprised by his own rudeness. He felt ashamed, but that feeling soon yielded to a surge of longing as he thought about Aimee and Crystal in the truck cab, on the drive back from the prison. That steady rock inside of Crystal had split so suddenly; her air had all rushed out as she'd hyperventilated. He had watched her calm down at the fingertips of her sister braiding her hair. He had been the intruder, then, and he'd tried to withdraw into himself but couldn't, so he'd just stood and watched, feeling half naked. And Aimee asked him for the rubber band from the cigarettes in the truck. He got it for her, and she went once, twice, then three times around the stub of hair at the bottom of Crystal's braid. He stood by, in love with the sisters' secret language.

Aimee had turned to him and said, "Aubrey, we need to get ourselves to the Heritage Fair." And they didn't speak again, Aimee driving, Crystal beside her, and Aubrey on the passenger's side, watching the wilted world blur past him and feeling the road wind, harsh on his bare arm since he still couldn't pull back into himself.

Aimee held onto Crystal's hand for the entire drive, except when she had to shift gears.

All three of them were silent, until they came up on King's Service Station, and Aimee pulled in behind Aubrey's Jeep. She stopped and waited for him to get out, but he didn't.

"Tell me why you're going," he said.

"You best not come, Aubrey," Aimee said. "Something's happening there ain't fit for you." She looked at the steering wheel as she spoke.

"What is it?"

"You got no part in it."

"What is it?" He knew he didn't have any part in this, but he wanted to stay. He had forgotten about Cord Lemley and about everything else except the part he longed to have in this truck cab with these two women whose pale skin struck him as too bright, everything like an overexposed photograph from which he could not shield his eyes.

"There's a boy gonna handle serpents at the fair tonight. Ronnie—you know, Arlene Sisler's boy. It's a fool thing some Holiness people feel they got to do. Crys wants to see him, so we're going. But you got no part."

It stung him when she said it again. "Handling snakes," he said. "It's something in a church service?"

"We Holiness people, too, but we never done it out at Glorybound. Daddy never wanted it. Not 'cause he was wise, though he said it like he was. A handler come to the church one time with a burlap sack full of rattlers, and Daddy kicked him out. Said it from Genesis, we was born to strike its head not pick it up. And that was that. Truth was, the snakes that preacher brung just scared the shit outta Daddy." Aimee laughed. "That was the real reason. I never expected Ronnie to get into it. He's gentle, you know?" She looked at Crystal, then at Aubrey, and he nodded. He did know that about Ronnie Sisler, because of what Arlene had said in class that morning: "More like a songbird the snake'd swallow up. He's a boy'd cry sooner than anything."

Crystal's fortress of silence, where she sat between them, was crumbling down into something frail and silky. Aubrey watched her profile, her hair pulled back in the braid he thought was pretty, and he half expected her to whimper out a sound, but she didn't. She didn't look at him, and he wondered if she was afraid he'd think she was weak for not being able to visit her dad.

"Just leave it," he said.

"Leave what?" Aimee asked.

"Just leave the Jeep here. I can get it later." He did not want to drive anywhere separate from Aimee. He did not want to let go of the girls' private love that excluded him but drew him all the same.

"You shore?" Aimee eyed him. She was trying to hide either mischief or relief.

"My first Heritage Fair," he said. "I wouldn't miss it."

Now, from their loose huddle, Louisa Felton broke off to go talk to her niece Jenny at the tent's entrance. Dotte pulled at her dress. Aimee leaned over to whisper into Crystal's ear. Hershel finally gave in to Aubrey and accepted the dollar, went off toward the French-fry booth. Aubrey was anxious as he watched Louisa, this woman who had quit his class either because he hadn't paid her enough attention or because she couldn't get along with her cousin Agnes. He was counting on her to get them in. He remembered that, before she had quit, Louisa had come to his classes with three newly sharpened pencils each night. She laid them out at the start of class, along with a plastic sharpener. She spent much of the class sharpening her pencils, starting to write something, then, finding the tip too dull, sharpening it. Why had she come to his class? Why did any of them come? To any of his classes? To the mildewed community-building room or to the sterile, windowless room in the prison, where everyone was so polite to him and distant, even Cord Lemley who that week had given him his bundle of papers? "Let it be record," Cord had said. He had all but bowed his emaciated body. Aubrey could feel that veil of politeness, now, because he could feel that veil tearing.

He looked at Aimee and thought, *Behind that veil, they enter a different world, both the people of Cuzzert and the inmates. They write letters to a dead brother, or they write about when they were children, when their mother taught them what was good, and they want to get back to that goodness. They write letters to themselves, of conviction one day, of vindication the next.* On a piece of loose-leaf paper, at the end of one of Louisa's love poems, she had written about how she had abandoned the man she loved because he'd lost his leg, and they were too poor to eat, and she got scared and came home. She was evil, she wrote. She'd planned to send him money, but now her mom needed her paycheck for pills. She had not heard a word. That was her last class, when she wrote that. Aubrey had feared the love poems were for him, but that was because the veil had still been intact. He saw more clearly now.

Louisa ambled back over to them. "Jenny says there's a gap in the back of the tent you could slip through. Front row, pretty much. There's no more seats prob'ly, but you can stand to the side up front." Aubrey nodded, ready. "Go on, now," she said. "It's 'bout five."

They threaded through the crowd toward the back of the tent. Aubrey let Dotte and Aimee and Crystal go first, Aimee taking her sister's hand, then he followed. But the crowd thickened; he bumped into Loyal Sisler and lost the Lemleys for a moment. The boy held a stick that glowed when he twisted it, which he was doing with fierceness.

"Won it when I busted the balloon," Loyal said, scratching at his freckles. He had come out of nowhere, and he looked frenzied. "I busted it straight, first goddamn throw." He was silent; then he poked Aubrey hard in the stomach with the glowing stick. "You gonna stop my brother in there?"

Aubrey didn't answer. He pushed past Loyal and turned the corner of the tent. Dotte's flowered dress was disappearing through the back flap, and he headed for her.

He was about to enter when he looked up and saw a truck pull in. *Patchwork,* he thought. Red with a black door, a white streak. A man in a black shirt got out and reached into the bed. Aubrey knew it was Ronnie when he picked up a dull, gold box with both hands and turned toward the tent. Ronnie wore his blond hair pulled back into a short ponytail. His eyes met Aubrey's. He looked familiar; his face had the same scruff as Aubrey's, a face that couldn't grow a beard, that looked younger than he might have wanted it to. Aubrey stroked his own face, then ducked into the tent.

Cord

....

#96309

June 23, 1999

What is the kindest thing anyone has ever done for you?

There is the kindness and the unkindness beside. Truly the kindest thing is Mama before she died. It was winter and me and my 2 sisters dressed by the fire. Before we waked up Mama stood there by the fire holding up my pants inside out. When I got up to put them on she give them to me so warm, then she went to put the biscuits from supper last night to toast them with butter. That is a kindness I still feel in my Soul. Beside it my Daddy done watched us dress. He was eyes on my sisters, they barely had time to get on a skirt and top before Daddy said to get out. He all but pushed them out the door to school, like he did not like to see them. I was not in school yet, he had the biscuits with me and not my sisters. He did not know nothing right. He knowed his drink. It is Mamas kindest thing beside a unkindness of my Daddys. It is like fire warm to dress in front of and have my pants so warm, but it is Fire I feel now that is more like my Daddy, like he waked me to real Hell Fire to be my trial. They say there is 800 beds in this here place. That is 800 Souls. They all Souls on Fire.

They pumped me full today 3 times like they said they was. I said no but they would not hear it. I spit up some after, cause my body knowed it was again God to have the liquid food. Now I am double hungry more than before, it is my <u>bitterness.</u> It is the evil in me trying to get out. The best thing Mama done was die to me, cause she knowed the evil in me but did not stay to see it. Glory.

One time my younger girl did a kind thing. She was little maybe 6 years. She give me a pouch made from a carton. It was one like grapes come on when you buy them. She bended it half over and put yarn in holes poked in the sides. I broke it soon with a book I sat on top so that is a unkindness she seen. I have 2 girls. I do not write about my girls. I been dead to them, though I dream. I do not know why I remember these type things now.

Aimee

....

THE CLOUDS HAD BROUGHT ON AN EARLY DUSK, and when Aimee
entered the black tent through the slit, she felt she had entered into night.
One blaring lantern, the kind Jimmy Shrout hooked to a raised hood when
he worked on an engine, hung from a lassoed rope at the empty front of the
tent. Everyone's eyes were fixed there, on the patch of lit grass where Ronnie
would stand.

She and Dotte and Crystal and sweet Aubrey—who she had worried might
chicken out till he followed them in—stood off to the side, all the seats around
them taken. Crystal no longer held Aimee's hand, and Aimee watched her
sister in the half-darkness, fingering the bottom of her thin blouse that now
had all its buttons.

The suffocation that had pitched Crystal from the truck cab outside the prison
was coming on her again; she bent down and up, less violently than before,
but still desperate for air. Crystal rocked her upper body like a clumsy dancer,
and nobody seemed to see but Aimee, not even Dotte who, like the rest of the
crowd, gawked at the empty, lit-up bit of grass with an anxious fascination.

Ronnie's hands had touched Crystal in her most secret places when the two
of them had lain in the corner of the basement church. Hands that had not
touched her again, except to soak and wipe her feet in the metal washtub at a
footwashing at Glorybound a week before he'd taken off for Charleston. Those
same hands tonight would grip a serpent by its never-ending neck. Aimee knew
it wasn't fear that suffocated Crystal, but yearning.

That rocking motion—up and down fast—put Janey Close in Aimee's mind,
Bud Dixon's girl, how Janey had acted at the wake of her stillborn baby, laid
up in a shoebox painted gold and sitting on the TV stand in the Dixons'

living room. People had trickled in and out of that trailer all day, and Janey didn't speak. She was kin to no one in Cuzzert, a thin girl from Biggs who showed up at Painted Rocks one day like she'd walked there. It was summer when she first walked down the gravel lane from Route 40. Folks sat out on front steps, and Janey said to no one in particular that she'd be damned if Painted Rocks wasn't just like her place outside of Biggs. She got to talking with Bud Dixon, and it made Crystal and Aimee sick the way he went all gentlemanly. "Janey Come Close," he joked, and she did, and that summer he got her pregnant in the fair's freak tent that was a hoax. The baby was born dead the next spring.

At the wake in the Dixons' living room, Janey Close rocked herself fast, working for breath, and no wonder—there were so many fake flowers, the room stank and choked you with more sickening scent than fresh ones would have given off. And Janey Close said, when Bud grabbed her shoulder, "I wanna die, I wanna die." It was the only time Aimee saw the fear of God in Joshie Dixon, who sat right beside the gold shoebox. She felt sorry for his pocked face then, till he looked at her and stuck his forefinger in and out of the hole he made with his other hand, grinning filthy. Janey disappeared before the funeral and the chicken dinner. She never came back.

That's how Crystal was moving now, like she was mourning, mourning Ronnie before he died, and Aimee reached out to calm her sister's motion.

Aimee tried to stop thinking about Janey and the dead baby, half afraid it would bring about Ronnie's death. To get her mind off it, she said, "Shore smells like a damn cucumber patch in here. The stink of a copperhead." Then she was sorry she said it, but nobody heard, and nobody spoke—not Dotte, not sweet Aubrey Falls whose face had lost color, not Crystal, of course, and not anyone in the crowd that was holding fast to their fascination.

But Janey Close rushed back into Aimee's mind quick when Ronnie Sisler entered the tent, walking down the center aisle. Though it was dark, she could see he wore the same black shirt from the day before, with a white tie, and he held the same baby-turkey box. But he'd spray-painted it ugly gold so all she could see was Janey's stillborn baby in the gold, shoebox casket.

She took Crystal's hand even though Crystal didn't give it. She had stopped rocking, stone still.

"I delayed myself, good people of Cuzzert, people of Biggs," Ronnie said as he walked. "I delayed for an anointing tonight. I waited, good woman," and he stopped mid-stride to put his hand on the shoulder of Chloe Shrout, who all but melted and cooed, "on the Spirit of God 'fore I come in here."

"Time you got on with it, Ronnie!" Joshie Dixon hollered from the back. He was drunk. "We done paid to see it."

Ronnie left Chloe Shrout to sit like a wilted poppy in her polyester dress, and he bounded up to the lit patch of grass at the front. "The Holy Ghost don't wear a wristwatch, and he come in his own time." He faced the crowd where they sat in dimness. Aimee feared he would see Crystal where she stood because the lantern's halo of light nearly reached her, but he didn't. Crystal drew back a step.

"What you got in the box, Sisler?" Joshie heckled, and somebody else said, "Shut up, stupid," but Joshie went on. "Why you got all black on? Looks like you dressed up for your own funeral."

Ronnie had changed in those five years. He'd lost that nervous manner of a skittish deer; he'd grown thicker. But those were the same sad eyes. They held a tenderness he could not altogether hide.

Ronnie undid his ponytail and let his hair fall down his back. He set the box on the ground, stretched out his arms and went into a slow spin, as though showing off his black clothes.

"This here suit, good man, it's got a purpose," Ronnie said. "What do you see when you pitcher the devil? Eh? Buddy, you see big horns on a red face? A pitchfork and a spiky tail like in a cartoon? Well, that ain't what I see. No sir, I see Satan wearing a suit and tie, good people, that white collar shirt, so white it burns my eyes. He's got the slick, black tie that's tied perfect. And he struts around like the coal boss—I ain't afraid to say it—like the coal boss who come to the wake in our house when my daddy died in the mine up here, God rest him. That coal boss come in my house in his white shirt—I was just a boy, and he give me a ten dollar bill and said for me to buy myself a ball glove. His eyes was short on kindness. He tried to buy my young-boy soul, but Jesus bought me with a greater price, praise God."

"Praise God," Joshie barked.

"But it ain't just the coal boss wearing that there white shirt—it's the crooked politicians, too, it's the schoolteachers teaching us we come from monkeys, they the ones in the fine suits. It's the preachers and the popes who say we don't got a direct line to the Almighty, *they* the ones in the white shirts, *they* the ones doing the devil's work. So I got me a *black* shirt and a *white* tie. I'm a counterdicting him. I'm a playing the devil's own game, good people, and I mean to win, by the power of the blood. Amen?"

A few shouted *amen*. One woman whooped. Dotte whispered for mercy, and a man sitting behind Aimee said, "Horseshit," but not loud enough for Ronnie to hear.

Ronnie started rolling up his shirt sleeves, and people muttered and hissed. He held his right arm high and showed that scar he bore, the deep pink scar, wide and twisted. "I been playing the devil's game, folks, and you can see he plays mean." He slapped the scar hard with his other hand. "But I done beat him so far."

The tent was silent then. Even Joshie Dixon.

Louisa Felton's niece Jenny sauntered down the aisle, and Aimee could hear the swish of the girl's dress. She sat cross-legged, holding her ice-cream bucket of cash, on the ground right in front of Dotte.

"Thank you, honey, for taking up the love-offering," Ronnie said. When he looked toward the girl, his eyes lingered in the space just behind and above her. Aimee felt her face get hot. Ronnie could see them, she knew, could see Dotte's body gone wide, could see Aimee holding the hand of the ghostly silent woman beside her. He stared at the silent woman and said nothing for a moment.

Then, "Let me ask you for a song," he said, still looking at Crystal. "I got myself a humble choir, just me, no tambourine. But join me now, good people. There is pow'r, pow'r, wonder-working pow'r—come on now—in the blood of the lamb." His voice was sweet as ever, untouched. "There is pow'r, pow'r— come on, I need to hear you—wonder-working pow'r in the precious blood of the lamb. There is pow'r—come on, you don't need no hymn books, you got the words by heart. You don't need no piano to tell you 'bout that power in the blood."

Nobody joined in but Chloe Shrout, who stood and swayed. Ronnie looked right at Crystal as he sang, but not with meanness. The wild water in his eyes threatened to roll down his face. Aimee didn't look at her sister; she let Crystal have her privacy where she stood, in the heavy half-darkness, touching her braid. Ronnie held his right arm outstretched, waving it back and forth like Queen Coal used to do from the float, waving at the crowd.

Ronnie broke his gaze then, and his song, and he spoke louder than before. "Maybe somebody's a needing that power tonight. I'm here to testify to the power. I'm here to tell you I *been* there, I been in need. I been on the lonely road, walking, yes, and God picked me up, praise him, but I done backslid. Good people, I got turned out to that dark place, and, don't you know it, God drug me back to his throne of grace. He pulled me out of the pit by that *power*."

Now the crowd started to stir, like horses in a barn before a storm. Ronnie could sense it, and he kicked at the gold-painted box on the ground.

Aimee let slip the memory of Janey Close's dead baby in the shoebox and watched the holes in that turkey box, watched the brown-rust color pass by the holes, then the dirty white stripe, passing quick.

"It's that power on high that come down to those first disciples on the day of Pentecost, good people, when Jesus said to them men waiting there, 'Go ye into all the world and preach the gospel to every creature.' I can't tell you chapter and verse, but I got it wrote out on my heart, amen? The good Lord said, 'He that believeth and is baptized shall be saved, but he that believeth not shall be damned. And these signs shall follow them that believe—in my name shall they cast out devils, they shall speak with new tongues, they shall take up serpents,'" and Ronnie kicked at the box again, "'and if they drink any deadly thing, it shall not hurt them.'"

Ronnie pulled a cloth from his back pocket and wiped his forehead. Then he dangled it at his side. Aimee recognized it as an old prayer cloth from Glorybound. Cord and Dotte had made them for a healing service once, to lay overtop of wounds to be healed. Cord had airbrushed them with the same purple and gold *Jesus Saves* that he'd sprayed on the T-shirt Crystal always wore.

People stood up in the crowd now. A woman in the back yelled, "Show us what you got, holy roller!"

Ronnie folded the cloth, calm, and put it back in his pocket. "They shall lay hands on the sick, and they shall recover," he went on. "And after the Lord had spoken unto them, he was received up into heaven, and sat on the right hand of God." Ronnie kicked the box so hard it flipped onto its lid and the brown-and-white pattern flashed through the holes in a blur of mad movement. "And they went forth, good people, and preached everywhere. The Lord worked with them and confirmed the word with signs following. Amen."

At the *amen,* Loyal Sisler ran up the center aisle waving a stick that glowed in his hand. He stopped at the edge of the hung lantern's light. "There's some don't want you doing it," Loyal blurted at his big brother. "Some don't even want you here."

Ronnie looked like he'd expected Loyal to show up right then. He nodded, looked at Loyal with peacefulness, but regret too. "Loyal Dye. You gone and growed up on me." Then to the crowd, "A prophet ain't got no honor in his homeplace, good people."

"You ain't no prophet," Loyal said. "You a damn thief."

Ronnie looked hurt, but he grinned and said soft, so only Loyal and a few in the front row could hear, "Now, that there's a thin line you walking, brother." He bent his neck far forward, like he meant to pray or meant for someone to chop off his head. Then he bent down all the way and picked up the box spray-painted gold. He held the box up to his face so the holes were at eye level.

"A very thin line," Ronnie said.

Aubrey

....

RONNIE SISLER OPENED THE LID as though the box were real gold, so gently and with reverence.

"No!" Loyal yelled from the aisle, without moving except to wave that glowing stick he'd won at the game booth.

Aubrey couldn't tell what was real—what was Ronnie's show, and what was his devotion. Aubrey's own shirt had soaked through with sweat.

Ronnie held the open box out in front of himself, tilting it toward his face and peering in. He looked like he might weep or run, but he did neither. Aubrey thought for a moment that the box was empty, but then, in one quick motion, Ronnie let the box drop and scooped up a snake inside it with his left hand. He grasped it around its thick middle, and it twisted its head and tail wildly in midair.

Ronnie hummed, seemed lost to the crowd that was all standing up now, to be able to see or to be ready to bolt if the thing got loose. Ronnie hummed the same tune of the song he'd been singing, the one about the blood. A flutter of white moths caught up to the lantern and danced around it.

Crystal took a step closer to the patch of light, straining her hand-hold with Aimee till they broke from each other. Crystal opened her mouth wide. Aubrey waited for her sound, but nothing came. The lantern light touched the glow inside of her and joined with it, as a water droplet slips into a pool. He saw the glow that he'd first seen inside the Lemleys' trailer, at the stove with the blue flame, when he thought she might catch on fire like a piece of paper. *Inside her,* he thought, *are the purest of sounds, surely.* She could stop Ronnie if she wanted to.

Ronnie began to speak quietly. His words addressed the crowd, but he seemed to speak only to the snake, intimately, almost lovingly. The copperhead opened and closed its mouth and flickered its tongue. Ronnie spun in a circle and disoriented the snake in twists and turns, his large body somehow conjuring a young girl clumsy with a dance partner. He spoke quickly and evenly, just for that snake to hear, but Aubrey could hear too, even as the crowd grew louder.

"That's right," Ronnie said, "you all got the fears of the world, but not me. The serpent be a carrier of evil, the devil's arm, outta that fine white sleeve. But me and the serpent, we partners in this game, cause together we prove God's blessing. That God be sovereign, no fear in it, no fear, for in the gospel it's writ we will not be harmed, we masters over it. We need not fear no broke-down mineshaft, no death by fire, by water, by wind. No, we masters over it." The snake reared back its head and struck out toward Ronnie's right arm, toward the pink scar, but Ronnie hid the arm behind his back, bowed forward. The snake went limp as though tired; it swung down its back end lazily.

Loyal, still standing in the aisle, backed away from his older brother. Then he turned and ran out of the tent without another word.

"You know I kill the black snakes," Ronnie said to the lethargic copperhead, "but I keep your kind. If you ain't got no killing sting, I ain't got no use. For I'm here to say there's a wonder-working power. Protect me, Jesus, amen, we victors over death, Jesus. We got us the *sweet* victory."

With his right hand, Ronnie pulled the cloth from his back pocket again, wiped his wet brow and his neck, thick like his mother's. Something about the cloth startled the snake, and it whipped its head back again and lunged for Ronnie's right arm, but he dropped the cloth and repeated the same movement as before: hid his right arm behind his back and bowed low, bowing to his dance partner, and the snake fell slack again.

Aubrey felt sick and strange. Ronnie smiled almost mournfully as he held the snake, his eyes deep, blue wells that extinguished the light of the lantern. No one could really see down inside those eyes. Aubrey touched his own face again, the scarce stubble on his chin wet with sweat. He'd been drawn into Ronnie's unfathomable eyes and transfixed there. Aubrey's stomach turned with each twist of the snake's head. When he'd first entered the tent, he'd heard Aimee say it stank like cucumber, but right then he thought it stank like everything at once: like the sharp tobacco the man chewed and spit behind them, the woodchips spread in the auction tent so many yards away, the quick shit of the animals nervous for their turn at auction time. Mostly it smelled of dirt—dry, trampled dirt. He dug the toe of his shoe into the ground as Ronnie Sisler bowed again, so reverently, to the muscled body he handled.

Aubrey recalled, in a rush, the smell of the dry Midwestern sod that he had pried up with the toe of his shoe in a park in North Heights. He was twelve, his dad newly dead. A recent tornado had ripped through the park, and his friend Todd called to say it had felled the biggest trees. Could he sneak off, Todd wanted to know, to climb on the trees, even though there was caution tape everywhere. When Aubrey got there, Todd was already scrambling onto a fallen oak, uprooted like a tiny plant. Come up, Todd hollered, but Aubrey just stood there taking in the ruined park. He smelled the dirt on the tree's upended roots, dark earth smelling both ancient and new. He stood watching and dug his toe into the dirt as Todd explored the network of branches, his red jacket disappearing then reappearing among the leaves. Aubrey stayed safe, observing from the ground, his shoe soon covered with sod and with bits of glass and garbage that he was careful with. Then Todd climbed to the top of the tree's root system, tall as a basketball hoop. Come up here, you pussy, and Todd took off his red jacket and swung it around. Aubrey crawled into himself, as he was just beginning to do at that time, without wanting to. He stood still, except for his burrowing shoe. Then Todd slipped from the tree and fell hard to the ground. He lay there screaming in front of Aubrey, the break tearing through the skin of his knee. Aubrey couldn't move or speak—he thought he was yelling, but it was only inside his head. He just stared at Todd's bloody leg as if it were a dream. A jogger heard Todd and came running. He looked at the statue-like Aubrey with his one foot buried deeply in the dirt and said, "What's the matter with you?"

Aubrey had broken out of it then. He'd run for help through the park's debris. *What's the matter with me, what's the matter with me,* he'd yelled inside his head.

Now Aubrey inhaled the stench of everything in the black tent, as though breathing in the sweet, suffocating face of a flower, and he let the stink fill his pores, his blood. He felt the familiar urge to withdraw, away from this wild man and the trembling snake. But he resisted.

Ronnie looked into Aubrey's face, then, and said, "You come on up here, brother." Aubrey kept his eyes locked to Ronnie's but didn't speak or move.

"You," Ronnie said. "I seen you outside the tent, remember? You seen me, too." He beckoned with the body of the snake to come forward, his right hand still tucked behind his back. He looked crazed, his grin fixed but unreal, like a sad clown's painted mouth.

"You come on up here," Ronnie said again.

Aubrey felt a tingling in his arms, a slight pain, as though his nerves were suddenly exposed. *Too close to the bone,* he thought.

"Come on up," Ronnie repeated. "You a new face 'round here. Maybe you know these here girls." He pulled out his right hand and pointed vaguely at Aimee and Crystal. It was the first time he had mentioned the Lemleys' presence.

"You just keep still, Aubrey Falls," Aimee said, stepping into the lantern light. She was a burst of red dress, too much for Aubrey's eyes, and he had to look away.

"He kin to you, Aimee Lemley?" Ronnie asked. She must have been too bright for him, too. He looked away from her as he spoke, into the eyes of the copperhead that was rippling into *S* after *S*.

"He ain't kin to *you*, Ronnie, and he ain't coming up there." Aimee didn't look at Aubrey, just wrung her hands. The crowd hooted, and Dotte asked for mercy, oh mercy. Crystal opened her mouth again, staring at Ronnie, but then closed it like a heavy door, trapping her voice inside.

"I can tell you itching to come up here, brother. See how I call you 'brother'? Maybe we know each other. You come on up and show these good people there's power. This ain't no trick, and you know it."

"Stop it, Ronnie," Aimee said, and she reached for Aubrey's hand. He let her take it, but he took a step forward into the lantern light, watching his shoes on the dirt as the light brought them into being. "Aubrey," she said.

He moved farther forward, dropping Aimee's hand. The snake faced away from him, waved its head into the hot air of the tent as though trying to get breath. Aubrey felt the burn under the lantern's hot bulb. He looked up at it, at the frantic moths.

"That's it, brother," Ronnie whispered. "There's victory for him who claims it of the Lord. Don't back down now. I seen you. I seen you want it."

The back half of the snake's body drooped low and barely moved. Aubrey saw the copper scales, nearly golden up close, and the thick white stripes pulsing, contracting and expanding in a bulge. Aubrey was going stiff with fear, but he resisted it once more, and before he knew what he was doing he reached out and touched the copperhead's body.

The snake flung its head around in a spin of brown and white, so close to Aubrey's face he leapt backwards, tripped over the open, painted box and fell to the ground. The snake coiled its tail tightly around Ronnie's left arm, and Ronnie brought up his right arm, palm open, in front of the snake's exposed fangs, waved his hand as though to charm the snake into submission. It withdrew, weaved back and forth and grew rigid, like a piece of sculpted metal in Ronnie's hand. Then, in a flash, the snake lunged and sank its fangs into the pink flesh of Ronnie's scar.

Ronnie howled and fell. The snake unwound from his arm and flopped its body loosely, fangs still deep in that scar's flesh, drawing no blood. The crowd spilled into the aisle, some screaming, but Loyal Sisler broke through, with a garden hoe from somewhere on the fairgrounds. He ran to Ronnie and swung the hoe to the ground, slicing into the dirt but missing the snake. He pulled up and struck again and caught the snake just behind its head so that it let go of Ronnie's arm and looped its body into one defensive spiral. Loyal held the hoe in place, pressing down, until it finally severed the head from the thrashing body.

A barrel of a woman followed after Loyal. It was Arlene, shrieking then muttering, "Son of a bitch, son of a bitch," then stopping cold when she saw Ronnie's body on the ground. She gave a hoarse wail. "My boy? Not my boy there?" she called out, as though trying to convince herself it was someone other than Ronnie who was dressed in black and seizing up in the dirt.

The snake's body kept flopping without its head, without method, and it leapt onto Aubrey's leg where he lay. Aubrey jumped up and caught it beneath his shoe. The tail flickered up like a flame, licked his pant leg. He searched out Aimee's face. She was near, and her face was twisted so that her black eyes wounded him.

"You all killed him, Aubrey," she said.

"I didn't mean to," he said. "I didn't mean to." He looked at Ronnie drawing his legs up to his chest and moaning.

"The snake. You and Loyal Dye killed that snake," she said.

"I killed him," Aubrey whispered. The tail kept rippling, pinned by his heel. All he could smell was the burning bodies of moths caught too close to the hanging lantern.

Crystal

....

THE DARKENING SKY seemed to fill with smoke. Crystal smelled for smoke in the air but smelled only the pickup's exhaust. She felt around Ronnie's body in the bed of the truck and grabbed the *Jesus Saves* T-shirt that she had thrown in there after she'd changed into her blouse. The T-shirt was still damp with rain; she bunched it up and slipped it gently under his head.

Someone had given Aubrey a denim jacket, and he held it as a compress on Ronnie's right forearm where the bite had split the skin of his scar. Crystal felt no suffocation now; she inhaled all the road wind she could as Aimee drove them down Route 40, then, through town, down Manheim Road toward Biggs. Crystal breathed deep, took Ronnie's left hand and willed her breath into his swelling body. He sucked air through his teeth.

Aimee flew down the road pocked from the pressing tonnage of coal trucks, from the freezing winters and the spring thaws that had widened the cracks nobody filled. Each pothole shook the three of them, Ronnie lying down in the truck bed, and Crystal kneeling, Aubrey kneeling. Crystal stared at the swollen right hand that stretched out beyond the denim jacket that Aubrey held in place. The skin around the fingernails had turned black, like someone had rubbed them with soot. Ronnie's eyes were squeezed shut, and she shut her eyes, too. She was with him in the darkness—like in the basement church so many years before, singing, and he had touched her leg, then between her legs—just her cotton dress skirt and underwear separating their skin—and she had not wanted him to stop, so he hadn't, and Dotte had stayed upstairs forever making fake-flower bouquets for Easter morning.

She pressed her two knees to Ronnie's side, her jeans against his black shirt.

She opened her eyes. Aubrey let his tears drip onto Ronnie's chest because both his hands pressed the denim down.

"Son of a bitch," Arlene had muttered over and over, looming over Ronnie in the black tent. "Don't you touch him—I knew it—just leave him be," she yelled at Aubrey, when he tried to lift Ronnie's head. "Leave him lay, boy." She spun around, checked herself, maybe as a student in front of her teacher. "No, Mr. Falls, you take him. You take my Ronnie to hospital in Biggs." Dotte came up behind her and took her arm, as though it were the most natural thing in the world, as though the two women took each other's arms every day, like sisters.

"You take him, hear?" Arlene said. "Damn ambulance runs a good half hour—take him fast. Damn, fool, son-of-a-bitching Ronald."

Loyal had stood beside her crying, clutching the hoe, ready to strike again. Art Shrout came forward to help Aubrey carry Ronnie's seizing body out to Route 40 where the white pickup was parked. Aimee and Crystal ran ahead of them, like little girls under the strung-up Christmas lights. They cleared out the truck bed, heaving the spare tire into the ditch.

The truck passed under the only street light in Cuzzert, out front of the Methodist church. It lit up Aubrey's childlike face. Crystal wanted to wipe the tears that trickled off the end of his nose, but she didn't.

"Ah, what a sight," Ronnie said with his eyes still shut. His voice was thick; his throat clutched at it. "What a sight, what a time, buddy. You done good. Good man."

"I'm so sorry," Aubrey said. "I'm so sorry I scared it." He sobbed now. His nose ran, and he cocked his shoulder forward to wipe it, his hands holding steady, as though that arm might split apart if he let up on the jacket compress. He looked through the back cab window at Aimee in the driver seat, at her black hair. Maybe he was crying for her, too, the snakebite a wound that pricked all other wounds in its vicinity.

"Nah, buddy, you done good. Who are you?"

"I teach here," Aubrey said, and he winced when Ronnie winced from the pain.

"That's good, yes." He did not say Crystal's name. "I fly from this world, Teacher. I know it's coming. I done flew with him 'fore now, above the town and strip jobs." Ronnie sucked in air with effort. "It's quiet—I been there—like I been to heaven and hell both. Bit two times, my arm once, my leg. I could show you. Doc says one more, I'm gone."

Crystal squeezed Ronnie's left hand, and he squeezed back, feeble.

"But God'll save me," he said. "I'm low as they come. Ah—" and he drew his legs up in a fit and knocked Aubrey off balance. Aubrey lost hold of the jacket for a moment and Ronnie's arm, deep blue now, met the wind flying past them, and he cried out. Aubrey recovered, held the denim back to the arm with one hand and helped Crystal hold down Ronnie's legs with the other.

She had to turn from Ronnie's grimace of pain. She looked up to see the sagging roof of the Cool Springs shop-and-diner as they passed. She couldn't find Balaam anywhere in that smoky darkness. He would gnaw on the corner of the shed when he got hungry for the oats chop. He'd go wild. She lost sight of the place as Aimee took them around the hairpin turn.

"Jesus, Jesus," Ronnie hissed through his teeth. "I stole from Mom, Teach. You know? I mean low."

"My name's Aubrey. Aubrey Falls."

"I make money offa the Lord's signs, Aubrey Falls. Low-down. Funny, me thinking he'll bring me to. Might not this time." Ronnie tried to thrash his legs again, but Aubrey kept steady.

"Lord *God* Almighty, it burns sweet, it burns," Ronnie said, his voice going faint. "Worst one, this one. Might not pull out, good man. Down for the count. I know it's dark."

"You're going to make it, Ronnie," Aubrey said weak.

"If he don't bring me 'round, I'm still going up. Funny, me thinking that, so low-down. But I'll get in, buddy, hair's breadth 'fore Judas. Hung hisself. Skin of my teeth, by the grace of God." Ronnie grinned and twisted his face. "If I turn a little profit, Lord God don't begrudge. I just show him off some, three dollars a head, coming north that way. Made my way back here." Ronnie clutched Crystal's hand tighter but didn't look at her.

"I know it's dark," he said again. Her heat rose up to meet the wind that whipped around them in the truck bed. They passed the first gas station just outside of Biggs. They'd be at the hospital soon.

Ronnie looked into Aubrey's eyes. "I seen you, good man. You know me?"

"Know you?" Aubrey asked. "I think I do." He nodded and looked shy, embarrassed.

"I love it that close," Ronnie went on, soft and raspy. "Times I near died, and God pulled me back, I swung on a vine over the lake of fire—just 'bout burn up, but he swung me back. Enough to get you drunk, that close. You know my daddy died in a mine? Smothered up. I swore not me, ain't going that way." Ronnie shivered, rocked his shoulders and sucked air. "But maybe no difference how you go." He looked at Crystal then, and his eyes went all water. They spilled and poured out.

"You still got that cross of nails I made you?"

Crystal nodded, hot as a hearth by fire. His tears touched her and steamed. She could almost see the steam release in the darkness.

"Shh," Ronnie hushed her, "shh," he hushed himself. She could barely hear his voice. "These years, Crys. Maybe you could sing something. For Aubrey here, good man." She looked down at their hands.

"Is all our shame past now?" Ronnie asked. His jaw went limp, his lips still parted. He faded.

Crystal opened her mouth wide, as though yawning, and the hot wind filled her gaping. Deep within herself: these that go without saying goodbye, must they go without comfort, without mercy? Must they come back only to die?

The truck passed under the line of street lights in the Biggs Wal-Mart parking lot. Bright as day. The hospital would be the next left. Aubrey squinted under the lights and shook Ronnie's leg at the kneecap, trying to wake him.

Aimee pulled up to the emergency room doors. She braked so hard, Crystal and Aubrey had to let go of Ronnie to hold themselves back from the cab window. Aimee ran to the tailgate and worked it loose. She'd done her share of crying, too. She went to the glass doors of the hospital and banged on them, then came back to help scoot Ronnie's heavy body onto the sagging tailgate.

Two men came out with a stretcher and rolled Ronnie onto it.

"He got bit by a copperhead," Aimee blurted out. "He was handling and got bit." The men worked quick, got Ronnie inside. Crystal followed first and heard one of the men yell, "We got a holy-roller snakebite. He's lost consciousness." She followed close till they took Ronnie through a second set of glass doors, and a nurse touched Crystal on the arm.

"Okay, now," the nurse said. "Okay. Tell me who he is. You kin?" Crystal watched Ronnie's black shirt on the white stretcher till they took him around a corner. "Are you related?" the nurse asked her.

"Aimee and Crystal Lemley," Aubrey said to the woman. "I'm Aubrey Falls."

"The man's name?"

"Ronnie Sisler," Aubrey told her.

"And you're kin?"

"We're from Cuzzert," he said. The nurse eyed Aimee's short red dress, her bare legs, Crystal's blouse with the dirty front.

"You'll have to sit in the waiting room," the nurse said. "All of you. I'll get your forms." The woman walked toward the big desk and shook her head privately, but not too privately.

Crystal felt for her braid. The wind had loosened it.

"Come on, Crys," Aimee said, and she took Crystal's hand. "I'll fix it."

Cord

....

#96309

June 30, 1999

If you could have one wish come true, what would that wish be?

I wish God Almighty to bury my bones. I done read the Word last night when I could not sleep, cause I got a sore on my backside. A light stays on all the time to see by even late. In the Book of Deuteronomy I seen clear that no man buried Moses dead body but God Hisself. Moses did not cross to Overjordan. There is men here I do not want to bury me. I wish God Almighty to fold me up like He done Moses to put me in a sack or pine box for the ground. I wish God Almighty to bury me good so no birds will circle and pick my bones. I seen blackbirds at night in my dream, that is something else like the sore keeping me up. They come in my face dying and I seen the end of each one, like it is their appointed time. Then I feel them heavy upon me. I write here glory even now.

(Boy you write me on my paper—did I want to write more about my girls. I done said I been dead to them. Do not ask me that again. They are one that likes to sing and one walking everyplace free like a bird

Dotte

....

WHAT WAS WORST OF ALL was Loyal Dye Sisler taking the money from Jenny's ice-cream bucket.

"Gimme that here," he said to the girl. He tore it from her hands, and she started crying. His meanness just loosed what was waiting to come out of her. Jenny was pale as a sheet, but the snakebite hadn't been real to her till Loyal took that cash. The boy was lost inside himself. He couldn't help it. After Art Shrout and Aubrey had carried Ronnie off, most people had cleared out. Loyal had thrown his garden hoe into the middle of the folding chairs.

Dotte had come up behind Arlene and tried to calm her wailing. The two women had their split ways, but Arlene was Dotte's cousin by marriage. "Mercy, Arlene," Dotte had said into her ear. Almost like "Please have mercy," since Arlene looked mad as a hornet at Ronnie. He lay twitching on the patchy grass.

Truth was, the Sisler boys had been set wild ever since Hiram got killed. *Can't put the head back on the chicken.* That's what Dotte was thinking, but she didn't say it out loud.

Now she and Arlene sat in the tent smoking Dotte's last two Pall Malls pulled from her dress pocket. Arlene was dressed formal, in nice blue slacks and a rayon shirt with some gold in it. She was dressed like she was going to church, but she never went to church.

"It'd been easier if he died down there in Charleston, Dotte. But for him to come up here and steal from me, then to act the fool in front of folks? And then be marked for dead where I can see it?"

"You seen it?" Dotte asked.

"I seen it from the very back. My goddamn brother was taking bets."

"Mercy," Dotte said. They sat in silence and smoked as long as they could, till the cigarettes were all but ash. Dotte kept thinking on Ronnie's face and his eyes. They'd been wild, yes, but, my, the light in them. She understood that he knew he was meant to die that night, but she didn't say that out loud either. She said, "That girl who got queen, Charlene Marie Sparr? She ain't got no light in her."

Arlene puffed air out her nose. "You got a odd way, Dotte Lemley. But I thank you for the smoke. Might be the only sane thing you do."

Like a picture in Dotte's mind, Charlene's dark green dress filled out like a real thing. Like the girl was there in the tent with them. Puff sleeves and that trimming, the pretty set of sequins on the yoke. Dotte squinted at the ground as though to picture the dress more clearly. Then her sight gave way to something crumpled and white lying there. She didn't know if it was real. She blinked. It was still there, so she went to it.

It was the cloth Ronnie had wiped his brow with. It was still wet. She unfolded it. *Jesus Saves*, it said. My, it was a prayer cloth from the church, years old. She remembered she'd sewn a dozen of them for a healing service. They were real plain, made from muslin. She'd hemmed three edges, but she'd had to sew them quick, the day of the service. So she'd saved time and left the fourth side, the selvage, to hold. Cord had airbrushed them *Jesus Saves*. He'd passed them out that night at the service, put them over all their wounds and sore places.

Dotte wished Ronnie hadn't dropped the cloth. She slipped it into her dress pocket.

"Godsakes, we got to get that thing cleaned up!" Arlene said. Dotte thought she meant the prayer cloth but then looked where Arlene looked. A skinny rabbit sniffed at the dead hind end of the snake. Lying there like it was made of rubber. Maybe it was the same hungry rabbit that Charlene Marie had wanted to touch.

"Go on, git!" Arlene said, and she shooed with her big arms. She stood up and wrapped herself up halfway with those arms. "I'm gonna find a phone, Dotte. I know my boy's dead, but I need to hear it for shore." She walked out and left Dotte in the tent by herself, under that lantern hanging by a lasso.

Dotte set out walking home, back Route 40 the way she'd come. It wasn't cool out, but it was cooler than it had been. She didn't have to tug on the elastic neck of her flower print dress. She squeezed the cloth in her pocket. She prayed Ronnie Sisler had been wrong about his own dying.

Aimee

....

"WHAT'S THE MATTER WITH HER?" A nurse tapped Aimee on the shoulder with a pen. Aimee flickered her eyes open and raised her head from Aubrey's shoulder. She had slept like that, and the hard armrest between them stuck her side like a knife.

"What's the matter with this girl? Is she deaf?" The nurse pointed at Crystal who stood by the big desk clutching one arm. It was a different nurse than the one from the night before. Aimee looked at the clock in the waiting room. Almost noon.

"Do you know what she wants?" the nurse asked. She worked her jaw hard on a piece of gum.

"I might," Aimee said. She touched her cheek, still warm from Aubrey's shoulder and imprinted with the crease of his shirtsleeve. He was waking now, too, and he rubbed his neck.

"You might," the nurse said. "Well, if you'd be so kind—the girl's been hovering round my desk like a stray dog, and she won't speak her mind. What's wrong with her?"

"Nothing," Aubrey said. "She doesn't talk. We're here for Ronnie Sisler. How is he?"

"Ah. The snakebite," the woman said, and her eyes narrowed. She wore a dark blue skirt too heavy for summer. She made Aimee feel the cool of the air conditioning.

"If you wanna know what my sister wants, it's to see Ronnie. We slept here all night." Aimee remembered the cocked head of a whitetail deer. She had dreamed of a deer in the road while she had pressed her head to Aubrey Falls' shoulder. She'd been driving in the dream, and the deer had run from the dark trees into the headlights, and Aimee couldn't remember if she'd hit it or not.

"I can't speak of Mr. Sisler's condition with none but family," the nurse said. "I assume you're family?"

"Is he dead?" Aimee asked.

"No. He's not." The nurse held back, likely aware they weren't kin to Ronnie, but then she let out the information as though sharing gossip. "The doctor said he's been bit at least twice before this. His body's all crippled up and aged. Looks like a swollen sixty-year-old in the face." She was fascinated by her own details.

"Can we see him?" Aubrey asked. He stood up, and the nurse backed away. As though sweet Aubrey Falls would ever harm a soul.

"It wouldn't be a good idea," the nurse said. "Wouldn't be wise. He's not conscious." She leaned in closer to Aubrey and glanced at Crystal. "You don't keep playing with that voodoo fire after you get burned. The doctor's pretty sure this one'll kill him."

Crystal heard. She knocked her knuckles on the reception desk like a child and jiggled a jar of pens.

"God, girl, get a hold now," the nurse said. "Like some kind of animal." She smoothed her white sleeve, glanced at Aimee's legs. Aimee could see the woman make judgments—they formed quick, like the hot liquid that hardens into Christmas candy.

"You eyeballing me?" Aimee said too loud. She was worried about that deer and worried about Ronnie.

"It's okay, Aimee," Aubrey said, but she stretched her ruffled skirt over her knee as far as she could, then let go, let it spring back and show the bright skin of her upper thigh. "You go ahead and do your looking." She slapped the rubbery seat of the waiting room chair. "We'll be right here, just a rooting around like little piggies. Sooner you let my sister in to see Ronnie, ma'am, the sooner we leave. Let her in, and then we'll get the hell out."

The nurse glared. "You can't act like that in here."

"She's ready to go—see her?" Aimee pointed at Crystal. "She got her hair all nice and braided, got her good blouse on. You just take her on into that room Ronnie's sleeping in. Go on. Me and Aubrey'll wait here, nice and quiet."

The nurse kept glaring as she backed over to the desk and put down her pen. She waited, shook her head, and walked to the glass double doors. "Well, come on if you're coming."

Crystal followed through the doors. Aimee watched the cornsilk braid disappear down the hallway. The braid looked as neat as it had the night before, when Aimee had reworked it in the waiting room. Crystal hadn't rested at all.

Aimee and Aubrey sat up stiff in their chairs, as though they hadn't slept touching each other. The haze of noon came in through the single window in the waiting room, but the air conditioning raised gooseflesh on her legs. Aubrey rubbed his hands together and looked young. He always looked young, with that patchy hair on his face, so different from the full beard Bud Dixon could grow by the time he was fifteen. But Aubrey looked even younger now and farther away.

"I didn't hit a whitetail last night, did I? When I was driving?" She had to be sure.

"I don't think so," Aubrey said, only half listening.

She felt sweat in her armpits, like a nervous teenager, even though she was cold.

"Why do you think Ronnie does it?" he asked. There was something buried deep inside sweet Aubrey Falls, and he'd pulled into himself in search of it. Aimee studied that something as best she could from a distance, but she couldn't help but tug at him. She grabbed his thumb and pulled him toward herself. He let her, as he had let her take his arm when Ronnie had called him into the circle of lantern light in the tent. But he worked his thumb loose and smoothed his hair.

"He told me he knew one more bite would kill him," Aubrey said. "So why would he do it again? It's suicidal."

"It's faith."

"But you said you thought he was a fool for doing it."

"He is. He's a damn fool."

"Then why do you call it faith?" Aubrey's voice went tight.

She didn't take his thumb. "One time," she said, "Ronnie stood up at a Glorybound service to speak. This was after that day Jesus didn't come back for us—it was after Daddy skipped town. Ronnie always shook real bad when he talked in front, so it was quick. He said, 'We can't just wait around for Jesus to come get us. We gotta fly to him.' Then he sat back down. I remembered it when he went down south for auto-diesel school. I hadn't thought about it since, till I was driving the pickup last night. Maybe that's what he's doing when he handles. Flying to Jesus."

Aubrey shook his head, shook off any mention of Jesus, and that hurt her. He stood. "I need to call and cancel class at the community building."

"No, they'll know," she said, taking his thumb again, insistent, and pulling him back down. "They was all there last night."

He was quiet, then: "Your mom said Jimmy Shrout called for you yesterday.

You won't lose your job because of this, will you?"

"Nah. Jimmy won't fire me. He's just like Art and Chloe. He's the one give us that white pickup. Crys kept asking him how much, and he said he'd think on it and then never told us. She finally swallowed her pride and took it for free. It's always run good."

Quiet again. The nurse returned without Crystal and settled behind her desk, not looking at them. When they spoke again, they whispered.

"Aubrey, I think we'll need to call us a prayer vigil at the church tonight. Will you come out for Ronnie?"

"Do you think it was my fault?" Aubrey stuttered in his whisper.

"That snake was fixed on biting him."

"But I startled it. I broke its trance." His eyes filled up, and he turned from her.

"It was fixed on biting. But you come out tonight. Pray with us."

"Aimee."

"You think you don't like it, but you never been out at Glorybound. My daddy'd call a prayer vigil anytime somebody'd get in trouble. He even called 'em for people who never come to church. We prayed over Janey Close's baby who died, you know, her and Bud Dixon's baby. When somebody was near dying, he'd call a vigil for 'em and it went all night. Lotta times they pulled through."

"And lots of times they didn't." Aubrey's whisper was too loud, and the nurse looked up sharp.

"Lotta times they did. Damn—you a case for hell." Aimee's gooseflesh smoothed, and she felt a soft fire inside. Her daddy would pray so hard, even after everyone else in the church went home. He'd walk into the trailer early the next morning with dark bags under his eyes and would eat just a scrap for breakfast. The only time she'd ever seen him cry was after that vigil he kept for Janey Close's baby. He held the vigil even though the baby had already died, and Aimee had wondered all night what her daddy had prayed for. He sat the next morning, silent, at his bowl of oatmeal and looked like he'd gone ten rounds in a boxing ring. And he cried. She had nearly forgotten that.

"We're gonna hold us a vigil tonight, Aubrey Falls, and I'd like it if you was there." She looked down at her black shoes worn gray on the toe.

"Why?"

"I'd like it." She wanted to touch his face, that face she sometimes called his savior face, but she felt a pane of glass between them. She wondered if he felt it, too. "They laid hands on me once at a healing vigil, and they healed me from the stomach flu. That's the truth."

"But you're a prophet, Aimee Jo Lemley." Aubrey smiled sad.

"Just about," she said. "But not quite."

"Close enough. I'd be dead weight. Your prayers are better off without me."

"You never been out to Glorybound."

"You never asked me to come, before now."

"Well, I'm asking." She watched her toes tap. "I'd like it if you was there."

Aubrey looked at her, and she raised her face to his. He spoke so soft she almost had to read his lips. "I know why Ronnie does it," he said. "It's like I can get inside him."

"How you mean?"

"How many moments of real living do we get, Aimee? When my dad died, I felt like a stone. I've been that stone most of my life, just watching everybody else and not feeling too much about anything." Aubrey spoke in a stream. "I was friends with this kid—I just remembered him last night in the tent—this kid Todd. He wanted me to climb a tree with him, and I couldn't. I was too afraid; I was too small. He fell and broke his knee open. It was a bad break, all the way through the skin—blood everywhere. I just stood there watching. I don't even know for how long." Sweet savior face of a boy who needed saving.

"You was just little then, Aubrey. You didn't know no better."

"But I lived like that. For a long time." He studied the floor tiles, wall to wall, back again.

"Right here," she said after awhile, and touched his knee.

"Yeah. He broke it to pieces."

"'Be healed,' that's what we say. 'By the power of the Lord.'"

It was one o'clock when Crystal walked back through the glass doors, so gentle, like she was afraid she might break them. Aimee and Aubrey stood up, and Crystal walked over with her hands in her jeans pockets. She put her face close to Aimee's, right up to it. So Ronnie was still out, but not gone. Not gone. Aimee saw that her sister's lips were chapped, from pressing together that way or from mouthing silent prayers, maybe. The left sleeve of her thin blouse was dark with dampness.

Aubrey made sure the nurse had their phone number.

"Maybe we should call Arlene," he said.

"Arlene Sisler? His mother?" the nurse asked. "She's called three times today already. I'll let you all know if he wakes up." No doubt Arlene had given the woman an earful. The nurse came out from behind her desk as though to see them out. Like they'd been visiting in her living room. Her heavy skirt held her legs captive. She judged them all the same, the people of Cuzzert, population 335. She judged Aubrey, too, and Aimee grabbed his hand as they walked out.

Aubrey drove the pickup so they could sleep. Aimee sat by the window, and Crystal put her head down on Aimee's chest like a child. The loose strands of Crystal's hair tickled her skin where her red dress dipped low to her breasts. Aimee held her, stroked her wrist.

"When we get home, Crys, we gonna call us a prayer service. We'll get Miriam on the chain to gather folks. Aubrey here's gonna come, ain't you, Aubrey?" Aimee looked into the dirty dash.

"Yes. I'll come," he said. She looked at him, grinned, then went sober.

"See there, Crys? Aubrey's gonna come. Folks'll come out, you'll see. We ain't had a vigil for some time, but folks'll come." She whispered when she felt Crystal's breath get heavy and slow. "And we'll go into the night. Ronnie'll pull through. He'll give this business up and come back to us. He'll sing for us and play guitar. Remember that healing service we had when June Tatum was living and she fainted from her vision? Now, you remember that. It's when Elsie Felton first got the tumors and June had that sight of a clean river cutting up past the strip mine, even though there ain't been nothing there but sludge pond for years. We all went with flashlights a looking for that river, and, don't you know, right outside the sludge, there come a pool of clear water out the culvert. June dipped her hand in and touched Elsie's side. I remember that." She whispered so soft now, she thought she just spoke inside her own head. "I remember that. We stayed out there a singing till midnight. Then the tree frogs took over. Elsie had some good years after that, too, up walking around. That's right, that's right." She closed her hand around Crystal's limp wrist.

Aubrey drove without speaking. She liked seeing him drive their truck, his arm resting easy on the door with the window down. Aimee watched the Donnie Manse once Manheim Road edged up alongside it. It flowed without giving thought to their cares. When they passed the cemetery, the tallest marker, the cross for Janey's baby, looked like it had shifted, bending forward, closer to the river.

Aubrey turned in at Painted Rocks and parked the pickup in its dent in the dirt and gravel.

"What about your Jeep?" Aimee asked as Crystal stirred.

"You go on inside," he said. "I'll walk to the service station and get it. It's not far." Aimee felt the weight of her sister's head lift from her chest and felt her own weariness. The Dixons' husky barked like mad behind the doublewide.

She opened the door and got out. Crystal slipped out after her and walked around to the back, toward the clothesline. Maybe she didn't want to face Dotte, who would be waiting at the kitchen table. Aimee lingered by the cab. The three packs of Pall Malls she'd bought the day before sat unbound and crinkled on the floor mat, and she gathered them.

Aubrey watched her from across the truck bed. He looked into the bed at the crumpled-up T-shirt and the denim jacket he'd pressed to Ronnie's arm.

"I better tell Mom what's what," Aimee said. "She'll get Miriam Louks on the prayer chain." She grabbed the T-shirt with her free hand, flopped it loose to see the *Jesus Saves,* purple and gold. "It'll probably start 'round six or something. If you do wanna come."

Aubrey picked at a spot of rust. "I'll be there if you want me there." Then he walked down the drive, past the rocks with red paintings and onto Route 40, like he was taking her path, headed to King's to get some cigarettes.

Crystal

....

CRYSTAL WALKED AROUND THE CORNER of the trailer, and the husky's bark drowned out Aimee's and Aubrey's voices. The bony dog stretched its chain taut when it saw her, its collar nearly strangling it. She expected the dog to bark itself to death one day.

She sat on the steps of the back screen porch. She smelled smoke, didn't know where from, smelled the Tide in the sun-bleached towels that sat in the basket on the washer. Aimee hadn't put them away.

Joshie Dixon came out his front door. "Shut up, Rod," he said. He kicked the dog in the ribs, and it yelped. It hunched down and shook, and he petted it. "Shut up, little fucker. That's it." Joshie wore his usual flannel shirt over his white undershirt, even in the heat. Crystal noticed that the heat wasn't as heavy as it had been. She felt a breeze. He fooled with the dog for awhile without looking at her. She didn't think he saw her, but he had come out like he'd been waiting.

Joshie wore long sleeves to cover the acne on his forearms. It was worse there than it was on his face. She and Aimee used to say it was his bad soul coming out. Now she felt how cruel that was. Maybe it wasn't a bad or good soul coming out, but just a soul that was raw, that couldn't be hid.

"The Pontiac's up on blocks in back," Joshie said, still watching the dog and scratching behind its ear. "Bud's waiting for a new switch or something. Takes 'em goddamn long enough to ship it." He moved away from the dog and leaned one arm against his trailer, put all his weight on one foot so he looked posed. The siding gave a little, and he let up on the pressure.

"I got class, but, you know. Called off or something. Things got kinda called off after it happened." He looked at Crystal and met her eyes. After she'd gone silent ten years before, Joshie had kept clear of her, like he was half afraid to look her in the face, always hangdog and muttering. He showed all his vulgar boldness to Aimee. But at one time, back when Crystal and Joshie had been little, they would string up tin cans trailer to trailer and try to hear each other's voices.

Crystal stood to go inside the porch.

"You think Sisler's gonna be okay?" Joshie asked. "I mean, you been to see him or something?" His arm that held his weight shook a little; he let it drop so that he leaned on nothing. "I had a good bit to drink, you know. I mean, I acted a fool, I know that, but I didn't really want him getting bit or nothing. Well, I did. I mean, just some." He kicked a rock under the Lemley's doublewide where the aluminum was peeling. "Crys, I wanted to wish bad for him. I'm saying it outright. And I did bet a five on him getting bit—it was Paint Davis taking bets. I don't know why. But if you ask me straight, I'll tell you I didn't want no copperhead to kill him."

Ronnie had looked peaceful in the white bed under the white blankets, with tubes stuck into him, themselves like snakes. He'd worn a mask for air and looked so old. One arm bandaged up, the other one limp. She'd taken his hand and tugged it lightly, pictured them running like kids racing the river.

Joshie shifted his weight and ran a finger along the inside waist of his jeans. They were too tight. She felt the heavy denim of her daddy's jeans on her, meant for a man. Her legs could shake inside them and nobody would see.

"He'll make it, won't he?" Joshie quit looking at her and looked back at the dog who rolled now in the dirt. He stood so still, like he wanted somebody to come hold him.

What do people do, Crystal thought, *when they go untouched, when they ain't okay with being touched?* They cover their arms with flannel sleeves; they turn to ashes and go gray. They see red; they go wild. They set fire to their dresses and leave lace and a pink belt in the trash barrel to make other folks wonder. They get themselves thrown in prison, and they call the punishment down. They handle serpents just to feel the scales and the muscled-tongue bodies. They do any number of things.

The lazy spring shut the screen door without sound after Crystal passed through.

They quit their singing. They go without a healing.

Cord

....

#96309

July 7, 1999

Write a letter to someone, telling him what you have never had a
chance to say face to face.

A boy come in my head from down Roane, I do not know why. His name was Gene,
that is not a womans name spelling. He is dead now many a year so it is not a letter
I can post. Gene was a boy loved his horse too much to sell it. It was something pretty
with a all black mane and a all brown body looked like a mans skin. Gene was all the
time brushing it with a horse comb. So he kept hold of the horse come spring sale but
he did not have no money to feed it, or his family neither. They was bad off. He could
not keep that horse fed, so he stoled money from a gas station in town. The man run-
ning register kept a gun on him and shot Gene dead before he could get out. He never
could talk to people good, he was shy like that but not with his horse. I did not know
how to say things to him in the face. I would write to him—

Dear Gene,
   I was not saved by God when we was boys in Roane them same years. I lived near you
maybe 6 mile. If I done been saved I might say—Do not rob that fill-up station, cause
you will die. But there is more. It says it in the Word that if thy right hand offend thee
cut it off and cast it from thee, for it is a better thing that one of thy members should
perish, and not that thy whole body should be cast into hell. It was your hand that
done the thieving to cut off, but the deeper sin is you loved that horse too much. You
ought not love a thing so much. It is again God. (Glory)

Aubrey

....

AUBREY LOOKED DOWN the Cuzzert Pike turnoff at the stirring crabapple trees that bore no fruit. He considered walking the gravel road to the church, just to see what it looked like. A few cars had passed. The drivers waved lazily, and he felt the dust from their passing thicken the skin on his arms.

He walked on. A crow called out from a fencepost with barbed wire spiraling around it. It was a wonder the bird's wings didn't get caught in the barbs.

Each time he thought of the pink scar splitting apart on Ronnie's arm, he made a fist and shook his head to get the image out. He grabbed for other thoughts to overwhelm the jitters he felt, so when his mother came to his mind he let her in.

As a kid, when he hadn't been able to sleep one night, he had asked her to pray like the mother in a movie he'd seen. His mom told him that prayer was just a blanket a child wraps around himself to keep him safe, but of course the safety is only a delusion. She had raised her hands in silly mock claws—the monsters would still get you if they wanted to. Some people needed the blanket just to fool themselves, but she didn't. Even with his dad gone, she wanted to see the monsters when they came, in all of their harsh reality. Or so she'd said.

He remembered one night, at Loyola, when he'd been walking to a campus lecture. It had been raining, a sudden downpour, so he'd ducked into the chapel to wait out the worst of it. The sound of his footsteps on the white marble ricocheted into the cavern of the place, the high, white ceilings. Only the emergency lights were on, and they lit up the blue stained glass—attractive when the sun came through it but gaudy in this fluorescent light.

A woman in a big coat sat on a pew in the back row, not ten feet away from him. She didn't move. She held a figurine, and Aubrey stepped forward to see what she held and to make sure the woman knew he was there. He didn't want her to go through with something private while she had an audience.

It was a plastic Virgin Mary figurine, something you'd get at a junk store, and the woman held it at its base of cloud where Mary's bare feet perched. The plastic Mary held out her hands; she had a blue robe, yellow hair. Some of the flesh color had been rubbed from her palms, and when Mother Mary had gone through the assembly line, the rosy dots had missed her cheeks and hit her nose and ear so she looked like a clown with fudged makeup. Aubrey cleared his throat, self-conscious. The woman said nothing, but her hands slipped loose from their support of the white cloud. She almost dropped the figurine, dangled it by one of the rubbed-off hands, the way a little girl holds her doll.

He stayed and watched the woman while she prayed like that, holding the plastic hand. He missed half the lecture, and when he finally sat in the seat his classmate had saved for him, he said he'd been finishing a book, couldn't put it down. "Plus the rain," he said. "Yeah, the rain," the classmate said back. "This guy's brilliant; shut up and listen."

Aubrey plucked a weed from the ditch and played with it as he walked. He thought, now, that he should have stayed and listened to that woman pray all night long. He should have asked her if she believed in the soul, and if she did, what exactly she believed about it and how had she come to her conclusions. But such questions would have struck her as foolish, surely, the same way they would have struck the Reverend Cord Lemley. The soul cannot be abstract in the clasping of a plastic Virgin Mary or here in the town of Cuzzert that lay dying at the base of dead mountains—nor can it be sheathed or tastefully ignored. He understood that now. He was seeing things so clearly they stung his eyes.

Even in the prison, where everything was walled into concrete cells with four-inch windows, those men came for his feeble class, and all of them, from the meanest to the most timid, bled out their souls through their pen ink onto the page in a way he'd never been able to do. They postured themselves for meager protection, hunched over their writing. All of them except Cord, who asked for no shield. Cord's cheeks had hollowed like those of a corpse; his belt, cinched to the last hole, held up pants three sizes too big for his frail body; his collarbone was a blade that Aubrey expected to pierce through the skin at any moment.

The soul was a tender bird hatched without warning, and there was no going back into the shell. The exposure, the defending—and he thought of Aimee's bold, desperate gestures, like wings flapping—became a way of life. Aubrey wondered if his soul had ever hatched, or if he'd paid attention when it had. That wasn't quite the right wording—none of it was—but he didn't go back and revise it. He wrapped the ditch weed around his finger and quickened his pace.

He was about to walk around the bend that curved to King's Service Station when a pale blue car drove up. Aubrey stopped, and the car slowed to an idle beside him. Jim Louks. Aubrey felt Jim's eyes on his dirty arms, on his clothes still rumpled with sleep. He threw the crippled weed back to the ditch.

"Hi there, son," Jim said. "You look in a hurry." He draped his elbow over the car door and squinted into the afternoon sun.

"How are you, Jim?"

"I see you're not holding classes today. I was just by the community building. Nobody home."

"We had to cancel this morning." Aubrey thought over the faces in the class. Yes, they had all been there to see Ronnie get bit, except for maybe Gary Wayne who'd been waiting outside to auction off his overfed hog.

"And why's that?" Jim opened his door and pulled himself out with effort. He leaned heavily against the still-idling car. Aubrey didn't answer.

"She's a hot one," Jim said. "But we got us a breeze, just now and again." He looked down at the cracked road, then up toward the bend, toward the spot where the new pavement started. "You know, we're a pretty simple people 'round here, Aubrey. Decent, for the most part, but simple, and we're pulling ourselves up. You know, again' the odds. But there's them that holds us back a little, and we need to cut ties sometimes. We need to keep them in their place. You see what I'm saying?"

"Not really, Jim." Aubrey's arms felt like weights. His neck hurt. Jim rubbed his own neck as though he felt Aubrey's soreness.

"I mean, even with Mama I got to say enough's enough, and she's kin, see? Some people. Well. There's people think you ain't exactly holding up your end."

"What are you talking about? What people?"

"Just some folks."

"Has Reverend Angus said something?"

"I don't intend to name names, son." Jim stroked his stomach, sucked his lips. "I'd like to be straight. 'Cause I like you, Aubrey. You come in here from the Middle West, and I can see how some things could turn your head—and you got a *good* head there on those shoulders. You're a good man."

"I'm a good man, Jim?"

"You're a good man, and I'll be straight. I know you was at that circus last night, that godawful mess. Serpent handling's for loonies, son. You keep your head. And that Lemley girl." He spread his hand onto the roof of the car then drew it back as though the roof were hot. "You're here to help out, help us raise our heads high. Not to make us look the fool. There's poor folks who's decent, and there's poor folks who's trash. If you don't mind my speaking plain."

"I think I do mind."

"She *is* pretty."

"Who's pretty?"

"I mean, I can see it, and all." Jim grinned and shook his wide head.

"What exactly can you see?" Aubrey grabbed his own shoulder, as if someone had punched him. Aimee had put her head there and slept.

"I'm speaking for your own good, Aubrey. You get mixed up with trash, you start stinking. You get my meaning?"

Aubrey watched the flesh hanging from Jim's jaw. It jiggled as the man shook his head again, climbing back into the car. Aubrey's vision was sharp, sharp enough to see the pathetic stains on Jim's collar and the sweat of his agitation striping his temple.

"You know, Jim," Aubrey said. "I think there's a prayer vigil for Ronnie Sisler tonight. Out at Glorybound Holiness Tabernacle. In your mother's basement. Why don't you come out for it?"

Jim looked away, up the road.

"I'll be there," Aubrey said. "I'll see you."

Jim spoke without looking up. "You got assigned here one year, VISTA. One little year, then you get to go back to where you come from and keep moving up in the world, in a way people here can't do for themselves." He took the car out of park and looked hard at Aubrey. "Year's 'bout up, son. That Lemley girl know that?" He drove off, making a racket on the harsh road, then quieting on the smooth asphalt. The pale blue disappeared.

Aubrey walked behind the car's dust, kicking rocks. He kept looking over his shoulder, feeling watched and exposed. He felt a sting of guilt. No, he had not told Aimee he would leave after a year. He had forgotten about that altogether.

Around the curve in the road, the steel sign edged out from the clutch of spindly trees. *Cuzzert Correctional Facility for Men, 15 Miles.* Fifteen miles. It was so close, but it might as well have been in another country. He wanted to keep walking till he could see Cord Lemley and tell him about Ronnie Sisler, about the vigil, about his daughters who were trying to get to him across those fifteen long miles to the other world. They were trying. Aubrey remembered that he had planned the day before to read all of Cord's writings again, each page a piece of this strange man's soul. Each page somehow a piece of Cuzzert, too.

Is there a clue in there to all this? he asked the reverend in his head. The papers would still be there on the desk in his cabin, curved upward, bound with a rubber band. He needed to get home to clean up, maybe shave.

Aubrey got in his Jeep where it sat slanting halfway into the dry ditch. He saw the shape of Agnes Felton at the counter in King's. She'd be reading *The Star* and patting her permed hair.

He sat there without turning the key. A car passed, and he recognized it: Paint Davis coming from the beer distributor's. He decided to sit there till a car passed that he didn't recognize. He sat for a while.

Dotte

....

THE CALM CIGARETTE SMOKE filled Dotte's throat, then it slipped out and rose to the kitchen light that wasn't on. The window light was soft. It was around three, and she had a show at three on Wednesdays but wasn't planning to watch it. Aimee had brought in these beat-up cigarette packs. Dotte had opened one of them like she was starving and it was food.

She didn't like it when Aimee smoked with her. It made Dotte feel dirty. But it was peaceful too, so she allowed it. Aimee was on her third.

"You and Crystal wash," Dotte said. "I can get a early supper going 'fore we go." Her Aimee girl sat with her at the table, fooling with the prayer cloth. She unfolded it and folded it back with one hand, the other hand for smoking.

"Crys's sleeping," Aimee said. Her red dress looked like a dead flower, all loose and crumpled. She still had beauty, though. Still like Queen Esther.

"You wash first then. Iron your peach dress."

"That the one I'm wearing, is it?"

"That's the one."

Aimee had come in there like on fire. Or she'd looked like fire in that red. She'd acted like she'd been through a fire and had run from it. She was so tired. But Ronnie was still living, praise God. Aimee opened the cup cabinet door where Dotte had taped up the prayer chain list of phone numbers inside.

"Call Miriam," she said. "We need to call us a vigil."

Dotte wanted to tell Aimee she'd kept vigil all night at the table with the prayer cloth, but she just said okay. She didn't think Miriam would be in favor of it, though. Miriam frowned on the fair and on handling and anything like it.

But Dotte called up Miriam Louks.

"Who?" Miriam said.

"It's Dotte. Did you hear about Ronnie Sisler?"

Miriam had heard. She said it served him right because he was testing the Lord's patience. And he shouldn't have been charging money on top of it.

"I went right out this morning," Miriam said, "and got to work a pinching off my geraniums. Yes I did, and I didn't think a thing of that boy. It serves him right."

Dotte said, "Well," and Miriam went quiet. Then she started crying, and she took it back.

"He had such a sweet singing voice," Miriam whined, "like sugarwater. Maybe there's hope for him."

And Dotte said, "Maybe there is." So Miriam would arrange it and would start the calls on the chain. Dotte would come early to do the flowers and help her sweep up.

She put the phone back on the wall. Aimee lit a cigarette and sat there thinking. Her eyes got blacker, so black Dotte couldn't see her thoughts.

"I might not wear the peach one. It's missing a button," Aimee said.

"You don't have no other nice ones."

"You don't like my dresses?"

"You mind, now."

"I'll mind, Mom. What you doing with this rag?" She lifted the prayer cloth with the tip of her finger. Dotte wanted to make Aimee a new dress that fit her right. She had been thinking on it.

"Nothing. Ronnie dropped it." She took the prayer cloth and folded it.

"I know that."

"Do you remember?"

"Yeah, I remember."

"I mean when we made 'em for healing cloths."

"I said, 'I remember.'" Aimee put her chin down on her arm. It shook ash from her cigarette onto the table.

"Well. I thought maybe it was a sign."

"A sign of what?" Aimee asked, lazy.

"Of your daddy's coming back." Dotte pulled at the elastic neck of her dress. She'd sat up in it all night at the table. She knew Aimee didn't believe in signs anymore, not deep down, even if she did play the woman-prophet.

"Maybe you're right," Aimee said.

Dotte thought she was teasing. "Maybe I am." She patted the cloth on the top fold where it showed the *Jesus* part.

"I think I will wash up, Mom. We got us a long night ahead." Aimee got up and walked down the hallway, still holding her cigarette.

They think I don't know things, Dotte thought. *They think I can't read signs. I can read some. I can read Crystal's signs of love for that boy. And if he dies, there's a part of her that's like to die with him. They think I don't know what she and Ronnie done out at Glorybound that night when they practiced for the Easter singing. When I was up doing the flowers with Miriam. They didn't hear me come down. I seen the two of them wrapped up in each other. I went back up and told Miriam I forgot my purse, even though she could see I hadn't.*

Dotte sat listening to the shower run. She could hear it clear as a bell from the kitchen. She sat till it was going on four. Then she started a pan of beans for an early supper, so they could get to the church and get it ready. Since she told Miriam she'd do the flowers.

Cord

....

#96309

July 14, 1999

If you could go anywhere in the world, where would you go?

I would stay right here. Buddy that is true. There is 800 of us here. I can see it is 800 places the men go to in their dreams or just thinking it. Most to get home, cause they come here from up New Jersey way and farther up too.

They said my kidneys is going to fail me inside if I keep up my fast. The liquid food is not to live on. They come around me like the flies on a dead deer. They said it to scare me but one thing only I fear is Almighty God. They think I am afraid to die. I told the man out front, he is the big one walks up and back, cause one night he done told us about the new fighter champ. I said—I believe the Lord God is like that referee that holds up the hand of the Heavy Weight Champ, he walks around the ring with him. That referee aint never taking a second look at the loser. We got to live like that is what I testified. But I have not. My kidneys failing is what it is. They force me to keep in this here world too long.

It might be there is reasons. I mark on a paper every day of my fast. It was 40 days I marked it last night.

Aubrey

....

A WHITE CROSS OF TWO-BY-FOURS stood like a grave marker on the side of the road. It was the only sign that a church met there. Aubrey might have driven past it if a few pickups hadn't already parked in the worn grass. Miriam Louks' house was small, with gray shingle siding and a yellow-and-white sloped awning over the front porch. The side door down to the basement stood open; low singing voices drifted out. Not a choir, more like voices trying to remember a song by singing through a few bars. The voices were nasal, like pressed tin.

Aubrey leaned forward on the Jeep's steering wheel to let the sweat on his back dry. He wore the blue-collared dress shirt he'd worn for his graduation, had almost put on a tie but decided against it.

He had pulled in line on the grass, late, since the church was farther down Cuzzert Pike than he'd expected and the washboard road had slowed him down. He watched Louisa Felton prop up her slight mother, Elsie, as they descended the stairs into the basement. Elsie's back humped up; she wore a white hat with a green ribbon around it. Louisa had on a sundress that was too big and white high heels she had to wobble in. She gripped the wrought-iron railing tightly till they disappeared inside.

Aubrey put the key back into the ignition. He didn't belong there.

Then, in front of the house, someone stood up. Joshie Dixon. He'd been sitting in the yard on a tire with red flowers spilling out of its center. Joshie stood slumped over, holding a bottle in a paper sack. His eyes narrowed in on a spot in Miriam's flowers, on a mini, plastic deer whose antlers tangled with the flower stems. Joshie looked up and nodded at Aubrey and looked away, both of them out of place. Aubrey nodded back and got out.

He walked to the basement stairs and touched the railing lightly, as if testing its sturdiness. He looked again at Joshie, who had fixed once more on the plastic deer. Aubrey understood that Joshie wasn't coming inside but he was there. Like Aubrey was there—as though being there made perfect sense and would somehow keep Ronnie Sisler from dying.

"You clean up good." Aimee's voice startled him. She came around the back corner of the house as if she'd been watching for him. She held some flowers and looked like a schoolgirl. He must have shown his surprise at the old-fashioned peach dress. "I know. So do I. Had to pin it here"—she pointed to a buttonhole—"but it's still fit for praying in." She came close and put her hand on the railing beside his.

"Who are those for?" He pointed to the white and blue flowers in her hand.

"They ain't for you, sweet Aubrey Falls." She grinned. "These is asters and bachelor's buttons for June Tatum. I put 'em on her chair every meeting, done it ever since she died." The dress narrowed at her waist in a V, and the skirt flared from it, swaying, as she pulled herself to the railing and fell lightly back, forward and back, shyly. "You shaved," she said and touched his cheek.

The singing inside ended, and silence like arms held the two of them in the doorway. It hushed them. Then, "Sweet hour of prayer, sweet hour of prayer." Chloe Shrout's voice came singly, a high bird trill. "That calls me from a world of care." A few voices joined in the song, a huddle of voices, and they reached out like arms, too, touching Aubrey on all the places where his skin was exposed.

Beside the door, in the window low to the ground and grown-over with grass, a stenciled sign that said *Tabernacle* leaned against the glass at a slant. Aubrey followed Aimee's peach dress inside.

In the front of the dim room, a table draped in yellow held a vase of flowers. The room smelled like coal smoke and old cement and strong lavender that Aubrey thought came from the flowers until he saw they were fake. He sat in a metal chair beside Aimee, two seats over from Miriam Louks, and it was her lavender perfume that stuck in his throat. Aimee put her flowers, tied with string, on the empty chair beside her. Next to that chair, Dotte crossed her hands over her stomach and mumbled the hymn with her eyes closed: "In seasons of distress and grief, my soul has often found relief, and oft escaped the tempter's snare, by thy return, sweet hour of prayer." She squeezed her eyes more tightly as they started the next verse, and she wiped her neck with a cloth. She put the cloth to her face and held it, as a baby does a blanket.

Crystal didn't sit beside Dotte, but stood up front, off to the side, as though she planned to address the tiny congregation. She looked into the vase where someone had propped a photo of a younger Ronnie Sisler among the stiff, fake blooms. His hair was short and combed to the side, maybe a high school graduation picture. Crystal's hair was wet, braided back neatly. She wore a blue dress as long as Aimee's but more squarish; it concealed her body the way her jeans and big shirts did.

Aubrey anchored his feet flat on the green carpet. He felt as though he'd sat down among bees that he'd been watching swarm from a distance. Among them, he heard their every hum and buzz, and he realized they were softly praying in this curve of metal chairs, while only two or three continued with the hymn.

Chloe Shrout sat singing beside Art, who had gotten hot and had removed his suspenders, stripped to his undershirt; his frail arms poked out from the sleeves, ready to snap in two. Elsie and Louisa Felton sat with Louisa's niece Jenny, the girl who had collected money at the mouth of the black tent. Jenny wore the same uniform-like outfit she'd worn for the handling but no shoes. She was the only child present, and she swung her bare feet, but, among the other faces, hers looked just as old and hard. Miriam Louks sat by herself with a large purse on the chair beside her. Two old men sat leaning forward on their knees like basketball players on a bench. Ashby and Tim Welch. They were the brothers Aubrey had seen only once before, when they had come to the community building one day with boxes of carpentry books for his class at the prison. The Welch brothers had gotten too old to see the print; the books were from the seventies, covers loose, and none of the men at the prison had shown interest. Aubrey knew the Welches lived somewhere out past the strip mine. They both wore insulated flannel, even in the hot basement, and they hummed the beehive hum of prayer through their barely moving lips. The chairs made a half-circle around the table with the yellow drape and the artificial flowers framing Ronnie Sisler's young face.

Aubrey counted seven portraits of Jesus hanging on the cement-block walls. Between the single window and a board with numbers recording nothing but the Record Attendance—26—hung the painting Crystal had picked up from Jim Louks' trash heap on Monday. The white, plastic frame; that thick darkness around the hovering head of Christ; the green thorns twisted on his head, catching the light of the two weak globes in the ceiling. Jesus didn't look at you squarely from the painting; he looked to the left with his kind but lordly eyes, out past the frame, as though he weren't paying attention. But, as Aubrey looked more closely, the painting reminded him of Cord's ashen face, its hollowed cheeks. Then he could nearly glimpse Ronnie's face and his sweat streaking like Christ's vulgar blood. Aubrey felt a chill and looked away.

The song ended, but the low hum of petitions kept on. The people seemed to float up into the sound. Aubrey kept searching for more people, people in the corners or on the stairs that must have led up to Miriam's tidy living room or kitchen, but there were only these few, along with Joshie Dixon outside maybe humming some kind of drunken prayer to the plastic deer.

Art Shrout stood slowly. "He who give us that song will give us another tonight, amen. But let's us testify some. Let's us lift up our brother."

"Hallelujah," Chloe said, with her hand raised, and the hum grew loud then soft again, like a wave cresting.

"We'll all have us a new body," Art said, his palms on his own delicate chest. "We know it 'cause the Lord said it and we believe it. We'll have us a new body and a crown of glory, and we'll go when you call us, Lord. We'll follow. But, Lord God, tonight our brother's a hurting, and we don't know if you done called him or not, Lord. Oh, there's one among us at the door of death, and we pulling him back, Jesus, won't you pull him back, Jesus. 'Cause he ain't lived long like I have, Lord. No, he's a young man who can yet bring you glory, Lord God, amen?"

"Amen," Aimee said with her eyes closed and her face so open. Aubrey felt his back wet with sweat again, and he leaned forward. He bowed his head to the green carpet.

"Ask and ye shall receive," Art hollered. "Seek and ye *shall* find—it's what you tell us in the Word—you say knock and the door *shall* be opened. Mm-hmm, yes." Art swung his brittle arms at his sides, as though preparing to leap forward. "'Where two or three are gathered,' says the Lord, 'there be my Spirit also.' It's something you can count on, brother; it's the rock, sister. The Spirit of the Lord God is here among us, real as rain."

The Welch brothers nodded, and Tim clapped. Dotte Lemley hunkered forward and wrapped her right forearm in the cloth she held. *Jesus Saves,* in purple and gold.

"Heela heela heela," she crooned. "Halamaha, keeya keeya," like nothing he'd heard before. She sucked in breath through her teeth and winced as if in pain.

"Keeya keeya," Chloe echoed in her bird voice. "Keeya keeya." She opened her eyes wide to the globe lights and saw something in them that made her nod her head *yes. Yes* to this quiet frightening flood. Aubrey did not say *yes,* or even know how to say *yes,* but it washed over him all the same, over even the tender white of his bones.

Art stomped his foot. "You feel him in your body, now. We the children of God; we come for the purifying of our flesh. You feel him on your outsides, now, and deep down in your insides, and all around us in the air of this here house Sister Miriam keep up for us. You feel him here like a wind." Miriam stood first, at the mention of her name, then the others stood up, and Aubrey sat there with a throbbing in his chest, his mouth dry, and his eyes burning from the coal-lavender swell in the room. Aimee grabbed his hand and pulled him to his feet.

"You feel him like a *wind*," Art said again. "There he is, brothers and sisters. Is the Lord a giving us a song now?"

"Oh victory in Jesus." Chloe started the hymn high and thin. "My savior forever," her voice stretching out like a piece of foil. "Well, he sought me and he bought me with his redeeming blood." A few joined her. The prayer-bees gently buzzed again, in between the verses, and Dotte waved the *Jesus Saves* cloth, jabbering on in her mysterious tongue.

Crystal held her place on the green carpet up front, staring at Ronnie's photograph. She had her hand in her front pocket; she swayed in time with the song and bent her knees before the refrain as though helping to lift it and carry it onward.

Crystal

....

IT WAS ELSIE FELTON who called for the foot-washing way past dark.

The young girl Jenny lay sleeping in the corner where Aimee and Crystal had slept as little girls when the prayers in the room had stretched over them like a heavy blanket.

Elsie clutched Louisa's shoulder and pulled herself up. The back hem of her dress hung a few inches higher than the front because of her hump. Her head sagged. When she raised it, her neck flesh tightened and she labored for air. She cupped her hands in front of her as if holding a baby bird.

Crystal watched Elsie's skin, bluish and paper thin. Death would soak through it soon enough and fill her. The others quieted to make room for Elsie's voice.

"It's time we take us a pail"—she stopped for breath—"and do like the Lord."

Art Shrout rose from where he knelt with his elbows on the seat of his chair. "Right now, Elsie?" She nodded and bent her body back down beside Louisa.

"Well, if the Lord's a leading your heart," Art said. Near the base of the stairs that led up to Miriam's, he picked up the overturned, metal washtub. He looked into it, studied it. "If the Lord's a moving you, then we'll snap to." He went to the bathroom to fill the tub at the spigot.

The small congregation lost hold for a moment. It was odd to practice a foot-washing at a prayer vigil. Maybe Elsie Felton was confused. Maybe she had no idea why they were gathered there or for whom they prayed. But Elsie lifted her face to Crystal, eyes lucid as starlight. Elsie saw inside her, to her inner parts unspoken of—she saw where Crystal kept the memory of Ronnie, the last time he'd touched her before leaving town. Elsie called it forth: he held Crystal's foot over the washtub, wiped this side of her ankle with his hand, now that side, wiped with cool water—tinted orange from iron and sulfur—and his hand made his kiss. He didn't dry her feet afterward, and she left wet footprints on the green carpet as she walked after him a ways. Then she let him leave.

Crystal felt Ronnie suffering.

She fingered the copper wire that bound the sixteen-penny nails in a cross in her dress pocket.

"We all got us the filth of the flesh," Art said, when he came back to the half-circle of chairs. "We all need washed. And Elsie's a saying it to us—wash clean so it's *then* God hears our prayers. Yes, I hear his leading, sister." Art set the tub on the floor, and the water sloshed. He slipped off his shoes, peeled loose his black socks and stood there barefoot. Chloe, the Welches, Louisa, Miriam and Aimee—each one followed suit. Dotte's black flats squeezed her feet tight, and she pried them off with the bottom bar on her chair. Her naked feet were red where the shoes had rubbed.

Crystal stayed still as Aubrey looked at her, helpless, his leather shoes firm on his feet. Everyone so full of need. Art went to Elsie Felton first, took off her knee-high nylons so gentle. "My," she said when her flesh touched the water.

Crystal felt a cry deep inside her, so low it ached in her leg bones, like some-one had turned on a faucet and all the water pipes rattled through the house. Pipes too thin for the water's flood; they'd split the walls. She would split the silence to pieces, rip it apart, but not here, not now. She left her spot beside the table of fake flowers and walked, slow and even, to the doorway, climbed the stairs up into night.

Crystal headed for the white pickup in the dirt and grass, her blue dress like a sheet wrapping her. She ran, and the sheet flapped.

Aimee

....

AIMEE FIDDLED WITH THE LOOSE STRAP on her shoe after she took it off. She felt an opening in herself, like someone had opened a window wide. Then she looked up and couldn't find her sister in the basement room.

Aimee grabbed Aubrey's hand and gathered her shoes, followed Crystal out the door barefoot. She ran after her, like she'd run after June Tatum the Sunday morning June had sewn that mismatching copper button onto her dress. Aimee ran with Aubrey to the edge of the road and saw the truck's taillights slip away down Cuzzert Pike.

She dangled her shoes at her side and kept hold of him, gripped him farther up on his arm, ready to lead him somewhere, but she wasn't sure where. She looked back at where the glow of the Tabernacle bled up to the grass. She looked to the dark porch and saw Joshie Dixon passed out in the flowers.

"Aubrey," she whispered, "take me home."

"She's going to the hospital," he said, "to be with Ronnie." His underarm sweat had spread to where she touched his sleeve. "Do you want me to get your mom? Maybe she'll want to stay." He looked to the basement door, hungry and pale, like he wanted to go back inside.

He had seen an old man wash the slack foot-skin of an old woman.

He had come here because she'd asked him to come. But he had stayed because he'd wanted to stay.

"No," Aimee said. "Take me home with you."

In the cabin, Aimee loved to see where wood met wood after Aubrey pulled the cord on the light above his kitchen table. Everything at Painted Rocks was plastic or cement. A world of metal and linoleum. His cabin floor hadn't been swept, but it was pure old wood and beautiful.

"You have lotsa girls in here?" she teased, but her hands shook.

"No. I pictured a certain girl in here a few times. Many times." Aubrey leaned up against the wall by the woodstove and rubbed his neck. "I never thought she'd come, though."

Aimee walked around the table to the stand-alone sink and touched the basin. She touched the funny rocker made from a pop can, rocking off-kilter. Papers were scattered over the kitchen table, and she touched them too.

"You been reading my daddy's papers?"

"Yes, I have."

"How's come? You done read 'em already."

"I wanted to remember them." He folded one of the sheets, then unfolded and smoothed it. Those hands were too gentle to stay around for long.

Aimee looked at the corner of the room, where wood met wood. "I want you to remember me," she said. "When you go from here."

Cord

....

#96309

July 21, 1999

Write about your earliest childhood memory.

*I smell the death on me. I am weak but I got a power come. I will lay it out here true
as I ought. There was one time I remember as a boy that I ought not remember. But I
do. It stuck like tar, it is one vision I never told, and there aint like to be forgiveness
for it. It aint my first memory, cause my first was for my Mama. But it is the one on
my Soul to write.*

*At the circus I seen this girl clown. Her face was white like washed in lye. Albino
they called her in the Big Top ring, they said her white face was real. I wanted to know
was that face paint or was it real so I followed her when the show quit.*

Aubrey

....

"WHAT DO YOU MEAN when I go from here?" Aubrey said. Maybe someone had told her his service assignment would last only a year.

"I know we're a passing-through place." She leaned down and put her elbows on the table, fixing her eyes on the loose papers. "I know you can't stay here. Ain't nothing for you here." Even with the close collar of her peach dress, he saw that she wore the silver camisole she'd worn the first time he'd met her, when she'd sold cigarettes to Esther Moats on credit.

"I never said I was leaving."

"You will. Everybody leaves here." Aimee touched her wrist, as though checking to see if it were broken. She traced its bare skin the way she had at the fairgrounds when she'd seen the high school queen's bracelet. Aimee flitted like a bird, opening his cupboard and touching the butterfly shelf liner.

"I never said I was leaving," he said again, but his voice cracked.

She walked away from him, over to the writing desk. She picked up one of his poetry books, set it back down, then pulled open the drawer. She glanced at him, seeming embarrassed that she'd infringed on his privacy, but she pulled a paper from the drawer and read it.

Aimee's face sank. "So you gonna be a doctor after all." She smiled sadly. "You'll make a good one."

He crossed the room and gently took the paper from her, one of the expired medical school applications that his mom had sent. He felt his loneliness hovering over him. It threatened to claim him and drag him into the cavern of himself, from where he would only be able to watch Aimee, as though from a great distance, as she turned in her childish peach dress to the black square of window above the desk.

"No," he said firmly. "You're wrong. I would make a horrible doctor. I can't even stand the sight of blood." He laughed softly, and he could tell from the way her shoulders shook that she laughed a little. "Besides. There is something for me here." He put his hands on her waist, her skin hot through the cotton dress. She flinched in her body, recoiled slightly. She turned and took his hand, ringing his wrist with her finger and thumb. At her touch, his wrist bone stung with a mild pain. Her living rubbed up against his living, so close, bone on white bone.

"You kiss lotsa girls?"

"No." He smelled the lavender that Miriam had swathed them in at the church. "Pictured it lots of times, though."

"Who'd you pitcher?"

"A girl who kissed me once."

"You wanna kiss her again?"

"If she'd let me."

"She might."

Aubrey shivered across his back though her hand was like fire. He kissed her open mouth and pulled back. "You sure?" he asked.

She pressed her lips and her body to him, filled the separating space with peach-colored cotton and flesh and her black hair that fell into both their faces. Their breath came heavily, and he heard it like a roar. He heard everything at once: the scrape of the floor as they shoved against the desk with their bodies; Ronnie Sisler's voice; the rush of the wind in the truck bed; the Donnie Manse River; the rain; the retreat of the rain; Chloe Shrout's whining hymn; the screen door shutting beneath the blue lattice each time Aimee had left him outside in the worn dirt, left him to ache for her out in the open where the cars passed on Route 40.

Cord

....

#96309

The albino girl had a pink dress on, I could follow the pink dress easy at dark. I was at the Big Top at night. I followed her to a truck with a pull trailer on it. I did not go in but just spied her through the back window. It was like her body blushed from my eyes on her. That was the pink dress. She was something <u>*pretty.*</u> *In the ring she done a baton toss, she done a twirl right in the trailer too like for practice.*

I seen her wash her face in the sink and it stayed pure white, it was real. I ought to left then and let her be secret, but she undid her top piece of the dress and I was full up with lust of the flesh. Then a man come in the pull trailer. I seen him in the Big Top too in a clown suit. His white face was paint and not real, cause his sweat took it off. She said—No get out. But he would not. He was stronger than her and he spoilt her right there. I mean he put her up again the wall to go into her over and over. It was the first time I seen a man and woman like that, I watched. I seen her white face when he done it. I seen her in pain.

Aimee

....

AIMEE KEPT HOLD OF HIS ARMS in the back room of the cabin, then spread her hands across his back still damp with sweat. He had a mattress on the floor, just a bed sheet over it. She said not to pull the light on, let it be, and he asked again if she was sure. He unbuttoned the pearl buttons with their fake, silver rims, buttons she loved. Her dress gaped open to her camisole and to the bare skin, cool across her belly where he touched her. He slid his fingers along the camisole's hem that frayed in places. She could see him dimly in the dark, his shaved face and wet eyes. She unbuttoned his fine, blue shirt, and he had no undershirt on. Her dress dropped to the mattress. He leaned away from her, looking at her, at her bare legs, at her underwear that she had a pad lying in, the warm blood blooming on it, her life blood.

"Don't look at me," she said, more sharp than she meant.

"Why?"

"Don't look at me," softer, but her eyes stung.

"Aimee." He drew her to his bare skin. Her forehead to the dip below his neck. She felt his blood pulsing.

"Please don't touch me," she whispered, but she wrapped her arms around him even so, put her hands to his ears, cupping them to block out sound, and held his face away from hers. "What if it's not for me to know? This thing." She let loose of him and crumpled down onto the mattress at his feet.

"Aimee." He spoke into her ear, on his knees, and she lay down on the cool sheet. Aubrey touched her on her shoulder that her silver strap had fallen from, and she felt the open doorway that led out into the rest of the cabin, still lit by the single bulb over the table where her daddy's cursive covered the shuffled papers in coiled letters. She felt his eyes on her.

"One time he seen me," she said.

"Shh," Aubrey whispered and kissed her bare shoulder, slipped his hand onto her back under the camisole.

"I was coming out the bath. I didn't think it was nothing wrong, from the bath to my bed. And I forgot my towel on the bed, so I went that little ways without no clothes on."

Aubrey moved his hand to her front, and his hand was a hot coal as he rubbed her. "Shh," he said again, and she felt a wild murmur inside, and between her legs a hum, and the light from the doorway of the bedroom seemed to fall over them hard, like something solid.

"He was in that hallway, Aubrey." She touched his arm and pushed his hand away. "Aubrey, you listening?" Aimee sat up, and he lay still, watching her with an awful look of sweetness and confusion.

"My daddy," she said. "He was in that hallway like he was waiting. And when I come out with no clothes, he stood there and blocked my way. He just stood there looking."

"Aimee." He had heard her now.

"I ain't good," she said. "I shouldn't of come out bare like that."

Aubrey sat up on the mattress. "Did he touch you?"

"He didn't lay a hand on me. He never did. He just looked, long and hard. I mean he looked at every part of me. Then he slapped his own face for it. And he run out. That's what happened. When I was bare, he didn't say nothing. Like a damn mute."

Aubrey looked away and bit his lip.

He can't bear me, either, Aimee thought. She stretched her camisole down over her taut belly. "He said I's evil. The next day, when nobody was in the house. I had the feeling he'd do something to me. I was afraid, and I hung 'round Crys till she went to the store with Mom. Then he come in the kitchen and said I's the woman in the street men should run from. From the Book of Proverbs—I remember clear as day—he said I's the woman who'd capture the trimming of your coat. I'd ruin you. I was bent for bad and a evil temptation."

Aubrey pushed her hair from her face.

"Don't," she said. "You don't know it. That time he seen me out the bath, that was 'round the same time he picked the day for Jesus to come back for us. Like Jesus was a coming to stop him from doing something he'd be sorry for. I wanted him to die, Aubrey. So I knew I was bad like he said."

"No," Aubrey whispered.

"Then I thought he did die. I told myself he did. I told Crys he did. And them papers there, and you teaching him, and him in that jailhouse so close. It's like he's back from the dead."

"Aimee, I didn't know. I didn't know." He curved his shoulders inward, as though protecting himself from a blow.

"I'm sorry," she said. "I wanted to be good. For you." She knew he saw her now and would not touch her. She should not be touched. "I don't always understand it." Her voice sounded far away. "Sometimes it feels like somebody done spent my life for me. So I ain't shore why I got born."

Aubrey's shoulders shook. He doubled over and held her foot. He looked up at her, silent, into her whole face.

"I want to be with you till the morning," he said. They lay there on the top sheet, half naked, and he cradled her foot like it was something breakable.

Cord

....

#96309

Before that night I thought aint no one or nobody that evil, but I done nothing to stop it. That is why I seen it was in me. I maybe wanted to do like that man done. I watched everything, I can still call it up in myself after many a year. It is a tar like I said. You can run from it but it stuck to bone. I still run

There is times it about catched up

After it the man went out and she lied there like she died. She was so little a broken white bird. But she had right to fly. I get a pain for her, the tiny pink dress. It is the one I baptized her father son holy ghost in the river.

If I bent I felt the sorrow

Her white face was real, not lye not some paint. I look in her window to see if the white is real

Crystal

....

THROUGH HER HEAD THE WATER POUNDED like the Donnie Manse
when it had rushed up against the insensible rocks then flooded the town of
Cuzzert, pounding the cement.

Crystal ran through the double glass doors. A nurse, a new one, said to wait,
but Crystal passed through anyhow, into the hallway that smelled cleaner than
salt and bleach.

She held still, hovering, and the glass doors shut silent behind her. She held
her breath, felt the broad tiles on the floor steady beneath her. She listened to
all who lay in the hospital rooms up and down that hallway, seven doors to
the corner.

Crystal had all but erased herself from the world's memory, like a silo in a
wide field when no corn came in, wind whistling through it. The people in
the seven rooms whistled up through her, their thin breath. She heard the
machines beep and chirr, soft and steady like the oats chop she poured from
the sack for Balaam. She heard a dry swallow down a throat, a hiss from a
needle sting, and the stir of a slack shape bending on a sheet. She heard the
hearts aching or the hearts not aching because they were not permitted to
ache. But even of them, she thought: *can't nobody go without the ache that
baptizes us.*

A doctor walked from one doorway into another without looking up at her.
He heard nothing, but she could hear the tile give under his step, his watch
tick. It was late.

Down a gravel road, people prayed barefoot, wet, for God to have mercy.

She'd taken in the world for ten years. Like taking in a stray. She took in the
sound and sadness that the world whimpered with. She was full to the brim
with coarse lives, and she let them spill from her now, down, down the hallway

onto the fine, broad tiles. Tonight she gave the world back its sorrow, because she wasn't meant to bear it all alone. She broke loose from her halt and sought out just one: she walked forward and listened for Ronnie.

Everything drowned him out at first, but, no, he must be there. He must still be alive. She moved her blocky blue dress through the white hallway, her dress a jangling blue against the walls.

Around the corner, slow, to his door, open just a crack. She pushed it all the way open and walked into his dark room.

Only the glow of a monitor lit his face, so pale, as though under ice.

Ronnie stirred. Awake. She knew he saw her shape in her square-edge dress, maybe in silhouette, maybe thinking she was a nurse come to read his vitals. Her hair was braided like a young girl's, dry now after Aimee had braided it wet and starting to come loose. A strand crossed her vision.

"Crystal," he said, weak. "They took my arm." His left hand gripped the metal bed rail. "I'd like better to have died."

The floodwater sputtered inside her, pounding and sloshing up.

She crossed the room. His mask was off now, and his breath came hard but sure, his flesh not so swollen. His right shoulder ended in a brief gathering of gauze. She went to his right side and touched his rib bones where his arm should have lain. His body through his white gown was dense, full of blood; it rose with breath; it would sing again. He had not died. Immodest though it was, she gripped his side and held onto him there.

"They give me these shots so I don't feel it, but I do. Something aching that ain't there. I woke up, and my arm was gone. Thought my time was up." Ronnie looked at his blunted shoulder. "I still feel it there, where the scars was. Crystal?" He said it like a question, like asking was it really her or was she that nurse checking his vitals. "Why is it through burning? Yet so as by fire? Why's the Lord make it that way?"

All the water of the river seeped into the fertile ground inside her. It pooled there, seeped down under rock, under foundation, under sandstone and deep coal seam.

"I'm freezing," Ronnie said. She pulled his white blanket up around his neck with one hand, kept her other hand lightly pressing on his ribs. If she lifted her hand, he might disappear. "Mom called up, they told me. Cussed 'em a blue streak and swore she wouldn't come get me even if they put me in a pine box. But I know she'll be up first thing in the morning. She'll die when she sees my arm cut off. I'm freezing."

A well shaft opened, down into her deep pools. A wood bucket, half rotted, was coming to dip clean, secret water.

"I'm so tired, Crys." He looked at her face and her hair so plain. She backed away from him, went to the door.

"Please don't leave," he said. "I won't ask you to say nothing." He lay quiet.

She shut the door and came back to his left side where his hand gripped the metal rail. She pried it loose and, from her pocket, took the sixteen-penny nail cross, bound with copper wire, and pressed it into his hand.

And she pulled water up out of the well, in the wood bucket half rotted. She pulled it slow. The water trembled as the ten-year vow let her loose.

It started like a newborn's cry, testing the waters of sound, or like a strange animal howling low, something other than her own voice. It was so easy for it to leave her when she parted her lips and her teeth. A pinched vowel beginning a word.

"In the cross," she started singing, hoarse, choosing the hymn sung at June Tatum's wake.

"In the cross." The higher note broke, and she cleared her throat.

"Be my glory ever." It was the refrain she sang, off key, she thought, unpracticed and crude, and she stopped—she had made a mistake. This was putrid singing like a coon dog's holler, horrible to her ears. But Ronnie broke into a smile and then a soft laugh with wet eyes, and matched her key, pulling her voice on in unison.

"Till my raptured soul shall find rest beyond the river." They paused, breathed, started again, this time with the verse. "Jesus, keep me near the cross, there a precious fountain," and it sharpened, tuned to the pitch. Something in her chest burst. This was her voice singing. Ten years older than when she'd last heard it, but it sounded like a young girl's.

Her voice going out like a strike of light—*it's water come into light,* she thought. *It's water come full into light.* She felt her skin color warm, as the water gave way to sun inside her, brought her leaf around to gold like a tulip poplar turns.

They finished the hymn, softer on the last refrain, and Ronnie laughed some more, showed his big teeth. He said, "Tell me where you been, girl. All those places you been."

"My," she said.

Dotte

....

EVEN THOUGH IT WAS OUT OF HER WAY, Louisa Felton drove Dotte home. Elsie sat in the car's back seat with her oxygen bag on. Jenny sat half asleep on Dotte's lap, and neither of them minded that—the holding and being held.

The vigil lasted till midnight, when everyone wore out. After Dotte's girls had left, she'd walked outside the church barefoot, thinking they'd gone out just for a spell, but the pickup was gone. Aubrey's Jeep, too. Dotte heard a rustle and looked for a raccoon, but it was the Dixon boy out drunk.

When they broke up the meeting, Louisa said she'd take him, too. Art helped him into the car. The boy could hardly hold himself upright.

"That's the closest you been to church, son," Art said to him, but the boy said something dirty and put his chin to his chest. He sat there by Elsie Felton.

"There's some come a hard way 'round," Louisa whispered to Dotte.

Dotte couldn't tell why her girls had left her, but she didn't speak on it to Louisa. Instead, she said, "I ain't had the Spirit come on with tongues since last winter." Ronnie's life was a heavy weight they all carried. He was alive, she was sure. They had prayed him through. She felt the tiresome weight of her own body, like she'd forgotten it for some time and now remembered it. She remembered her hands, sewing that prayer cloth. She now held the cloth wadded into a ball in the hand that held Jenny close to her.

"Is that right?" Louisa was too tired to say more than that about the Spirit. She tapped her fine, painted nails on the lit-up dash as they drove.

The older Dixon boy had to help them at the trailer, and he was sore.

The home lights were dark, but Dotte knew the girls weren't sleeping. They were gone. Louisa asked if she'd be all right, and Dotte nodded. She put Jenny's stringy hair behind her ear, like she used to do her girls' hair. *When the sun comes up,* she thought, *I wanna do for my girls.*

She walked the long hallway to their rooms, just to be sure. The thin board that split their rooms apart bowed something awful. Getting old. She would get a proper wall put in if they wanted. She would ask Ronnie to do it when he got well. He'd be around more now. She felt tired and heavy again, feeling like she'd held him up away from death all night, his young man self. Mighty tired. She passed into her room where the cigarette smoke hung thick, but she did not lie down.

She felt many things, and in her mind many things came clear. She thought on Charlene Marie Sparr who had no light and who lived locked up in herself. That girl had not felt free to stroke the thin rabbit at her feet. It was a rabbit like a frail lung, sighing out its last breath in a trash heap at the fairgrounds. What if the girl had picked it up and fed it something?

Dotte felt strange, but she let the strangeness wash over. Her Cord Paul was coming back. He was close as the yellow curtains on the window. He was weak as the frail-lung rabbit. She did not know how she knew it.

She spoke it out loud. "You're coming back soon. It must be."

When he came, she would have much to say. And she would say it. She said it now.

"These girls need to get outta the shadows," she said. "You hear me? Things is different. They need to start living." She bent down by the bed, slow. She pulled out a shoebox in a Family Dollar bag.

He had sent a package once, the year after he left. She had opened it in private and never showed Aimee and Crystal. It was six or so yards of material, soft, double-knit cotton. White with little violets all over. "For you and the girls," he wrote in cursive on a piece of cardboard. That was the only note. She'd kept it in its parcel paper in the shoebox and bag under her bed.

She opened it up now. Double-knit is a kind that doesn't wrinkle or keep the crease, even being folded up so many years. "Isn't that something?" she said.

There was enough for a new blouse for them both. "And you sent plenty."

She thought on Charlene Marie's V, the fitted bodice of the green dress. She thought on her girls' shapes as though for the first time, sweet woman shapes. She pictured them coming home through the screen door, how tall they were. How the trailer wasn't much, but she loved seeing them come through the screen door. She would have to guess at it since she didn't have patterns that would fit now.

Dotte walked through the TV room and opened the door to Cord's study, switched on the light. Her tin of buttons lay spilled all over the floor in a pretty puddle. "Well," she said. The cookie tin sat upright beside her Singer machine on the floor. The machine case was pushed partly off, ready for her. From the puddle, she picked a set of tiny, silver buttons still fixed to their paper. Never used. "These is fine." She cleared the desk stacked high and needed to wipe away the dust. She had that prayer cloth in her pocket, as good a washrag as any, and she wiped it clear. She spread wide the six yards of white with violets and measured and ticked it with a pencil.

"There was a time I could whip it up in a hour, but now it'll take me the night through. It's been some time. A body got to remember." She swayed a little, chose a light-color thread for the bobbin.

"And I'm a dreaming it up from scratch. Ain't got no pitcher or nothing." But she'd dreamed her own wedding dress from a magazine, and it turned out.

"That's right."

Cord

....

#96309

July 28, 1999

What would you like most to be remembered for?

It is come due, I say I been struck by lightning once. I could show you the mark on my side but I boast not about it. I been 10 years trying to figure why I lived. I missed out. I read all the signs wrong

I give you my name and place, if they like to mark my headstone but it is of a man long dead. Cord Paul Lemley once preacher of Glorybound Holiness Tabernacle on Cuzzert Pike, not 30 mile out. Wife Dorothy Jean was a Sisler and 2 girls heir Crystal Lee Ann, Aimee Jo. Route 40 Box 1 in Painted Rocks Estates. I do not know if my girls live there now or someplace

It is not me that be remembered, it is my memory of the world. One time my girl name of Aimee ask me at the fair can I buy a money bank of a fake dog of 3 feet a old junk bank but she did not want the nicer thing, I bought the bank for her. And for my girl Crystal can I get a black book for writing yes. I am sorry I did not get them more things and my wife.

I see it out I seen the whole world, winter rye and a wheat growing out the window now it is a season coming I will not see it come. Better that a seed of wheat go into the ground and die

I ask the Lord tell me one thing clear. Today He showed clear to mercy, I been dead to my girls 10 years. Now the sun come up on me and God will take me

Cord Paul Lemley 1958-1999

Aimee

....

THE CLINK OF A BUCKET HANDLE woke Aimee at dawn on Thursday. She heard water slosh like it was right beside her head. Aubrey lay asleep beside her on the mattress, and she felt the pressure of his hand on hers. She slipped her hand loose and still felt the pressure, and it grew to a throb, till she felt the deep ache, a prophet's ache.

Aimee took a T-shirt from his closet, *Loyola* in white on dark green, her dress a pool of peach beside the mattress. She pulled on the jeans he'd worn the night before, too big. She smelled the wood and river and her own skin. She tiptoed to the window above his desk. Melanie Angus hauled a bucket of water into the church building, clinking the handle. "Shh," Aimee said and wished Melanie would lay her body down for once, sleep half the day and dream.

Aubrey's key stuck her through the jeans pocket. On the mattress, he lay under the top sheet, his shape rising and lowering in breath. She knelt and kissed his leg soft through the sheet.

He had held her so hard, he'd worn out, and they'd slept side by side.

"You sleep, Sweet Aubrey Falls," she whispered. "I need to do this alone." She left the cabin barefoot.

Aimee parked the Jeep in the empty dip in the dirt in front of the doublewide. So Crystal had stayed with Ronnie. And maybe Dotte had slept over at Miriam's.

Aimee paused on the cinder-block steps, put her fingers through the holes of the lattice, then went inside. In the kitchen, the dawn light softened everything: the gas stove; the cupboards; the yellow of the floor. Her eyes adjusted, and she saw something white spread out on the table.

A white blouse with purple flowers on it and little silver buttons. She touched it—a double-knit cotton—and held it up to the light. It had a nice, scoop neck and capped sleeves that hung limp with no arms in them. Two darts gathered in the fabric under the bust. It was lovely and new, put out on the table like her mom used to put their Easter presents. Set them there to be found when they rose from bed like Jesus rose up from the ground.

Aimee padded down the hallway to Dotte's bedroom door left open. Dotte slept on top of the bedspread, a heap of woman, still dressed for the vigil, a quiet mound, breathing in her clothes like Aubrey's bare chest under his bed sheet. She had fallen asleep sewing another of the white blouses, not quite finished. She had been sewing on the buttons. A few lay loose like a trail of silvery water drops across the bedspread. Aimee shut Dotte's door, silent, to let her sleep.

The wall phone rang, and she ran to it, giddy, with her hand full of new, white blouse. She got it before the second ring.

"Hello," she said, and no one answered. "That you, Aubrey?" she whispered. Still nothing. "I need to do something, but I'm acoming back, Aubrey. Can you wait for me?"

"Aimee?" The voice on the other end was low, a woman. "It's me."

Aimee breathed in quick, put her hand to her cheek. She heard a soft laugh in the phone and followed the floor with her eyes. She traced the floor without speaking, traced the sink and the window, the framed embroidery, *I will lift up mine eyes*. She looked out the mesh of the screen door toward the road. She heard the laugh again, and she cocked her head to listen harder. She listened ten years back, heard a girl laughing, then two girls, running around to the back screen porch, chasing each other, yellow hair, black hair, making lists of things to do before Jesus caught them up for glory—things they still had yet to do—making promises and clutching each other on their slight wrists, holding on.

"Crystal," she finally said. "You sound like Crystal Lemley. You do."

"Aimee," her sister said and laughed again.

"I hear you," Aimee said. "You sound real good." She wiped her eyes with the back of her hand, and the white blouse waved in front of her. She remembered Ronnie. "Crys. Is Ronnie living?"

"He is. I wanted to tell you he is, but they had to take his arm clear off 'cause of infection."

"Clear off?"

"Yes, but he's okay. He's gonna live. You tell everybody that."

"Yeah, I will." Aimee smiled. "You can tell 'em too." She shook her head, waved the blouse around, strained to keep quiet to let Dotte sleep. "Hoo! You sound real good, Crys. Real good."

"Mom okay?"

"She's sleeping and"—she was about to say what Dotte had sewn, but she felt the ache and said—"and I gotta go. Listen, I gotta go, but Aubrey and me'll be up to see you."

"You'll come?"

"Yeah, 'fore noon, but I got something, first. Crys?"

"Yeah?"

"You sound real good to me."

Aimee got the sack of flour from the bottom cupboard, careful not to get any on her new top. It fit her close and perfect. Her neck breathed. She had tucked the blouse into the waist of Aubrey's jeans and found a leather belt to hold them up. Dotte still hadn't waked.

She put two cups of flour in the tin mixing bowl, lit the oven and set it to four hundred.

Crystal was speaking again, in that hospital room with Ronnie Sisler. It was like she'd been meant for it. She had done her meant-for thing. And Aimee was surer now of what to do.

She mixed the flour with a wooden spoon, salt and baking powder, half a teaspoon of soda. Then she lay down the spoon and mixed the fine dust with her hands. She found the canister of oleo and dipped some out for the flour mix, took a fork to cut it in till it looked right, like Crystal had taught her. Till it got good and crumbly. Then she made a well, deep in the center for the buttermilk, but there was none in the refrigerator—just regular milk—so she did like Crystal did sometimes: put a teaspoon of vinegar, something bitter, in the cup of milk to sour it. She let it stand five minutes while she spread a layer of tinfoil over the baking sheet warped and rusted.

It was going on seven in the morning when she poked the circles of biscuit dough with a fork, twice each on top, and put them in to bake. She got the tea towel ready to wrap them in and looked for jam, found only a jar of Flavorite grape jelly with just a spoonful left. For a moment, she felt the meanness—*old grape jelly is what he gets, and that's that*—but she shook it loose. She would stop for jam on the way.

The morning world was the same as every other morning world she'd seen on Route 40, the fencerow and goldenrod, the thin birds scuttling from the ditch as the Jeep passed. But when she hit the new paving spot and heard the tires hum, she felt herself shed things that had been the same for too long, like a creature shedding old feathers, old skin, old scales.

Cuzzert Correctional Facility for Men, 15 Miles. A cluster of blue bachelor's buttons sprayed up the side of the steel sign and made her think of June Tatum.

The biscuits warmed her lap through the towel. She was good and ready.

"Morning, Agnes," Aimee said. She headed for the canned goods in the service station.

Agnes Felton lifted her face from *The Star*. "Hey there, early bird." She leaned on the counter. "Shorely Dotte ain't through three packs, yet."

"No, I come for something else." Aimee chose a pint of home-canned strawberry with a gold-ring lid. The small sign taped to the shelf said it was from a Beverly with a Biggs address.

"You heard anything 'bout the Sisler boy?" Agnes asked.

Aimee set the pint jar on the counter. "He's gonna make it," she said. "Lost his arm, but he'll make it."

"Lord." Agnes gripped her shoulder.

"You give me this on credit, Agnes?"

"Shore thing." She pulled a yellow slip from underneath the register. "You get a new blouse?"

"Mom made it."

"No she did not."

"She did. One for Crystal too." She thought of Crystal's voice and smiled wide.

"She did it just right, I tell you. Sign here. Now you come in back, and I'll give you a permanent, Aimee. You'll be all good as new. I swear it'd set so nice on you."

"Soon, Agnes. I got someplace to be today."

"Where to?"

Aimee paused, licked her lips. "I'm gonna go see my daddy."

"Well." Her face went blank.

"In the prison. I'm going there today, right now."

"Well." Agnes touched her own hair and swallowed. She opened her mouth and shut it, and Aimee thanked her for the jam.

Before Aimee walked through the door, Agnes said, "Well. You tell him I say 'hello.'"

"I'll do that."

Cord

....

#96309

August 4, 1999

Describe the face you see in the mirror.

Aimee

....

AIMEE SAT WAITING at the metal table in a room all gray and hard. It would not be like she'd seen on TV—no glass between them or a phone to speak into. Just a table set with two chairs.

The man at the gate on Prison Road had said if you're Aimee Lemley, you can go on through. Aubrey Falls called ahead for you. Aimee had blushed at that, grateful.

They had run a metal detector all over her. They took the knife she'd brought for the jam and told her to leave the biscuits behind because you couldn't bring food inside. But she'd pleaded, calm and sure, knowing no one could hinder a prophet called out. When she said who she was there to see, they gave in, so she knew he must be bad off from the hunger.

She had not looked to the right or left, at the officer attending her, at the razor wire, or the barred doors she touched and gripped for a brief hold like gripping her blue lattice, because if she took in too much of the scene she might turn back. She didn't look around at all till she sat down in the gray room. She set her biscuits and jam on the cold, metal table and looked full at the walls with no windows, felt her throat close.

She watched the heavy door open. A broad-faced, uniformed man came in and stood to the side, next to her escort.

Then her daddy, Cord Lemley, stooped and shuffling. His hair was uncombed, as gray as the room, and the skin hung from his face like a balloon all out of air. He'd shrunk—small as a young boy—but aged and empty, not curious or full of any of his former fire. He sat down in a sigh, like a shriveled up seedpod. She did not think he recognized her.

"I brung you some biscuits," she said in a small voice. He didn't look up. "I hear you ain't eating, but they still warm." She pushed them across the table.

"I guess them men's gonna stay there by the door, then. That'll be fine."

Aimee touched her neck where the white blouse with tiny violets scooped to her chest bone. "Mom made me this here blouse."

Cord looked at his hands in his lap. "Why'd you come here?" he said.

She felt the shame like a sack of lead on her shoulders, the shame he'd heaved upon her without mercy. She let herself cry, but she would not howl and carry on. He looked at her and squinted, then looked away, like she was some bright light. His face lost even more color, and she understood that he was afraid of her. Her mighty, old daddy was afraid.

"The Lord," he said, with nothing after it.

Then he said, "I ain't been good to you."

"No. You ain't," she said and wiped her eyes. He had made her skin feel burned to charcoal and flaking, something ugly. "But you ain't the beginning and end of goodness. I walk free. And I had me near a week to think on it—would I come or not. And here I am. And I brung these biscuits. Feel—they still warm." She pushed them closer to him. "They wouldn't let me bring in the table knife, but I think that jam'll pour. I got it out at King's Service Station just up from home, put up fresh this summer." She unscrewed the ring lid from the jar, popped the seal with her thumbnail and set the jar in front of him. "Agnes Felton's still working there. She said to say 'hi'. You take this and eat it. You ain't gotta eat 'em all—that'd make anybody sick. But you need to eat one."

Cord lifted a flap of the towel, and a salty smell wafted out.

"No call for it, is there? I'm on fast." He spoke so quiet.

"Today," she said firm, "you meant for a meal."

He raised his face to her again, and she met his eyes straight on. His eyes deep black like hers, two pieces of coal. But, my, how hers had been pressed, pressed hard for a thousand years to diamond-shine. A diamond's just coal pressed down immeasurably, sweet Aubrey Falls had said. And it was time her daddy looked on her and remarked her diamond-shine.

She peeled the towel back farther and took a biscuit, pinched just a part of it off, like she would for a child with a mouth too small for a big bite. "Go on," she said.

He minded her, took the morsel and held it.

"Go on," she said again.

He tilted the full jam jar, so weak, and dribbled some on the table, a little on his bit of biscuit. He put it in his mouth.

"That's it. Chew it slow. We got time. They said we got twenty minutes today, but I'll be back, and Crys and Mom. And Aubrey, I believe he'll be by, and Ronnie when he's fit. Ronnie Sisler, my. There's lots to tell you after ten years. Lot's changed 'round here. But we got time. Time's a spreading out." She took the rest of the broken biscuit and poured out more jam.

"Here now," she said. He took it and ate. Their hands lay open on the cold table, not quite touching. "Now you gotta quit telling the Lord how to do. It ain't your time to die."

She watched him take a painful swallow, and he looked at her like she was the one who'd come back from the dead.

"You know me?" she asked.

His jaw hung weak, and his dry lips parted for a whisper. "You're Aimee Jo."

"That's right. It's me."